Jillian Hunter

USA Today bestselling
author of *A Wicked Lord at the Wedding*

The Wicked Duke Takes a Wife

Don't miss these deliciously sexy historical romances in the Boscastle series:

THE SEDUCTION OF AN ENGLISH SCOUNDREL

THE LOVE AFFAIR OF AN ENGLISH LORD

THE WEDDING NIGHT OF AN ENGLISH ROGUE

THE WICKED GAMES OF A GENTLEMAN

THE SINFUL NIGHTS OF A NOBLEMAN

THE DEVILISH PLEASURES OF A DUKE

WICKED AS SIN

Ballantine / Del Rey
Presidio Press
One World / Spectra

ISBN 978-0-345-50395-4

U.S.A. $7.99 CANADA $10.99

50799

*S*HE stepped away from him. He followed, his eyes smoldering with dark intent. Her heart was pounding in her breast. She bumped up against the library door. He raised his hand. His leather-encased fingers traced the contours of her jaw.

"What sort of beast do you suppose I am at heart?" he inquired softly. "A Caligula? A Blue-beard who murdered his wives? If you continue to spread these rumors of my bestial desires, there will be no one left in London for me to ravish."

Sweet mercy. His voice awakened the most ancient of all desires. She felt her body, her whole being, tense in expectation; whether she led or followed him into the library, she was unsure.

She only knew that once the door closed, he began to undress her, button by button, hook by hook, in the room where an hour or so ago she had sat in warm gratitude with his family.

"What if someone comes in?" she whispered, staring into the fire as he kissed her bare shoulder, then her breasts and her back, until she sank down upon the sofa, holding up what she could of her unhooked dress, shift, and simple corset.

"I have a lock on all my doors," he answered with a hesitant smile.

"Your grace has the advantage," she whispered.

"I don't think so."

Also by Jillian Hunter

The Wicked Duke Takes a Wife

Jillian Hunter

BALLANTINE BOOKS • NEW YORK

A Ballantine Books Mass Market Original

Copyright © 2009 by Maria Hoag

All rights reserved.

Published in the United States by Ballantine Books, an imprint of The Random House Publishing Group, a division of Random House, Inc., New York.

BALLANTINE and colophon are registered trademarks of Random House, Inc.

ISBN 978-0-345-50395-4

Cover art: Alan Ayers
Cover lettering: Iskra Johnson

Printed in the United States of America

www.ballantinebooks.com

9 8 7 6 5 4 3 2 1

For Beverly—

You were dressed as Dr. Frankenstein, dancing the "Monster Mash," all alone onstage in our school talent show the first time I saw you. I thought you were the bravest person in the world. Thank you for sticking up for the English nerd and re-creating her with Aqua Net and white lipstick. I would never have survived swimming with sharks—and grunions—without you.

The Wicked Duke Takes a Wife

Chapter One

"I agree with you," replied the stranger;
"we are unfashioned creatures, but half made up . . ."

MARY SHELLEY
Frankenstein

It had taken Miss Harriet Gardner two years of intensive training in the polite graces to become that mysterious creation known in Society as a gentlewoman. It took the stormy young Duke of Glenmorgan less than two days to undo months of discipline, of tears, of sweat, of French lessons, to reawaken every gutter instinct Harriet had fought to subdue.

The foundress of the elite academy for young ladies where Harriet was now gainfully employed would not be pleased. In fact, Emma Boscastle, the former Lady Lyons and current Duchess of Scarfield, would be the first to remind Harriet that a gentlewoman would sooner be caught in a swoon than in a sweat. Horses sweat. Gentlemen perspired. And ladies glowed, albeit only after a vigorous cotillion or lively ride through the park at the fashionable hour. Certainly a lady of the academy did not draw attention to this unfortunate bodily function. She merely applied her fan with a little more energy than usual. A well-bred lady should never speak of whatever embarrassment befell her at all.

Which was why no one at the academy ever mentioned that its foundress had abandoned every rule in her own book when *she* unexpectedly fell in love.

A handsome duke tended to wield a devastating effect upon even ladies who believed themselves to be above temptation. The Duchess of Scarfield's lapse in love's name, however, did not excuse those she had tutored from their obligations. Harriet would battle forth as her creator had intended.

For two years she had devoted herself to the study of deportment. She had turned down the dancing master's marriage proposal. She had laughed at the footman's clumsy effort at courtship.

Two grueling years, mind you, for everyone involved in her social edification. Days of rehearsing the nuances of proper behavior until curtsying to an earl came as easily to her as cutting a purse once had. Evenings spent practicing dictation until her tongue went numb.

"How many times do I have to remind you *not* to drop your aspirates, Harriet?"

"And how many times do I 'ave to tell you I ain't never dropped my—what you said—in my life?"

She cringed to think of what an utter ignoramus she had appeared.

Certainly Harriet's colorful past was not a Crown secret. But the fact that she had been rescued from the slums and had risen to the position of fledging instructress in the exclusive academy proved that one could indeed fashion a little monster into a suitable member of Society.

For, in a fond if morbid way, she regarded herself to be less a lady and more like the ill-fated fiend created in the recently published sensation *Frankenstein*. Having come late in life to the pleasures of literature, she took secret delight in comparing her own re-creation to that of Victor's hideous being. Not that Harriet planned to end up on a sled in the Arctic. A mate would be nice, though. That's all the misunderstood monster wanted.

Indeed, she hoped one day to meet the anonymous author and confess how the queer parts of Harriet's own nature had been similarly redesigned as a social experiment, not by a mad scientist but rather by a genius of the genteel arts. Harriet had been the academy's first charity case. Several others had been accepted since. This practice might have discouraged enrollment had the school not achieved unprecedented success in marrying off its graduates, known as the Lionesses of London, to numerous noblemen highly ranked on the marriage mart. One teacup, one viscount at a time, the girls of the academy were unleashed upon Society and set forth to conquer.

Harriet had worked harder than any pupil in the school's history to overcome her flaws, and a rough bit of work she'd proven to be during those initial months. She had been tempted countless times to revert to her former ways. Instead, she had risen above her past to prove that her Modern Prometheus's faith in her redemption had been well placed.

Yet therein lay the black magic of London's most beloved and infamous family, the Boscastles. One way or another, by hook or by crook—although usually by charm—the lords and ladies of the notorious clan not only won over their hapless victims, they mesmerized those invited into their inner circle so that bewitchment seemed an honor and seduction a benediction.

Unfortunately, Harriet's introduction to the esteemed family had not been of their choosing. She'd been caught red-handed in the act of robbing Grayson Boscastle's Park Lane mansion during a house party. Fortunately, it was not the marquess who had interrupted her amateur crime. It had been his wife, Jane, a woman possessed of emotional depth and unconventional daring.

Harriet might have inherited a penchant for vice from her father's ancestors. But the will of her Boscastle sponsors had proven stronger than the malicious influence of her own blood.

It was, therefore, what the Duchess of Scarfield would consider a regrettable irony that a member of the family that had redeemed Harriet would prove to bring about her final disgrace.

* * *

At precisely four o'clock every Thursday afternoon, Cook prepared a scrumptious tea of bite-sized ham, cheese, and watercress sandwiches served daintily between triangular slices of thin buttered bread. No sooner were these morsels consumed than scones, cakes, and cream-filled French pastries arrived to tempt the palate. The scullery maids donned fresh aprons and delivered the treats to the ravenous young ladies of the academy. The underbutler brought out the silver tea urn and polished it to a dazzling gleam to place it, steaming invitingly, on the sideboard. At last came the anointed chime of the long-case clock. The scuffle of slippered feet resounded in the musty drawing room like a stampede of deer.

It was Harriet's first opportunity to preside over the practice tea. She had not felt this nervous since she stole a necklace from the Prince Regent's mistress during an act of what she didn't care to remember. Not only were the eyes of a dozen students observing her for the tiniest infraction, but several of Society's stalwart matrons had volunteered their presence to ensure that the ritual went as smoothly as possible.

One might assume, from the gravity of those in attendance, that the torch of female knowledge was being passed from the hands of ancient priestesses to the uncertain grasp of an uninitiated white-gloved generation. The Duchess of Scarfield's etiquette manual was the sacred tablet from which her young priestesses read.

Harriet would count herself fortunate if she survived the ordeal without losing her temper or spilling tea on her new lavender silk frock. Today marked a milestone in her life. She breathed in the scent of pastry and honest-to-God beeswax candles like an elixir against her evil upbringing. A far cry, she reflected, from her former days of gin and card games played under the light of cheap lard candles.

It was her pinnacle of achievement. She was to be trusted to supervise the sacred ritual. Not even the thunder that rumbled over London could spoil the occasion.

"Miss Lucille Martout," she said in mild reproach, "do remember that the first lady to the table does not attack her tea with the brutality of Genghis Khan."

"Hear, hear, Miss Gardner," one of the ancients concurred. "Let us nibble in due time."

"Sorry, miss," mumbled the shamed girl, sliding her lacy triangle of buttered bread and watercress back onto the plate. "I shall not do it again."

The eleven other students, dressed by London's finest mantua-makers in gowns of dreamy spring pastels, giggled demurely. Their kidskin-sheathed hands settled like wings in their laps. Miss Charlotte Boscastle, the academy's current headmistress, walked between each table before returning to her place with the four young ladies who would make their debut this season. She nodded her fair head in approval.

Three of the accomplished quartet had received a

half dozen offers of matrimony between them, with others pending. The fourth was a shy Yorkshire girl with solid connections at court. Her family had confided to the academy that they had begun negotiations with an earl. The prospect appeared to interest their daughter far less than the thickly iced cakes adorned with fresh violets that graced the table.

Charlotte took her seat, her willowy frame silhouetted against the tasseled silk curtains. She sent an encouraging smile across the room. "A final reminder, ladies. Tea is not a game of tennis. Serve those closest to you first, and do not use the silver tongs to pinch one another. If you are pinched, seek retribution at a later time. I was a student once myself."

Harriet cleared her throat, then paused. It challenged the imagination to picture Charlotte as anything but a model of propriety—unless one happened to read the novel she was secretly writing, and that, indeed, was another story.

A brilliant display of lightning flickered behind the sash windows of the cozy drawing room. At once the skies that had bestowed a celestial blue upon the city dimmed. The candle flames danced as if to defy the elements.

"Taking tea is an art," Harriet began, raising her voice in competition with another clap of thunder. Hell's bells, what a clamor. Did she hear hoofbeats, or was the back door banging open? It sounded like the confounded apocalypse. She glanced

around the room in rising irritation. She was anything but a model of propriety. She still struggled to
shackle her tongue when something upset her. The
coalman cheating Cook, for example. A nob
whacking an apprentice with his walking stick.
The prospect of a ruined practice tea. The students
had started to wiggle, sensing that Harriet was not
paying attention to protocol.

One of the girls sitting at the window gasped.
"Oh, golly! Look at that."

The dowager at the distracted student's side
sprang out of her chair. As the gathering watched
on in happy apprehension, the distinguished guest
parted the curtains for the entire assembly to behold a jet-black carriage with enormous wheels
rolling to a dramatic halt at the pavement. A
spume of mud splattered the lacquered red dragons
emblazoned on the door panel. A man in a top hat
sat behind the carriage window.

"Who is he?" Miss Martout demanded, craning
for a look.

"I believe it is the Duke of Glenmorgan," the
dowager said after a pause. "I saw that same carriage pass through Berkshire two years ago when
his brother was still alive."

Harriet turned to question Charlotte, who had
half risen, shaking her head in denial.

"But he isn't meant to arrive until Thursday,"
Charlotte whispered in panic. "I wrote it down."

Harriet rolled her eyes. "This *is* Thursday."

Charlotte pushed away from her chair, white as

marble. "Assert your authority, Miss Gardner, lest we have anarchy on our hands."

Harriet clapped her hands. "Ladies, please remain in your places." That was futile. There wasn't a single girl left at the tables. "Girls! There is nothing worse than lukewarm tea!"

"You'll have to come up with a more dire threat than that to control them," a cheerful voice commented over her shoulder. "A duke will trump a cup of hot tea any day."

Harriet opened her mouth to reply, but it was too late. The stouthearted Lady Hermia Dalrymple had surged past the students to the windows as if she were a schoolgirl herself and not a widow in her late sixties. To look at her, one would never guess she was as celebrated for her painting circle, which featured half-naked Boscastle men posing as deities, as she was for her place in the family as a beloved aunt-in-law.

"Where is he from?" a younger student asked, climbing onto a chair to see above the other girls peering through the curtains.

"Why is he here?"

"No one has told me, but I saw him first."

"How could you? He hasn't even stepped out of the carriage."

"For all you know, he isn't even *in* the carriage." Harriet strode across the room, snagging a sash here, an elbow there. "That could be his valet or his uncle. Back to your seats this very moment. I shall not tell you—"

"He's stepping out of the carriage—"

"That's a lady's foot, you ninny," another student noted. "And all those lovely feathers in her hair are going to be soaked and leave her battered like a wet hen before she reaches the front steps. Where are the footmen?"

From where she stood, Harriet could discern neither bird nor beast through the rain washing against the windows. The temperature in the drawing room dropped. Few of the candles had survived the frantic dash of a dozen girls at once. Harriet's shawl had fallen to the carpet. A furtive shape moved in her peripheral vision. She turned to glimpse Charlotte sneaking toward the door.

"Where are you going?" she asked in alarm.

"I have to change," Charlotte said quietly, pressing her finger to her lips. "I'll only be a few moments."

Change? But everyone looked so fresh, so lovely. Like a watercolor of fairies gathered under a rainbow—before a big nasty storm appeared to ruin the day.

"I know the duke is a distant cousin," Harriet said in bewilderment. "But I thought he would only be leaving his niece at the academy, and—why do you have to change?"

Lady Dalrymple hurried after Charlotte, agile for a woman of her ample build. "It's his aunt, you understand."

"Understand what?" Harriet asked, suddenly feeling like the lone rat on a sinking ship. "Wherever are you going?"

"We have to freshen up, dear," Lady Dalrymple whispered. "Lady Powlis and I attended school together long ago. I'd never dream of greeting Primrose without putting on a fancier pair of gloves. She notices things like that. Charlotte, you don't mind if I share your dressing closet for a few moments?"

"Who is going to welcome the duke with all these girls gone wild?" Miss Peppertree, the academy's senior instructress, a spinster, and a sourpuss, asked in an aggrieved voice.

"Miss Gardner won't mind," Charlotte called back distractedly.

Harriet frowned, staring at the academy's finest shoving one another aside to stand on the highest chair. "I won't?"

Lady Dalrymple paused to deliver an unhelpful bit of advice before disappearing into the hall. "It's good experience, dear. One day you might be employed in a grand house and have to answer to a duchess."

"But in the meanwhile I haven't the faintest notion what to do with . . . a duke," Harriet muttered, feeling more abandoned by the moment. Even worse, she sensed herself to be in trouble. As subdued as her street instincts might be, they rarely failed to warn her when her well-being was at stake. In her experience, people who caused this much bother when they arrived only meant a load of work for everyone expected to please them.

Miss Peppertree propelled her toward the door. "Just be polite and let him guide the conversation," she said anxiously. "I'd go in your place, but one of us has to remain here to calm the girls down. It is quite clear they are not listening to you."

Harriet sighed in resignation. The duke, being a Boscastle, would undoubtedly disregard pretension and put her unfounded fears to rest. Lady Dalrymple was probably right. The social experience might prove to be a better lesson than teaching the girls to pour tea without spilling.

The students would witness that the calm reception one afforded a duke differed little from that granted an ordinary gentleman. Harriet had bluffed her way thus far through life. She should be able to pass this minor trial. Besides, the man had not been born who could make her lose her head.

"Wait." Miss Peppertree clamped a bony hand around Harriet's wrist. "It is only fair that I advise you to be on your highest guard."

"He's only a duke, Daphne." Harriet pried her wrist from the talonlike grasp. "Good heavens. All this fuss over a person none of us have even met. I shouldn't have to remind you of what I have dealt with in the past."

Miss Peppertree nodded unconvincingly, turning to confront what she clearly perceived a less dangerous duty. The drawing room had erupted into chaos. Dames and schoolgirls alike seemed to have fallen under some wicked enchantment. It disheartened Harriet to think that in the end a shove onto the path of holy matrimony mattered more than . . . a hot cup of tea.

She gave Miss Peppertree a reassuring smile. "I'll be fine, you silly goose."

"You don't know about him, do you?" Miss Peppertree was edging away, a frown of impending doom settling over her thin, pale face.

"What?" Harriet scoffed. "Are you going to tell me that he's a rake? That all the ladies fall at his feet? You ought to be used to that sort of nonsense by now. I have never known a Boscastle who was a saint."

"You have never known one who murdered his brother for a dukedom, either," Miss Peppertree whispered in a dire voice.

Harriet snorted at the warning.

Duke or darling. In her estimation, his grace's arrival would prove much ado about nothing. He wouldn't be the first nobleman to be accused of doing away with his brother for an inheritance. That was actually none of her business. What involved her was that he had chosen to darken the academy's door on the very afternoon she had meant to distinguish herself. To think she had purchased a new frock for the occasion with her paltry savings. The duke would not care.

No doubt he would blow in and out of the school as swiftly as the present storm. He would drop off his ward as casually as the morning post and expect her to be transformed into a proper miss by his next return.

And it might well happen. But not until everyone stopped oohing and aahing and got back to work.

"One more thing," Miss Peppertree said at her shoulder. "Do you know what he is named for?"

Lord help her. What a time for a history lesson. "Another duke?"

"Not his title—his given name."

"I shall hardly be on a first name—" Harriet gave a sigh. Far be it for her to spoil Daphne's small pleasures in life. "Go on. What is his name?"

"It is Griffin."

Harriet waited a few moments for further clarification. When none appeared to be forthcoming, she released her breath. "Well, I'm glad you told me. I shall bear that in mind when I bring him in from the storm."

"You have no idea what a griffin is, do you?"

Harriet hung her head. "You have caught me out again."

"It is a fabled beast."

She glanced inadvertently at the window. "And here I thought I was greeting an ordinary duke."

"There is no such thing," Miss Peppertree said, sounding oddly pleased.

"As a griffin?"

"A sharp tongue will not protect you from the world, Harriet."

"I know that better than anyone you have ever met."

Miss Peppertree sniffed. "I admit that when you first came to the academy, I thought you were a hopeless cause. But I have seen you transformed into a living young lady one could almost admire."

Harriet smiled. "That is high praise, indeed, coming from your lips. But I have to ask—Do griffins attack young girls in particular?"

Miss Peppertree blinked repeatedly. "I would imagine that they attack anything that attracts their notice. They have a lion's body, a beaked eagle's head, and—"

Harriet nodded thoughtfully. "That must make it difficult for him to drink tea, speaking of which—"

"—they have wings!"

Harriet had heard enough. "Then he should have flown here, instead of riding in a coach. Honestly, Daphne, a woman of your age should not believe such nonsense."

"He is a duke, Harriet. A *duke*."

Resigned to the whims of the nobility, Harriet hastened into the entry hall. To her surprise, half of the academy's staff had already emerged from the bowels of the house to observe the occasion. The portly butler, Ogden, proceeded at a sedate pace to the front door, as was his custom, in order to set a proper example to those who served in lesser positions.

"His Grace the Duke of Glenmorgan has arrived!" the head footman, Trenton, shouted back to the underfootman, Raskin, who was hurriedly tying one of his knee breeches with a trio of maidservants trailing amusedly in his wake. Harriet would have scolded the lot of them had she not suddenly lost her voice.

Chapter Two

I wield the flail of the lashing hail,
And whiten the green plains under,
And then again I dissolve it in rain,
And laugh as I pass in thunder.

PERCY BYSSHE SHELLEY
The Cloud

❧ ❧

He stood in the doorway, utterly silent, his presence so imposing that Harriet felt as if time had taken a step back to assess him. Suddenly the butler, the footmen, the maid bringing another platter of sandwiches for tea, seemed at a loss as to how they should proceed. They stared at Harriet, awaiting her direction.

But she was staring at the cloaked duke, who must have wondered whether he'd arrived at a house of eccentrics. Raindrops slid from the brim of his black silk hat and ran into the faint lines carved into his cheeks. He glanced back at the carriage parked in the street. She studied his profile. He had a sharp blade of a nose, a cleft in his chin. When he turned again, his metallic-blue eyes cut straight to Harriet, riveting her to the spot.

He's young, she thought. *And he looks a proper beast.*

He wrenched off his sodden top hat. The thunderclap that accompanied this impatient gesture deepened the tension that had gripped his spellbound audience.

"Is this or is this not Lady Lyons's Academy for Young Ladies?" he demanded.

The butler passed the soggy hat to one of the footmen. A maid ran forth to take the dark one's cloak, only to realize she was still holding a tray. Her hands trembled. The tray wobbled. Harriet was afraid she would scatter a carpet of her watercress sandwiches at the duke's feet.

He stepped into the hall. A spray of cold wet air and indescribable energy accompanied his entrance. Harriet noticed that there were raindrops caught in his indecently thick eyelashes.

"This is not Lady Lyons's Academy for Young Ladies, is it?"

His voice, a rich, melodious lilt, reminded Harriet that it was her duty to give him a proper reception, not to admire the length of his ducal lashes. He had brought his niece all the way from the Welsh–English border to the academy with the assumption that it was well worth the trouble. Harriet had been entrusted with offering him a courteous welcome.

"Your grace," she said, sinking into a curtsy, "we are called the Scarfield Academy now. And—"

She broke off in embarrassment. The butler was bowing, the two footmen following suit, with the three maids dipping up and down in jerky motions that made her feel dizzy. What had come over everyone? They looked like a collection of windup toys whose springs had gone askew.

"Well, whatever this place is called," the duke said over Harriet's head, "I hope that my aunt and niece might be allowed to take refuge from the storm."

Harriet glanced up from his muddy black Hessian boots and straightened instantly. Through the curtain of rain that shimmered in the open doorway, she could see his coachman conversing with the academy's stablemaster. From the carriage, a silver-haired lady was waving a lace handkerchief at the house like a naval officer flagging down a ship in distress.

"I do apologize, your grace." She darted toward the door. "I shall bring them in straightaway."

He stepped in front of her. "Have a footman attend to the task. With umbrellas if possible." His disgruntled gaze seemed to absorb every detail of her appearance. "I'm in no mood to hear another lady complain that the wretched rain has ruined her hair."

A test, Harriet told herself, inhaling quietly.

This was one of those social trials that sooner or later a woman in her position must face. She would remain unmoved by his curt manner. She would stand, in her mentor's words, as *a beacon of civility when battered by a storm of rudeness*.

What misfortune that Harriet had loved thunderstorms since her earliest years.

Despite living in the miserable garrets of St. Giles

and Seven Dials for most of her life, she associated storms with the few moments of family closeness she had ever known. She and her half brothers had often been forced to huddle together for warmth, sharing ghost stories to distract one another from the perishing cold. On some nights they might hide under a blanket from their father, predictably too drunk to recognize the sniggering dark shape in the corner as his own offspring.

Occasionally, after begging a pie vendor for his unsold wares, she and the boys would sneak into a swell's carriage or scramble over a garden wall to take shelter in a summerhouse. Harriet would dub herself the Duchess of St. Giles, while her halves would alternately laugh at her or pay her court. When the storm ended, it was every urchin to himself. Weeks would pass without Harriet knowing where they were or what mischief they had followed.

And now here she stood with another storm raging, having no idea what to say to this gorgeous young duke, who apparently wasn't inclined to make the situation the least bit easier.

The cultured voice of Charlotte Boscastle floated down from the top of the stairs to rescue her. "Griffin!" she exclaimed warmly. "How sad we were to hear of Liam's passing. And please excuse us for not giving you a proper welcome. We thought you wouldn't be here until . . . Thursday next."

The reluctant smile he gave in answer disappeared before Harriet could recover from its impact. What did she know, anyway? Perhaps grief over his brother's death had turned him hard. To look at him, it was impossible to judge whether he had committed murder for an inheritance or not. Miss Peppertree often proved to be an unreliable source of gossip. And while Harriet could not envision the well-mannered Charlotte changing into a fancier gown to impress a killer, Harriet had known of stranger reactions.

"I shan't be long, your grace," Charlotte added, her disembodied voice fading away. "Have Miss Gardner take you to the red salon for fresh tea."

Harriet felt a surprising tug of resistance. The two footmen crept around her, umbrellas sprouting open like giant mushrooms. She gazed up at the staircase, calling out like a coward, "Perhaps I should stay with the girls and ask Miss Peppertree to do the honors."

The duke's voice mocked her attempt to elude her duty. "What's wrong with you? You are here. She is not."

She pressed her lips together. His imperious stare irritated her. So did the giggling whispers that escaped the drawing room where she had been about to make her own debut. She turned to see Miss Peppertree peering around the door at the duke with the intensity of a barn owl. Twelve students twittered in the background.

"That is Miss Peppertree in the doorway," Harriet said, lowering her gaze. "I assure you, she will be able to satisfy your grace far better than will I."

"I doubt it," he said in unconcealed amusement, his gaze flickering to the figure in the door.

Harriet felt her face heat. Duke or not, he deserved to be taken down a notch for that. The butler edged to her side, whispering, "You don't want to tangle words with a man like him, miss."

No, but she might want to strangle him.

"Whispering to a guest is common, Miss Gardner." The duke peeled off his black gloves and unfastened his coat. "Furthermore, I dislike tea. I am, however, in grave desire of a brandy and a moment's solace. And you, in my estimation, appear more than capable of meeting those needs."

Chapter Three

My first care was to visit the fire.
I uncovered it, and a gentle breeze quickly
fanned it into a flame.

MARY SHELLEY
Frankenstein

❧ ❦

"As you wish, your grace," she said, straightening her shoulders. "The salon is not far. Walk this way."

"I assume there won't be another coven of schoolgirls lying in wait for me there," he said as he followed her hurried steps through the hall.

She drew a deep breath through her nostrils. It must be hard on the poor fellow, having women hiding behind doors wherever he went. "I apologize if the girls have embarrassed your grace. I shall guard you against any such further intrusions on your privacy."

"*You* shall guard me?" he asked, looking her up and down in interest. "You won't need a shield or teaspoon to defend us?"

"I have other weapons at my disposal."

He smiled. "Do you, indeed?"

She marched her fastest to lead him into the room at the end of the hall reserved for special guests. He outpaced her with ease, his manner infuriating. "And what is my guardian's name again, if you don't mind refreshing my memory?"

"Miss Gardner. Harriet Gardner."

He stared at her. "And do *you* have a guardian? Or are your hidden weapons enough?"

Heat stole into Harriet's cheeks. Had he just asked her if she had an arrangement as a mistress to another man? Who did he think he was, asking her such an improper question? Did being a peer give him the right to pry into her personal affairs? And on the first day they'd met, too. She bristled to think what he'd want to know next week.

"It was a joke, Miss Gardner," he said, shaking his head with the rue of a man accustomed to being misunderstood. "I was trying to put you at ease."

"At ease," she echoed.

He frowned. "It appears that I make a fearsome first impression. I don't know how I do it. It isn't intentional. But . . . I do."

She nodded cautiously. "Yes."

"And I *am* hard to please."

She swallowed. "Well, I do hope our brandy meets your standards." She flung open the door to the private salon, which she had previously visited only as part of her academy training. She had never entertained an important visitor by herself before. However, as the daughter of a drunkard, she knew how to pour a measure of liquor when it was demanded. And she could bluff her way through most situations. "Does your grace—"

"Dear God!" he shouted, in a voice that took a year off her life. "The blasted room is on fire!"

Harriet gasped. So it was. She slipped around him to seek out the source of the noxious banks of smoke swirling around his tall form. The duke coughed, rather dramatically, in Harriet's opinion, and rushed to open a window. Harriet winged to the fireplace, having quickly perceived the problem.

One of the academy's staff, obviously terrified of displeasing the "Duke of Thunder," had hurriedly lit a fire to warm the infrequently occupied room. In his or her haste, this well-meaning servant had tossed a wad of newspaper onto the grate as kindling, with disastrous results.

"Nothing to worry about, your grace," she called over his discordant gasps for breath. "I'll have it put out before you know it." And she waited until his back was turned before falling to her knees to beat down the inferno with a brass shovel.

Horrible idea.

The smoke not only billowed, it blew soot everywhere, including into the unfairly beautiful face of the man who was suddenly bending over her in an apparent effort to help.

His voice thundered in her ear. "How could *any-one* possibly be so inept?"

That was it. Thus tested for the first time, she failed. She dropped the shovel onto the hearth, muttering, "Well, I *beg* your stinkin' pardon."

He picked up the shovel, leaning around her to smother the rest of the flames. He completed the task with an efficiency that made her efforts look like a pantomime. He laid the shovel down on the hearth. Then he settled onto his knees beside her.

Silence then.

Foul smoke and silence.

She sank onto her heels. Her eyes burned like . . . hot coals. Could she hope he hadn't heard her impolite outburst? Should she distract him by pointing out that rain was splashing through the window he had opened and was saturating the wool peacocks that were woven into the elegant Brussels carpet? How was she going to land a position as a governess or stay on at the academy if she couldn't hold her tongue?

She knew the rules. They had been drummed into her head often enough. If the duke wanted to admonish her, she was supposed to listen meekly and think of . . . well, of anything except how handsome he was or that, if he kissed her, she would at least have a plausible reason to accuse him of ruining her debut.

He turned his head. It was obvious by his expression that kissing her was the last thing on his mind.

He narrowed his eyes. "*What* did you just say to me?" he asked, looking like Lucifer in the dissolving drifts of smoke.

She lifted her gloved hand to her heart, replying steadily, "I said that I beg your pardon for your grace having to breathe in such a . . . stink."

A glimmer of understanding lit his face. The transformation reminded Harriet of that deceptive lull during a storm when the sun glances out through the thunderheads and gives false hope.

False proved that hope, indeed.

In the next moment she was staring into inscrutable darkness. His gaze dropped in slow deliberation.

She glanced down and immediately discerned the source of his enrapt scrutiny. Her battle with the fire had left an ugly smudge on her lavender bodice. The forget-me-nots that had sweetly adorned her bosoms stared up at her sadly with filthy, accusing faces. Their disgraced state dealt her the final blow. She had spent a pretty penny for this dress to celebrate her debut as a reformed member of Society. What a waste. She couldn't let the girls see her like this. With a sigh, she pulled off her gloves and balled them up in her fist.

"I suppose it could have been worse," he said, examining the rest of the room.

Harriet did not see how, at least not from her perspective. "Let me make sure that there's a clean spot for you to sit," she said quietly. "The smoke tends to settle everywhere. I do hate coal."

"I should probably close the window." He grasped her hand, an act she was too flustered to protest, and lifted her from the hearth. "And I shall take that brandy now, if you don't mind."

She nodded, staring past him to the marble-topped sideboard. If the glasses were dusty, she'd have to wait again until he wasn't looking to give one a quick swipe with her sleeve. A drink would not help her dress, but it might put him in a better mood.

"Right. Brandy."

"A double measure, please."

She was only too eager to put a safe distance between them. From the corner of her eye, she watched him close the window. Odd how the mundane act suddenly absorbed her attention. How many times had she seen the footmen at the same task? Not once had she admired the pudgy butler helping to hang pictures on the wall, either.

But then, none of them claimed good shoulders and a lean torso that tapered into parts one presumed were equally strong and nicely proportioned. The duke's muslin shirt had gotten damp. So had his black hair. No doubt it was her fault for blowing soot all over him, but suddenly she thought he looked a little slovenly. Perhaps even decadent. Still, he was as fine-looking as any man ought to be without causing a riot in the streets.

She carried a brandy to him. "Is this enough?"

"For four or five sailors." He took a few sips from the goblet, then set it on a low folding table. "Are fires a usual occurrence in the academy?"

"Absolutely not. But then, neither are dukes," she added before she could stop herself.

His chiseled mouth curled at the corners. "One relates to the other in exactly what way?"

"Unpredictable elements of nature."

"In that case, it's fortunate you know your way around a shovel."

"I'm sorry," she said ruefully. "I've never greeted a duke before—not properly, I mean."

"I can tell." He sighed and let a moment elapse. "But we are human, you know."

Harriet's heart pounded in her throat. The sultry humor in his eyes suggested he was too human, indeed. She might have noticed if she hadn't been trying so hard to please him.

"Well?" he said, clearly expecting a response.

She swallowed. "Well, what?"

"I think you were supposed to make a reassuring remark to soothe my wounded feelings."

"Are your feelings wounded?" she asked in surprise. "An influential man like you? A man who has to hide from his hordes of admirers?"

He cleared his throat. "You see, that is exactly what I mean. No one has sympathy for a person of my position."

"Your grace must suffer greatly."

"You have no idea," he said wryly.

He subsided into a thoughtful silence. Then, slowly, he lifted his hand. Harriet should have known he was up to something. Soft as night, he traced his thumb across the smudge that was emblazoned on her breast. She didn't dare breathe. Demon. If she even flinched, he'd be touching improper territory.

"It is quite a mark," he mused. "I am not a laundress, but I'd venture a guess that the dress is ruined for good. I suppose you can't afford another. Ask my cousin Charlotte to have a new one billed to my account."

Quite a mark.

Not as indelible as his touch.

It was a good thing she had put down that shovel.

"I'm ruined," she whispered. "If I knew how to cry, I'd be gushing like a fountain, not that it would help. It's all ruined: the tea, my dress, my gloves—"

"If you're going to prattle and expect *my* sympathy, you'll have to speak so I can hear."

"This is all your fault," she said loudly, deciding that if he was even indirectly the cause of her dismissal, he should at least be named.

He put his hand to his neatly folded neckcloth. Which, upon closer inspection, Harriet realized was not meant to be a dirty shade of gray. "*You're* the one who brought me into this smoking Hades."

Funny, she'd have thought he would feel right at home. "Your grace is right, of course. It is all my fault: the fire, the smoke, the—"

"The fire was lit before we entered the room," he said matter-of-factly. "If anyone is to blame, it should be the idiot who stuffed the grate with newspaper."

Thunder. Lightning. Rain pummeling the roof. There were certain powers it was useless to resist.

Harriet took her soiled gloves and efficiently swept up the ashes that had fallen on the hearth. Everything else, disregarding her dress, looked in order. The duke had left the curtains parted to emit only a flattering glow into the room. The flocked chinoiserie wallpaper, the delicate armchairs, the Queen Anne clock, appeared to have survived the conflagration unscathed.

The duke reclined, his eyes half closed, on the red tufted couch. Except for the bitter tang of cinders in the air and a brand upon her breast, there was little evidence to raise suspicions when, a half minute later, Charlotte Boscastle escorted Lady Primrose Powlis, Lady Dalrymple, and the duke's young niece into the room.

Chapter Four

I fear thy kisses, gentle maiden,
Thou needest not fear mine;
My spirit is too deeply laden
Ever to borthen thine.

PERCY BYSSHE SHELLEY
To–. I Fear Thy Kisses

🙙 🙚

Griffin could barely remember the last time he'd felt like laughing. Certainly not in the fourteen months since his brother's death.

Nor during the eternal journey to London with his meddlesome aunt and his morbid young niece, Edlyn, whose guardianship he had inherited along with a dukedom he did not want. It was assumed that his cousin's academy would draw the girl out of her gloom and introduce her to a glittering world. He hoped for her sake that such a miracle would be wrought.

It was also assumed that he would take a wife. More than a miracle would be required to bring that momentous event to pass. Before Liam's death, Griffin had led a charmed life. He'd served his obligatory stint in the cavalry and returned home to the family castle with the full intention of doing absolutely nothing. Liam would inherit the dukedom, and a damned good thing, too.

Griff had no aspirations to either a peerage or the responsibility that went with it. His brother, however, relished the role, riding day for night across his lands, playing the dutiful lord to those who for centuries had depended upon the duke's largesse.

If a pretty lady crossed his path, Liam thought nothing of taking her to his bed. If a love child resulted from some forgotten affair, he would assume responsibility. What was another benefactor added to the list of a duke's retainers? Yet as the years passed, the family elders, composed primarily of aging aunts, closed in to curb his reckless ways.

A boy could pursue wicked pleasures for only so long. Did he intend to fulfill his duty as the Duke of Glenmorgan or not? If so, the time had come to leave sporting to his younger siblings and settle down.

He resisted.

His factors had made an unofficial offer of marriage on Liam's behalf to a young lady in London in the months that followed his father's death. Liam had met her during a family holiday in Italy. Her beauty was the stuff of legends. So was her fortune. And yet after he came home, he ignored the stream of letters from her family solicitors that first invited and then insisted he step forth to announce his intentions.

Griffin thought it was all a game. Liam was playing everyone like a pack of cards. Why should either of them settle down? Why should he believe the rumors whispered in the village that another woman had captured Liam's heart?

The answer arrived one early April evening when a castle servant discovered a little girl of seven years or so abandoned on the drawbridge. She had jet-black hair and eyes an unearthly shade of blue that in a certain light looked almost violet. All that could be coaxed from her was that her name was Edlyn and that her mother had left her here to live with her father, who was a duke. She knew, or refused to reveal, nothing else of her background.

Father and daughter loathed each other on sight. Edlyn grieved her mother with a vengeance that seemed unnatural in a young child. She threw fits and refused to eat. She threatened to jump off the turret. She bit her nursemaid's finger clear to the bone.

Her very existence eclipsed the lives of those who struggled to care for her. Her young aunt Ravenna and the two great-aunts who ruled the castle stopped reassuring themselves that she would outgrow her sorrows.

She ran away the day she turned thirteen and twice a year thereafter. She gave her best gowns to the gypsies and dressed herself in the black crepe of perpetual mourning. She grew her hair to her waist, only to cut it off above her ears one Christmas Day. She sat at the dinner table like a wicked sprite.

Her father forbade her to utter another word about the mother who had abandoned her.

And for reasons he could never fathom, Griffin became her champion. She never confided in him, and for that he was glad. But he was the one she ran to when she was upset, the one who hoisted her on his shoulders and let her swing from the wrought-iron chandelier while he ran around the hall three times, then shouted, "Drop!" And she did, safely in his arms.

It wasn't that he considered himself to be the family peacemaker. He merely seemed to be the only person in the castle who did not incur her wrath.

"I hate you. I hate you. I hate you," she was chanting with her usual malevolence for her father as he sauntered through the passage screen one morning. "I hate you so much that I would burn my bones in acid for a potion to make you die."

Griffin grabbed an apple from a bowl on the banqueting table. "I hate him, too," he said genially. "What has the knave done to upset our beautiful Edlyn today?"

Liam, slumped on a bench by a blazing fire, snorted in disgust. "Beautiful? Both of you belong in Bedlam."

Then, when she stormed off in her usual melodramatic fury, the armorial swords mounted above the fireplace dropped to the stone floor with a clatter that sent the three dozing hounds into a howling frenzy. Liam jumped out of his chair. Griffin fell against the table laughing like the lunatic his brother had just called him. It never occurred to him that Liam might not be immortal. No one in Castle Glenmorgan had died before his time. An unhappy girl's curse could not alter the course of history.

Liam knelt to the fallen swords. "If I didn't know better, I'd swear she did that on purpose."

"Perhaps she did," said Aunt Glynnis, studying the tiny spider that dangled from a gossamer thread above her pianoforte.

"She's definitely inherited the Welsh talent for strangeness," Aunt Primrose said in concern, the three hounds settling in her tiny shadow.

Liam looked up in vexation. "Is she going to behead me if I don't obey her nasty little demands?"

Griffin gave him an evil grin. "You'd better start wearing a helmet, or I'll be the duke, and everyone will be in trouble then."

"Take the dukedom," Liam said, touching one of the swords to Griffin's shoulder. "I dub thee the Most Wicked Duke Who Ever Was. Anyway, I'd rather ride horses in hell than stay in this moldering castle and have a girl who may or—well, damn her, anyway. The next time she runs off, I will not chase after her."

The two aunts drew a simultaneous gasp that frightened the spiderling up its thread into the blackened rafters. "Don't say things like that, Liam," Aunt Glynnis whispered. "That spider might weave your words into the devil's own web."

Griffin raised an eyebrow in mischief. "Then *I*

wish I could marry an Irish princess who would make me laugh every night—"

"Unfeeling fools," Aunt Primrose said from her chair. "Don't you realize that the girl wants her mother more than anyone in the world, which is hardly a surprise considering that her father is a rude young rakehell who cannot even behave when his elders are in the room?"

Griffin and Liam straightened, bowing this way and that at the aunts, at the dogs, at each other, until Aunt Glynnis picked up a pair of apples and stuck one apiece into their grinning mouths.

In the months following Edlyn's outburst, Liam reluctantly made plans to travel to England to court the woman brave enough to be his wife. He and Edlyn still clashed whenever they spent more than a few minutes together. Griffin, their two aunts, and their twin siblings, Ravenna and Rhys, were still forced to intervene more times than the allied powers completing the peace treaty.

Was there a woman in London, in the whole of England, strong enough to bridge the family divide?

Edlyn withdrew until she became a shadow. Everyone wondered why she seemed agreeable to accompanying Liam to London. Could she be growing up at last? She didn't object when Aunt Primrose explained that she would make friends her age at school and no longer be allowed to wander about with the gypsies who lived nearby. A week before the journey, she had already packed her own bag and talked the guards into promising to feed the crows that nested on the parapets.

Griffin challenged his older brother to one last ride through the woods and over the river wall. Liam never refused a dare. Griffin had never lost a race.

Not a day had passed since that Griffin didn't picture Liam standing in the stirrups with his wind-blown hair bristled up like a hedgehog. "Come on!"

Griff guided his horse down the incline. "I'll go first."

"No, you won't. You challenged."

They stared across the river, absorbing the beauty of Glenmorgan, young pagans who preferred wild-ness over London's pleasures, warriors at heart.

Griff lifted his face to the sky. The light was swiftly fading. The mystical irradiance that bathed the battered castle stones would soon disappear. Storm air drifted in the breeze.

"Let's do it tomorrow," he shouted to Liam.

"Giving up already? I'll jump," Liam said, wheel-ing. A dying ray of light caught his smile and out-lined his agile figure as he set in his spurs.

A crow flew toward the castle turret. Griffin felt the drum of his brother's hoofbeats through his bones. Invincible.

His brother's mare had never before balked at a jump or thrown a rider. Not that anything could hurt Liam. The great vital lump that landed in the water had steel woven into his body and soul.

"Duke! If you want to cede the race right now, I won't tell anyone what a bloody fool you've made of yourself." Griff waited, then dismounted. He knew as he slogged through the water that at any moment his brother would tackle him by the knees and half-drown him to prove he could. This day would not be different than countless others.

"Liam. Get up, idiot."

The head groom, who'd been following at a distance, splashed up beside him in his thick riding boots. "Move aside, my lord."

The mare scrambled up the embankment. Griffin grabbed his brother's riding coat at the shoulder, turning him onto his back. "Please," he whispered.

The groom pulled off his jacket. "His neck is broken. It was an accident. Let me lift him onto the rocks."

Griffin sank to his knees. "Did you see it?"

Their eyes met.

"Aye," the groom said. "And so I shall swear."

He hadn't seen. No one but Griff had witnessed what happened. It was inevitable that some of the villagers in Glenmorgan would ask themselves if he'd done more than entice his brother into taking that fatal jump.

Wasn't that enough?

He would be the one who had to tell Edlyn and the rest of the family. She had lost her mother, and now he was responsible for her father's death.

After the funeral and a suitable period of mourning, they would travel to London together—he, the seventh Duke of Glenmorgan, to find a wife, and Edlyn, to learn the rules she would break for the rest of her life.

Chapter Five

It was a strong effort of the spirit of good
but it was ineffectual. Destiny was too
potent, and her immutable laws had decreed
my utter and terrible destruction.

MARY SHELLEY
Frankenstein

❦ ❧

The red salon filled in moments. Ladies buzzed
about, footmen swarmed, and a sharp-eyed scul-
lion at the hearth swept up the few ashes that Harriet had missed. Griffin would never have recognized
Charlotte Boscastle, as they had both been in the
cradle at the time of their only acquaintance. She
stood almost as tall as he, her blond hair drawn off
a delicate oval face that could have graced a
cameo. Miss Gardner was easily the most arresting
person in the room, with her tightly knotted red
hair, piquant features, and marked lavender dress.
Her disheveled charm drew his eye so often he
feared he would be caught.

She did catch him once as he looked up from the
fireplace.

Her brows rose. Calmly, she turned to the tea
table, concentrating on the cups as if one of them
contained a gold sovereign. His gaze slid down her
creamy décolletage to the damning brand above

her bosom. Not only did it appear that the smudge had darkened, but the ruffled hem of her ruined dress had not escaped the soot, either.

He gazed down into his goblet at his reflection. He'd made another fearsome first impression, and he hadn't even tried. It seemed to get easier every time.

"Are you looking in the River Styx?" a throaty voice asked at his elbow.

He glanced around in hesitation at his niece, who never missed the chance to spread her personal gloom around.

As was so often the case, it was his aunt, Lady Primrose Powlis, who quickly intervened before anything worse could erupt.

"Do I smell smoke? I hope something hasn't gotten caught in the chimney. You weren't puffing on one of those vile cheroots again, Griff?"

He glanced good-naturedly at his aunt. She was a small woman, whose spirit increased as her physical self diminished every year. Her booming voice could chill his blood. Her sweet wrinkled face was a beloved comfort. The rain had fortunately destroyed her atrocious hat. Her silver-white hair was flattened beneath an intricate netting of tiny ivory pearls, showing a bald spot here and there.

Annoying, intrusive, she manipulated her family without a thought, making up stories and heart-rending fibs as served her purpose. And it was because her purpose nearly always derived from a genuine concern for those she connived that Griffin adored her.

He rarely admitted this to her, however. She took enough advantage of him as it was.

She was also uncannily observant. He was not at all surprised when in her next breath she accused him of setting Miss Gardner on fire with an imaginary cigar.

"Did my nephew drop ashes on your dress, Miss Gardner?" she asked in a horrified voice, leaning from her chair for a closer look.

Griffin smiled. The River Styx might need to be refilled tonight.

"It was my fault," Harriet said quickly. "I fanned some papers I hadn't noticed in the grate. His grace was good enough to air out the room."

Lady Powlis settled back in her chair. "Hmmph."

"But everything is fine now," Griffin added, suddenly afraid it was anything but. Thanks to Aunt Primrose's meddling, his cousin Charlotte now appeared to be on the scent.

She had excused herself from chatting with Lady Dalrymple and was making a quiet assessment of Harriet's crumpled gloves, her dress—and heaven only knew how Charlotte put two and two together, but all of a sudden she was looking right at Griffin's cravat.

He coughed into his fist. "I hope no one will take offense if I slip away for the rest of the day? There are matters of my aunt's comfort that I have promised to attend on Bedford Square."

Charlotte turned to him. "Of course. No one has

stayed in the town house for years. I should have thought to offer Odgers."

He lowered his hand. "I would appreciate a few hours alone, to be quite honest." As only a man who had been trapped in a carriage with Aunt Primrose and Edlyn could understand. He'd rather have walked the distance to London, in fact, than have listened to his aunt prattle on about his future wife, about when they would have Edlyn's debut, and about how she prayed Edlyn wasn't going to make pets out of the pigeons in London as she had the crows in the castle turret. Yet while Griffin looked forward to a private evening, he would not have minded spending another hour or so with the young instructress who had unwittingly entertained him.

"Edlyn will do well here," Charlotte assured him as they walked to the door.

"I hope so. She is not . . . easy."

She gave him a knowing smile. "If you doubt our success, you have only to look at Miss Gardner for proof."

"Proof. Of?"

"The academy's ability to resurrect the sensibilities of one who might otherwise be considered dead by Society."

Griffin didn't know what to say. Harriet Gardner seemed anything but dead to him. She had certainly enlivened his arrival.

Charlotte bit her lip. "When you look at Miss Gardner, what is it that you see?"

He couldn't very well answer, *A winsome face with wicked hazel eyes,* or *A smudged dress.* So he said, as gamely as he could manage, "A perfectly . . . perfectly . . . well, a gentlewoman." Which was a safe reply that shouldn't earn him or Miss Gardner a scolding.

"Did she give you a spot of trouble at first?" Charlotte asked shrewdly.

He grinned.

"If she did, I probably deserved it."

Harriet unstrapped the single traveling trunk sitting up against the bedchamber window. It didn't occur to her that Edlyn had dragged it there herself until a few moments later.

"Shall we unpack and have your clothes pressed?" she asked.

Edlyn shrugged and wandered like a wraith to the window. The girl's drab gray frock hung on her thin frame like a shroud. Thoroughly versed in the art of furtive escape, Harriet realized that Edlyn was assessing how dangerous it would be to drop to the garden. "You'd shatter your kneecaps and probably your back. It's impossible since they cut down the old plane tree."

"How do you know?" Edlyn asked, kneeling on the trunk.

Harriet hesitated. "One or two of the girls tried to see how far they could go without being caught."

Edlyn glanced at her. "How far *did* they get?"

"Don't you dare say I told you, but Miss Butterfield was brought home before she got past the gardeners. Miss Ruston landed in the philodendrons just below. They've taken a while to grow back."

"And you?"

Harriet smiled. "I'm growing nicely, thank you."

Edlyn slid backward on her knees, off the trunk. "I don't care if it's ever unpacked." She curled her fingers over the windowsill. "Are there always that many people in the street on a rainy day?"

"That's nothing." Harriet came up behind her. "London doesn't come to life until after midnight in some places."

"What does one do during the evenings here?"

"Those would be for sitting by the fire, practicing the spinet, or reading."

"I hate it in this house already."

"That's your right, I suppose." Harriet rubbed the heel of her hand across the glass. "Still, you don't want to be walking about London unescorted, if that's what you're thinking."

"Would you like to escort me? I shall pay you." Edlyn ventured a smile. Insincere as it was, Harriet decided that the girl would be beautiful if she didn't go to so much trouble to make herself look like a corpse. She had to spend a fortune on rice powder, bleaching cream, and beetroot lip salve.

"You do know London?" Edlyn prompted.

Better than the landscape of her left ear. Harriet knew London from the vice-ridden alleys of the East End, where she'd been born, although no one had ever produced a certificate of birth to prove she existed at all. She knew the riverside docks where her father had worked when capable of rousing his soused arse into action. She knew the dirty warrens, the church bells, and the House of Corrections, at whose doors she'd waited in the rain for her half brothers to be released.

She'd gotten to know the West End, too, the elite squares and mansions of Mayfair where her father had finished her unwholesome education by introducing her to larceny.

"I know the city well enough to entertain you," she said evasively. "As a student here, you'll participate in many adventurous outings. There are circulating libraries, operas, and—"

Edlyn twirled a black curl around her half-bitten fingernail in an attitude of bored disinterest. "Will we see any duels?"

"I certainly hope not. Trust me, there's nothing exciting about seeing a man bleed—you know, breaking the law. But we'll go on rides in the park, attend dances, and shop on Bond Street. And there are champagne breakfasts that don't even begin until three, and supper parties—"

"What about Vauxhall Gardens?"

"A duke's daughter would never set foot in a disreputable place like that."

"I'm not even sure that I am his daughter."

"A duke's niece, then," Harriet amended, deciding it was high time to slip downstairs for an emergency chat with Charlotte. "I'll bring you up some tea and cake while you rest."

"Lots of cake."

"Very well."

"Miss Gardner?"

A tinge of foreboding inched down Harriet's spine. "Yes?"

"Leave my tray outside the door. I don't want to talk to you again tonight."

Chapter Six

I never was attached to that great sect,
Whose doctrine is, that each one should select
Out of the crowd a mistress or a friend.

PERCY BYSSHE SHELLEY
Epipsychidion

❧ ❧

When a long-lost family member returned to the infamous Boscastle flock, it was cause for his brethren to rejoice. When that black sheep happened to be a duke, it was an excuse for Grayson Boscastle, the fifth Marquess of Sedgecroft and anointed leader of the fold, to host as many parties in the prodigal's honor as could be crammed into a season. He had already been inundated with requests for an invite to meet this new sensation.

Only two days after the young Duke of Glenmorgan's arrival in London, Grayson feted him at a ball in the Park Lane mansion that had been best described as a small-scale palace. After all, it was not every day that one could display a peer.

As a chosen favorite, Harriet had been invited inside this spacious house on numerous occasions. She wished she could forget her infamous first visit, however.

By some miracle she had managed to elude the

senior footman's coterie of guards and infiltrate
Lady Jane's private closet. The moment she'd
stepped into the room, she completely forgot what
she had come for. She felt like a princess getting
ready for her first ball and not a thief whose half
brothers had sent her to do their dirty work.

The closet had seemed bigger than the crumbling
pile she shared with seven other people. The huge
gilded mirrors that hung on the walls reflected her
astonished face and shabby appearance. Piles of
painted fans covered a blue silk chaise. She had
never seen so many shoes strewn about in her life.

The marchioness must have spent the entire day
selecting the perfect costume for the gala. Harriet
went to pick up a gold hairpin from the floor. The
next thing she knew, she'd slipped one foot into a
diamond-encrusted shoe and the other into a dancing pump with a pearl-inlaid heel that made her
ankle look devilishly attractive. Then she spied a
collection of tapestry shoes in an adjoining room.

"Cor," she'd exclaimed, walking unevenly toward
the door, "so this is where the cobbler's elves work
all night."

"Wrong," said the snootiest voice that to this day
she had ever heard. A tall footman dressed like an
enchanted frog plucked a shoe from her fingers.
"This is where you shall remain until the police remove your person to the station."

She snorted. "I don't 'ave a person. I work alone."

He had leaned down, his mouth pinched like a
clam. "You are going—"

The chatter of female voices interrupted whatever dire threat he'd been about to make. "Heavens above!" he muttered, his hands lifting as if he were about to tear off his wig. "The marchioness is here! And—" He made a menacing noise in his throat and snatched the gold hairpin from Harriet's hair.

It was at that moment that his mistress, the Marchioness of Sedgecroft, and her sister-in-law, Emma Boscastle, the widowed Viscountess Lyons, had walked through the adjoining door of the closet. Neither of them screamed, although Lady Lyons blinked when she noticed the cashmere shawl Harriet had stuffed halfway up her sleeve.

"Who is this young woman, Weed?" the marchioness asked, eyeing the mismated slippers on Harriet's feet in amusement. "One of the new scullery maids? Remember that we forgive the curiosity of the first week."

"She's a thief, madam."

"Oh," the marchioness said, "I see."

"I shall have her removed immediately from the premises," Weed vowed, lowering his hand to reach for Harriet.

"Wait," Lady Lyons had said, in a powerful voice that halted the footman's hand. "She cannot be observed by anyone at the party. For one thing, her hair has not seen a brush in at least a week. For another"—she fanned the air—"she smells so strongly that my eyes water."

The marchioness took a delicate sniff. "That's

the new perfume Grayson bought me for my birthday."

Harriet gave her a frank look. "Lovely, ain't it?"

More than two years had passed since that ignominious day. Since then, fortunately, Harriet had never been caught in anyone else's closet. Although Lady Jane teased her from time to time about her crime, she did so with a fond twinkle in her eye. She also paid Harriet the high compliment of seeking her confidence as concerning family secrets.

Within a half hour of her arrival tonight, Lady Jane had taken Harriet aside to whisper, "What is your opinion of the duke and his relations?"

Harriet admired Lady Jane. She was not merely pretty, generous, and kind, she was also a devious schemer who had sabotaged her own wedding, only to fall in love with her scoundrel of a marquess. "Lady Powlis is a double-edged sword," Harriet whispered after a moment's reflection. "The duke's a moody one, and I'd be afraid to guess what Lady Edlyn's got locked up in her turret."

"Darling," Jane said, drawing Harriet deeper into the shaded alcove. "What do you mean?"

"She hasn't been at the academy long enough to get into trouble, I swear. But every time I've gone to her room she's been sitting at her window as if she's waiting, for whom or what I've no idea."

Jane's green eyes darkened in worry. "Poor lambkin. Could she have met a young wolf so quickly?"

"I wouldn't think so. I've got a sense for that sort of thing."

"Perhaps she is still grieving her father," Jane said quietly. "Is she close to the duke and his aunt, or are they estranged, as the gossips say?"

Harriet peered out into the vestibule. "Lady Powlis couldn't love her more. But as for what Miss Edlyn and the duke feel for each other, well, your opinion would be better than mine, madam."

Jane patted her on the arm. "I never fail to think of you whenever I buy a new pair of tapestry shoes. Now, now. Don't blush. We all have our skeletons in the dressing closet." She stepped out into the vestibule, gasping in pleasure as she spotted the tall masculine figure who stood in front of an enormous queue of guests. "Is *that* Griffin?"

Harriet stood on tiptoe to peek over Jane's elaborate headdress. Somewhere between the thicket of ostrich feathers, she made out a bladed nose that belonged to a lean man in a black evening suit. Oh, dear. The duke appeared to have been caught in a receiving line and looked none too happy about it. Perhaps he had not been exaggerating when he'd complained that he had hordes of admirers.

"My goodness," Jane whispered. "How handsome he is! And you never said a word. I always wondered what an infusion of Welsh blood would do to the line. I imagine the castle drawbridge had to be closed every night to keep him safe from the village girls."

Harriet dredged up a pleasant smile. Never mind

the village girls. The marchioness must have given every eligible debutante in London an engraved invite to meet the duke tonight.

Jane's delicate face grew pensive. "I should have known. Why would I think the family could escape even one season without notoriety? My, my. We do have our hands full, don't we, Harriet?"

"The Duke of Glenmorgan has—"

He had not even been properly announced by the majordomo before a swell of guests, ladies primarily, surged forth from the line to surround him. He'd lost sight of his aunt and Edlyn. He suspected that they were watching from the balcony above, where only family or the most favored guests were taken for a private introduction. He felt like a human sacrifice being fed to a flock of harpies in evening gowns.

He looked about for someone to rescue him. The only person he recognized in the crush was the flame-haired Miss Gardner, who sent him a wicked smile and promptly disappeared.

"Condolences on your brother's untimely and cruel demise, your grace."

"Congratulations on your calm grasp of duty."

"Your grace, it is a privilege."

"What a tragedy, your grace. All of London wept."

"My daughter Anne-Marie has composed a poem in honor of your loss. If your grace could spare an afternoon this week to have it privately heard . . ."

Condolences. Congratulations. An arena of London's weepy and conniving mamas sharpening their claws and quills with a ravenous appetite that gave him heart palpitations.

He knew he had promised his family that at some unspecified time in the future he would carry on the line. But he also knew he wasn't about to marry any of the ambitious debutantes who were eyeing him like a supper course. In fact, it was all he could do not to shout something unforgivably rude to scare the lot of them away. And when one of them suddenly had the unmitigated gall to sneak up behind him to grab the tails of his coat, and another to slap her hand upon his shoulder like a sledgehammer, he ground his teeth and—

"Isn't he pretty?" a hideous voice cooed as its owner tugged again on his evening coat.

"He's the belle of the ball."

"Ooh. Feel his shoulders. How strong he is."

"I want the first dance."

He might have known by the deep laughter accompanying this assault that he was being set up by his cousins. He swung around, expelling a sigh of relief. "I don't want to dance, as flattered as I am by your attention."

"Not even to save yourself?" the tallest of the three men surrounding him asked.

Lords Heath, Drake, and Devon. He would have recognized the three black-haired, blue-eyed demons as his cousins even if they weren't grinning with the wicked intentions that distinguished a Boscastle male from other gentlemen. Unfashionably faithful to their wives, they still dabbled in mischief every now and then. Lord Heath, it was said, had a hand in something of an undisclosed nature for the Home Office. Their propensity for brewing scandals was as legendary in London as was their loyalty to the clan.

"Which one of you wants to dance with me first?"

Drake, dark and cynical at heart, nudged his older brother in the ribs. "Heath has always been lighter on his feet. And he's a perfect gentleman."

Devon, devil-may-care and friendly, said, "He's more graceful, too. And he can whisper Egyptian endearments in your ear."

"But Drake is more rugged," Heath protested. "A man's man. I know I'd feel safe prowling an alley with him at my side. Just don't let him lure you out onto the terrace."

"I have a brilliant suggestion." Devon threw his arm over Griffin's shoulders. "We could form our own set, and share you."

"That seems a rather drastic way to take myself off the market," Griffin said with a faint grimace.

Heath lifted his brow. "Anyone in particular on your list you're hoping to avoid? Or capture?"

"I've only been in London a few days."

"That long?" Drake gave him a skeptical grin.

"And you haven't found a woman to pursue yet? This might call for a family cabal."

Odd. Griffin thought suddenly of Harriet Gardner. She was the first woman he'd met in London. And even though he had been introduced to quite a few others since, she was the only one who had come close to setting him on fire. He smiled inwardly. He had wondered quite a few times since what would have happened if they'd been alone a little while longer.

"My wife mentioned something in the papers about Lady Constance Chatterton," said Devon, who was not the most discreet member of the family. "Fact or fiction?"

Griffin frowned. That was a woman he hadn't thought about at all. "We made a brief acquaintance in Venice when our families were visiting."

"Ah." Heath, who *was* discreet, nodded. "And this was the start of what the papers are calling the Season's most heart-stirring romance?"

"I don't think I would go that far," Griffin said quickly. "Our gondolas passed in the same canal. We looked at each other. Or perhaps I looked at her. I believe she had her eye on Liam. I was only the duke's brother then. Liam may have seen her afterward. I wasn't interested in her enough to ask."

There was a silence. He was relieved they made no attempt to offer maudlin sympathy for Liam's death. But then, they had lost a brother, too, in a vicious ambush, and Brandon Boscastle's body had never even been recovered.

Devon withdrew his arm from Griffin's shoulder as the band assembled on the dais to play. "I don't mean to break your heart, but we're going to have to find another time to dance. I've a wife and little daughter waiting for me at home. Come and meet them, won't you, before the ton takes over your life?"

Griff laughed. "Believe me, I'd rather stand on a scaffold than stand out in Society."

Drake slapped him on the back. "Too late. You're a duke. Society has already claimed you as its next victim. Do call on us if you need help. We have all of us been in your place before."

Chapter Seven

I quitted my seat, and walked on,
although the darkness and storm increased every minute,
and thunder burst with a terrific crash over my head.

MARY SHELLEY
Frankenstein

❧ ❧

Harriet drank her lemonade, perfectly content with her position between Lady Powlis and the assembly of wallflowers and chaperones observing the guests who gathered at the edge of the ballroom floor. A ruddy-cheeked young gentleman, who had been waiting for a quiet moment to approach, had just asked Edlyn to dance.

The girl looked stunned at the offer, glancing at Lady Powlis for advice. "What should I do?" she whispered behind her fan.

"Dance with him," her aunt replied, nodding encouragingly at the gentleman.

"But I don't want to. I'm in mourning."

Lady Powlis released a long-suffering sigh. The official mourning period had long since passed. "Then refuse him nicely."

"Fine," Edlyn muttered with a mutinous look. "I shall dance with him."

Harriet took another long sip of lemonade.

Lady Powlis frowned, tapping her closed fan on her knee. "Stop slurping, Miss Gardner."

"Pardon me, madam."

"No, pardon me," the older woman said.

"For what?"

"For snapping at you."

"That's all right, Lady Powlis. I understand."

Lady Powlis stopped tapping her fan and searched Harriet's face. "Do you, indeed?"

"I might," Harriet said evasively, and hoped she wouldn't be asked to explain what she understood. Or thought she did. She sensed that the old lady deeply loved both the duke and Miss Edlyn, and it made Harriet a little sad to see all of them so miserable. Of course, it would be unseemly to admit any of this. So, as to seem agreeable, she settled for a banal smile and said, "Would your ladyship like another glass of lemonade?"

"I've had three already," her ladyship replied illhumoredly.

"If we're counting, you've had four," Harriet said before she could stop herself.

That might have been the end of her right then and there. Lady Powlis could have insisted the academy dismiss Harriet for impertinence, had the duke not sauntered up to her chair. Her ladyship brightened, and Harriet breathed a sigh of relief.

Saved. By the rake. At least, if what the gossips like Miss Peppertree said was true. He had not revealed himself as such in the short time Harriet had known him. The entire collection of wilted-looking wallflowers cheered up as he honored them with an elegant bow. As he straightened, his eyes lingered on Harriet.

Elegant beast, she thought in grudging pleasure. All the ladies around her were sighing, smiling, or murmuring vapid remarks, which he gallantly acknowledged with a few evasive nods. There was an uninhibited honesty about females who for various reasons had abandoned all hope of snaring a catch. Having discarded their illusions, they could appreciate a stunning man for what he was.

The duke, however, seemed a little at a loss over the fuss afforded him. Suddenly the thought occurred to Harriet—no, it wasn't possible. He couldn't be shy. He knew the value of his masculine appeal. And he certainly had not been shy with her the day they met.

Still, his haunting beauty, his tragic past, the identity of the woman he would marry, would be discussed by this audience for many weeks to come. Harriet realized that her own status had suddenly risen simply because she could claim his acquaintance. And even though she doubted he would ever have reason to confide in her, she felt an obligation to protect his secrets, whatever they were, from the world.

The Boscastles had favored her. Heaven knew she might even learn to care for the snippy old tartar sitting beside her.

And then, right before Harriet could go floating away on a cloud of sentiment, Lady Powlis said to the duke, "You look elegant in black, dear. Be a good boy and dance with Miss Gardner here."

Harriet willed herself not to react. If she had obeyed impulse, she might have emptied her lemonade glass on her ladyship's head for making such a preposterous suggestion.

The duke's silence only intensified her annoyance. Another woman might have been mortified. Having shed her pretensions early in life, Harriet wondered why she felt the slightest humiliation. Lady Powlis, she decided, was not a woman to be pitied. She was a double-faced harridan who bedeviled others to alleviate her boredom. The duke, one assumed, had developed tactics to elude his aunt's traps. Still, he was taking his sweet time to employ one if he had.

"Did you hear me?" Lady Powlis asked in a voice that rang across the room like a cathedral bell.

Harriet couldn't bear it. She said, "I wouldn't dream of leaving you by yourself, Lady Powlis."

The duke gave his aunt a strained smile. "And why," he asked evenly, "should I torture this innocent young lady by dragging her into that foray? What crime has she committed that I should punish her with my abominable clumsiness?"

Harriet's lips curved in acknowledgment of such a gracious rejection. One could learn more from an uncaring adversary than from a devoted friend. Another young woman might have taken his refusal as a sign of modest character. The duke didn't want to dance with her. And why should he? He could have his pick of anyone in the room.

"Do as I say, Griffin," his aunt said again.

He leaned down to address her in a stern but respectful voice. "I came here tonight to please you and the rest of the family. Have you ever known me to participate in a public affair of my own volition?"

"You're known well enough for participating in a few private ones," Lady Powlis replied tartly.

Harriet finished off her lemonade. She enjoyed a lively quarrel as well as the next girl. In fact, she was debating which of the pair would come out the winner when the duke looked at her unexpectedly and said, "Dance with me, or we shall never hear the end of it."

Almost immediately, a footman appeared and whisked her empty glass away. The duke reached down for her hand. She stood, vaguely aware that Lady Powlis had risen beside her. For a moment she wondered whether the three of them were going to dance together. She faltered. What the dickens was that dance called, anyway? Harriet couldn't be expected to recall every minute detail of what she had been taught.

"I don't waltz," she said faintly.

Lady Powlis subjected her to an irate stare. "It is a Scotch reel, my dear." She nudged Harriet in the ankle with her cane. "And it will be over before I talk sense into the pair of you."

The duke took Harriet's arm, almost protectively.

"It is you, Aunt Primrose, who appears to have taken leave of your senses."

"Don't you understand?" she asked in a low, worried voice. "Edlyn has disappeared from the dance floor, and her partner has just walked off by himself."

"Well, why the devil didn't you say so?" the duke asked.

"And let everyone in London know?" she whispered.

Harriet glanced around. Now she understood. There wasn't a lady in sight whose ears had not pricked up like Puck's to eavesdrop on the conversation. "But I just saw her dancing right by the door to the supper room," she said, straining to pick out Edlyn's gray silk dress.

Griffin's height gave him the advantage of looking down upon the assembly, whereas Harriet and Lady Powlis could barely see above the shoulders of the other guests. "She isn't by the door now," he said grimly.

"She might have run off again," Lady Powlis said, gripping Harriet's free hand. And then Harriet started to feel sorry for her all over again.

The duke gently pulled her toward him. Harriet's nape tingled in pleasant warning. Submit? Disobey? Did she have a choice? Would she have denied herself this experience even if she could? His eyes smoldered with concern, if not with a justifiable anger. She wouldn't want to be in Edlyn's slippers when he found her.

Where had she gone, anyway? If something had upset her, she should have at least told the old lady. Her misbehavior as a student at the academy made Harriet appear negligent in a duty not entirely hers. Still, she felt a twinge of compassion for the girl. Edlyn had buried her father and gained the arrogant duke as her guardian. No wonder she acted unwisely. She'd lost her way in life.

Therefore, Harriet decided, she would sacrifice what small dignity was hers and dance with the duke. After all, she had acted unwisely often enough in the past, and the Boscastle family had guided her onto a better path.

At least, this was what she believed until the moment Griffin swept her into his arms and she lost her way all over again.

The moment he took her by the hand, Griffin knew he ought to have run for his life instead. The mistrustful look on her face suggested she felt the same way. If he followed the instincts that she had awakened in him, one of them—and he wasn't sure whom—could very well end up ruined.

He placed his hand around Harriet's waist to guide her between the vigorous figures swirling in every direction. She resisted, and rightly so. She wouldn't have let herself be caught within a mile of him had she guessed how his body was reacting to being close to her again.

He inclined his head to hers. "I apologize for making you dance with me."

"Is that what we're doing?" she asked as they assumed their positions among the other dancers, neither of them in step. Another couple darted through the space between them. The duke frowned at this apparent breach of etiquette. Was he expected to emulate the intricate footwork of the other male dancers? He could barely hear himself breathe above the din. Worse, he practically required a horn to speak to his partner.

"No wonder my niece disappeared from the dance floor," he said in a loud, disgruntled voice.

Harriet shook her head to indicate that she couldn't hear him. He reached for her hand again and missed. He did, however, manage a few half-hearted hops to bring them closer together. Some overenthusiastic oaf bumped into Griffin's back. He turned to address this insult, thwarted by the sound of Harriet's uninhibited laughter. Suddenly he was laughing, too, moving toward her with a determination that impeded the progress of the dance.

Her hazel eyes shone with delightful mischief. "I don't see her anywhere. Do you?"

"Do I what?"

"Your niece. I don't see her."

"Neither do I."

He knew he should insist she return to his aunt. He could damned well find Edlyn by himself. But he hadn't felt this . . . alive, entertained, attracted . . . well, perhaps he had *never* felt like this before. He found it oddly comforting that she seemed to recognize him for what he truly was. Why that made her so appealing, he couldn't explain.

"I owe you another apology, by the way," he said.

"What did you say?"

"I said—"

He wove her in and out of the formation with haphazard grace. The other dancers, at first offended by his presumptuous behavior, gradually appeared to realize that they had the scandalous Duke of Glenmorgan in their midst and attempted to follow his impromptu steps.

Harriet nudged him down the line. "I think you'd better sit this one out, your grace, before you cause an accident. What did you want to apologize for?"

"I was rude to you the day I arrived at the academy."

The lively notes of the violin quartet rose dramatically as if to underscore his admission. The dance ended before Harriet could reply. He noticed the other guests drawing back to watch them. He was tempted to sit down in the middle of the floor to see how they would react to a ducal temper tantrum. Fortunately, Harriet turned toward the opened doors of the crowded candlelit supper room before he could act upon this impulse. His glance moved past the guests standing at the buffet table. A row of ladies and older gentlemen sat against the far wall, chatting and nibbling away. A raven-haired girl in a gray silk dress occupied a corner chair. She appeared to be listening attentively to a gentlewoman who stood with her back to the ballroom. Her dance partner was nowhere to be seen.

He felt a flash of guilty relief.

"There sits my sullen niece in the supper room, with nary a rake in sight."

"Well, there's certainly one in my line of view," Harriet said frankly. "And now that the reel is over and we are standing alone on the dance floor, would you mind if I went to check on Miss Edlyn for myself?"

"Yes. In fact, I would."

"I'm sorry," she said slowly. "I don't think I understand."

That made two of them. He searched his mind for a plausible explanation. "You'll never plow through the crowd at the buffet table without my help."

She glanced around him. "That's what you—"

He claimed her hand before she could finish and pushed a path rather imperiously through the throng of astonished guests, leaving her with little choice but to follow. He'd have the devil's time finding another reason to enjoy her company. After all, a man could rely on his aunt to provide excuses only to a certain point.

"There are side passages in this supper room," she said breathlessly.

"How do you know?" he asked without turning around.

There were some secrets that a woman took to the grave. If discretion were the better part of valor, Harriet decided that she would not satisfy him with an answer. In fact, for a man she had begun to think of as shy, he was causing a scandal with his ungracious entrance into the supper room, shouldering aside bewildered guests and hauling about an academy's instructress in the bargain. She glanced up into the astonished stare of the usually unflappable senior footman to the marquess, Weed. His shrewd gaze cut sharply to the duke. Without blinking an eye, he snapped his fingers, and three other footmen appeared as if they existed for no other purpose than to await the duke's every desire.

Not that the duke needed anyone's help to command an antechamber. He had the attention of the entire assembly. Even the small glasses of syllabub trembled as he strode past the table.

Upon recognizing his ducal personage, the guests who had gathered in the room parted to allow his progress. A few called his name in the hope of being acknowledged. Several of them stared enviously at Harriet for having captured his attention. She would have stared back, except she was more intent on keeping her eye on Miss Edlyn in the corner. The girl seemed to be watching a matronly woman in a green muslin gown escape into one of the private corridors, which Weed and the other footmen would be guarding had they not been chasing the duke around the room.

The duke sighed. "All is well. Neither of us shall be scolded by my aunt. By the way, she goes into a panic at least once a week. It's nothing you should take personally."

Harriet frowned as Miss Edlyn rose suddenly from her chair, ducking away from the guests who clamored to coax a look from her. The girl had apparently never bothered to put her Boscastle charms to the test. Her young uncle had probably been exercising his since the day he was born.

"You may let go of my hand now, your grace," she said, when it became clear he would not do so by himself.

He turned, a thin smile playing on his lips. "But I have a reputation to uphold."

She shook her head at him in reproach. "Mine will not be helped if I'm reported to be remiss in my duties or to be so smitten by—"

Oh. Hung by her tongue again.

"By?" he inquired, widening his heavily lashed eyes as if he didn't have a clue.

"I shall be tarnished," she explained in an undertone. "You will shine like a black diamond."

He paused briefly as Edlyn walked past him without a word. "It isn't fair, is it?"

Harriet sighed. "Not at all. But there's nothing to be done for it." She lowered her voice. "Please, your grace. People are staring. We must separate before they draw certain undesirable conclusions."

He glanced around in resentment. "What are they waiting for, anyway?"

She bit her lip, her gaze following Edlyn's progress back into the ballroom. "An introduction to you."

"All of them?"

She smiled. "So it appears."

"Where does that side passage lead to?" he asked her suddenly.

She laughed, pulling her hand from his possessive grasp. "If you want to get in trouble, I shall not be the one held responsible."

"I saved you from the inferno, remember?"

"I remember," Harriet said, as if that were an experience she would ever forget. She backed away before he could stop her. "Now, if it's all the same to you, I believe I have to save myself."

Chapter Eight

Lost Angel of a ruin'd Paradise!
She knew not 'twas her own; as with no stain
She faded, like a cloud which had outwept its rain.

PERCY BYSSHE SHELLEY
Adonais

❧ ❧

Edlyn was sitting at the window again when Harriet entered the room with a bedtime offering of hot chocolate and warm currant buns. She set down her tray on the circular rosewood table. The girl had at least traded her dreary gray dress for an embroidered white nightrail, but somehow the change only made her seem thinner and more ethereal.

"I love hot chocolate on a rainy night," Harriet said cheerfully, if only as an antidote against the somber atmosphere in the room. "Which, living in London, means I drink it all the time."

Edlyn sat in utter silence.

"And Cook makes the most scrumptious currant buns you've ever tasted. I ate five in a row when I first came to the academy. I almost blew up like a balloon. It's embarrassing to think of it."

Nothing. She might have been talking to the bedpost. Charlotte had urged her to persist. "You aren't unwell, are you?" she asked. "Perhaps we should—" She broke off. Harriet had never possessed much patience. "What *are* you looking for from that window? Whatever it is can't be more enticing than Cook's buns."

"You talk too much," Edlyn said unexpectedly.

"That wouldn't be because I have to talk for two, would it?"

She waited. Then, more curious than offended, she went to the other end of the window and peered down into the street. It was empty. Edlyn turned her head and subjected her to a wrathful scowl. Having received and given worse in her tender years, Harriet disregarded this affront. She thought she heard the echo of hoofbeats from the corner. She might even have perceived the rear end of a hackney coach. But there was nothing unusual about that. It was almost as if the girl could see ghosts. Harriet shivered pleasantly at the thought.

"Have some hot chocolate," she insisted, returning to the table. "This room is colder than I can ever remember. Perhaps we're going to have another storm."

Edlyn finally deigned to speak. "It stormed the entire way from home to London."

"Did it? Mind you don't burn yourself. The drink is piping hot." She carefully handed her the bone-china cup.

Edlyn took a reluctant swallow. "This is good," she said grudgingly. "Bitter and dark, the way it's supposed to be. And it always storms when one of us is in a mood. My great-aunts think Uncle Griffin attracts thunder and lightning."

"Nonsense," Harriet said, her scalp prickling. "Nobody has that sort of power, except in stories. What you probably mean to say is that he—I don't know—that he stirs up his surroundings."

"Does he stir you?"

Harriet blinked. "A woman in my position does not allow herself to be stirred."

"Would you admit it if you were?"

Harriet gave a reluctant laugh.

"I saw you holding his hand tonight."

She cut one of the buns neatly in half. "I was *not* holding his hand. We were on a hunt. Your aunt was frantic because she couldn't see you, and if I appeared to be upset, or stirred, that would be why. Now, then. I'll leave you in peace. I have to go and settle down the other girls. Some of them have never attended a ball before, and they'll be up half the night talking."

She waited again. At least she had tried. "I sleep down the hall if you need me during the night."

"Why should I?"

"Ring if you want anything," she said in resignation.

She turned. Harriet could hardly escape the room fast enough. Then, just as she reached the door, Edlyn's voice stopped her. "What do *you* do when you're alone?"

Harriet knew she should not give an honest answer. But she did. "I read."

"An etiquette manual?" Edlyn asked in disdain.

Harriet turned slowly. "No. Not when I'm alone. I have a favorite book—"

Edlyn turned her head. "I'm tired. Go away."

Harriet paused. "Fine. I hope you have pleasant dreams."

When she left the room a moment later, she realized that she knew nothing about Edlyn but that she had revealed three things about herself. One was that she loved hot chocolate on a rainy night. The second, that she had once eaten five currant buns in a row. Third, that she read when she was alone. And if she had not admitted it in so many words, it was obvious that she had allowed herself to be stirred by Edlyn's horribly handsome guardian.

She almost screamed when she encountered the horribly handsome duke in the middle of the stairs. At first she thought it was only a tall shadow that darkened her path. Then the shadow moved up toward her. A pair of strong arms reached out to firmly entrap her. The duke's eyes gleamed with dark amusement. She pursed her lips, doing her best to look disapproving. He wore a black cloak over his long-tailed evening jacket. The satin-lined wool bore a pleasant scent of damp that wafted to her as he shifted his weight evenly on the step beneath.

"If I'd had a tray in my hands," she said in a precise voice that she hoped would put him in his place, "I would have dropped it and disturbed the entire academy. Shame on you, your grace. You shouldn't be sneaking up here like this."

The darkness lent his chiseled features a danger-ous appeal. "I know," he whispered with a con-spiratorial smile. "But I won't tell anyone if you don't."

She gave him a politely discouraging frown. "I assume that you were looking for Miss Edlyn. I have in fact just left her. She's still awake but ready to retire. I'm sorry, your grace, but gentlemen aren't supposed to be upstairs. You will have to wait until the morning to make a proper call."

"Oh." He didn't appear particularly disap-pointed or surprised. "Well, in that case, perhaps you can give her a message from me."

She nodded graciously. "Of course." But only be-cause it was a duke asking and there was some-thing beguiling about his voice. If any other fellow had come creeping through the house, Harriet would have tackled him for all she was worth. "I'll go right upstairs and deliver it before she goes to bed."

He frowned.

"Your grace?" she prompted.

"Yes?" His large body pressed against hers, a pleasant if awkward position that gave little chance to move.

"I can't very well deliver a message unless I know what it is."

He gave her an abashed grin. "I don't know what it is, either. Do you want me to make one up?"

That was her cue to escape.

She knew it.

But did she try?

He studied her face, obviously interpreting her hesitation as a sign of encouragement. In the next moment he was leaning over her. Even then she could have squeezed under his arm and slipped down the stairs. She could have resisted the soft kisses he sprinkled against her neck and denied how nice they felt. Instead, she stood, utterly mesmerized by the sensations that took her by storm.

"*This* is your message to Miss Edlyn?" she managed to whisper in chagrin, her chin resting upon his clean-shaven cheek.

"Not exactly." He lifted his head. Suddenly his firm lips rested ever so lightly on hers. His arm locked around her waist. She waited, then expelled a breath.

"Your grace," she said firmly, "you are *not* allowed upstairs. Or past my guard. Or—"

His mouth captured hers. His arms held her before she could fall. Thunder. Lightning. A force so remorseless and elemental that it torched not only a woman's senses but the entire world. Electricity shivered through her veins. He wedged her securely between the railing and his body. Her lips parted, softened, sought, allowing his tongue to slide deeply into her mouth. *Nobody has this sort of power.* But the power gripped her harder, possessive and assured, guiding her into temptation. For several inarticulate moments, she was too nonplussed by the maddening ache that rose inside her to recognize it for what it was: passion. Subtle. Persuasive. To think she had been born in sin and managed to elude this. No wonder the girls in the academy were forbidden to talk of kissing and what it led to. Harriet had never before received such an insightful lesson in the art.

Griffin gave Harriet the barest chance to breathe, afraid that she would make him stop. His cloak had gotten trapped between them, buffering the intimate heat of their embrace. Her mouth had tempted him all night. He had deceived Charlotte when he'd left her downstairs with his aunt, promising he would seek a servant to make sure that Edlyn had settled into her new room.

Worse, he had deceived himself. He realized it the moment he spotted Harriet on the stairs. If she hadn't set them both on fire earlier, she did so now with the purity of blue flame.

His mouth sought hers again. He tore off his gloves, catching one of her hands in his. Before he knew what he was doing, he lifted the bare fingers of his other hand to her cheek, to the curve of her throat. Her skin felt warm, enticing. He could spend hours drawing constellations from the tiny freckles that dipped from her neck across her shoulders. Untouched. Unexplored. From the depths of the house, voices rose, intruded, impinged on his awareness. He groaned softly in protest. *Not yet. Go away.* He hadn't realized that a woman's kisses could bring him to his knees. A dark haze blanketed his brain.

"Your grace."

Her voice. Her mouth. Her—

"Duke," she whispered urgently, giving him a sharp poke in the ribs. "Get hold of yourself right now."

He drew away, shaking his head. His blood was on fire. "Please tell Edlyn that I was here. There's no point in making her come down if she's ready for bed."

She hesitated, then reached down behind her with a reproving sigh.

"The academy will do its best, your grace," she said, handing him back his gloves. "You'd be surprised what a difference the proper influence can make. Now do us both a kindness and leave before one of the girls realizes you are here. There seems to be something about you that disrupts our sheltered world."

Chapter Nine

Learn from me, if not by my precepts,
at least by my example, how dangerous is
the acquirement of knowledge.

MARY SHELLEY
Frankenstein

❧ ❦

Harriet slept late and went by rote through her morning ablutions. It was to her advantage that today was Sunday and that the previous night's ball had, as she'd predicted, kept most of the students up into the wee hours, whispering of amours imagined and observed. At least they would sit in chapel too weary to get in trouble chattering.

Monday morning, however, was another thing.

She walked slowly down the stairs, straight past the spot where the duke had kissed her. The memory still lingered in her mind as she entered the classroom a few moments later. She hoped the young devil's conscience had prevented him from enjoying his day of rest. To think he'd bluffed his way past her guard. It wouldn't happen again, even though she accepted half the blame for playing into his hands. Yet it wasn't altogether the worst thing that could happen to a woman, being kissed for her first time by a duke.

She dropped her book down on the desk.

Today's lesson covered the proper attire for garden parties. Linen was the preferred fabric, and a bonnet was de rigueur. What would the well-prepared lady do in the event of rain? Was it true that a gentleman could wear any shade of gray, while his female counterpart would be accused of bad taste? And why could a duke get away—

She pressed her fingers to the bridge of her nose. He had a lovely mouth and strong, gentle hands.

She heard her name. The girls were whispering about . . . *her*.

"Do you think poor Miss Harry will be dismissed because of what happened at the ball?"

"That wouldn't be fair. I heard old Lady Powlis ordering her to dance with the duke."

"Is he here?"

"In the academy?"

Several heads turned.

Miss Edlyn strolled into the room, her black hair streaming to her waist. "He isn't. The old one is, though."

Harriet glowered at the girls. "I hope you're all proud of yourselves. It's one thing to talk about me, but you are never to disparage another student, not in her presence or behind her back."

"It's all right," Edlyn murmured, slipping into the empty chair that had been saved for her. "Everyone talks about us."

"It isn't all right," Harriet said in a curt voice.

She opened her guidebook, wondering whether

the chapter on funerals would be more appropriate than the more cheerful subject of garden parties.

Dismissed? Was it possible? Not for obeying a frantic lady who was also a family member. However, if Charlotte or anyone else in the house had glimpsed the duke kissing Harriet on the stairs, a dismissal would not only be possible but completely deserved.

Charlotte Boscastle smiled cordially as she served tea in the yellow breakfast room. She wished she knew of a polite way to request that Lady Powlis lower her voice. The subject of their conversation happened to be Harriet Gardner, who, according to some reports, had created a delightful scandal at Saturday night's dance. Charlotte saw no reason to admonish Harriet. She had not witnessed any impropriety on her young assistant's part. Still, for the life of her, she could not understand why Lady Powlis had insisted that Harriet be brought to her immediately. To what could this tête-à-tête be leading?

Had Lady Powlis learned of Harriet's unfortunate upbringing? No one at the academy spoke of it, although one could not bury what could be so easily unearthed.

"Oh, for heaven's sake." Lady Powlis set down her cup. "You must be wondering why I have come today."

"Well, at first I assumed you came about Lady Edlyn," Charlotte said cautiously. "But then—"

"Yes, of course," Primrose said, a trifle testily. "Edlyn is always my primary concern."

"And she is the reason you asked me to summon Harriet from class?"

"No." Lady Powlis frowned. "It has come to my attention that Harriet debuted as an actress at an early age. Is this true?"

Charlotte fidgeted. "Well, yes, but she was very young, an orange girl, and she got her first part—"

"—when the leading lady broke her nose."

Charlotte sighed. "She was very young."

"And very busy afterward, from what I've heard. Miss Gardner has lived quite the eventful life."

Charlotte put down her tea. "Are you afraid she will have a bad influence on Edlyn?"

"Good grief, no. Edlyn is the one who taints the well water. Trust me."

"Then what in the world do you want with Miss Gardner?"

"I want to employ her as my abigail."

Charlotte's blue eyes widened in astonishment. "You want to what?"

"Do I not speak loudly enough, dear?"

"Quite loudly," Charlotte said with a frown.

"Then what is confusing about the nature of my request?"

"Well, I—that is, the *academy* needs her."

Lady Powlis balanced her cane between her knees, her voice creaking like a rusty hinge. "More than one lonely old woman?"

Oh. Charlotte knew she had backed herself into

a corner. Harriet and Primrose. What an impossible association. She had always assumed she would be having this conversation with a gentleman who sought to be Harriet's protector. But how did one refuse an aging relative who had spent an entire life exerting her will? "I shall have to speak with Emma about this, and she and the duke have not arrived in London yet."

"My nephew is a duke," Primrose said craftily.

"No one is likely to forget that."

"Well, do you own Miss Gardner?"

"Excuse me?"

"Stop pretending to be such a corkbrain, Charlotte. Did Miss Gardner sign a contract with you or not?"

Charlotte blinked. A corkbrain, Griffin's sweet-looking aunt had called her. Who was the one who needed instruction in manners? "I don't know that she and Emma actually made—"

"I'll buy it off Emma. The price is of no consequence. Are we agreed, then?"

Charlotte shook her head. "I am not empowered to pass Miss Gardner off like a pawn. Harriet has a say in this, too. And, oh, you have really pushed me into revealing what I promised to keep private." She hesitated. "Harriet's past is—"

"—interesting?" Primrose flipped her cane against her chair. "I gathered that. Why else do you think I want to employ her? Do you imagine I want to spend my final days being dusted like a museum piece? I have hopes for my dotage. Your young instructress gave me a giggle the night before last, and I am a lady in sore need of upliftment. One of these days I intend to travel, and I am *not* dragging along a dull, stodgy companion who spoils my fun."

"Interesting is one thing," Charlotte sputtered. "But let me be clear when I say that Miss Gardner has spent more of her life in the rookeries than teaching the rules of deportment."

"Yes, yes. One can hardly help noting her flaws. However, I shall soon be alone to contemplate my own deficits. Griffin will marry. By the grace of God, Edlyn shall, too. I would rather pass my final years in laughter than mourning the child and husband I have lost."

Charlotte felt rather as if she were being trampled by a runaway cart horse. Not that one could compare Lady Powlis to—Perhaps she was worrying for nothing. Harriet felt at home in the academy. She and Charlotte had become close friends. It was Charlotte who had introduced Harriet to literature. It was Harriet who stayed up with her late at night, listening to the stories Charlotte wrote. Why would Harriet want to give up her safe shelter to work for a woman who would—treat her like the daughter she had lost?

Charlotte didn't want to lose Harriet, either. Without Harriet, the academy would revert to the boring, disciplined institute it was meant to be.

But in the end, the choice would come to Harriet,

and Charlotte could only be glad she was staring down into a teacup instead of a crystal ball.

Harriet could not believe what she had been asked. She stood in a daze, until Lady Powlis insisted she take a chair. Then she plopped down so ungracefully that Charlotte closed her eyes in mortification. "Sorry," Harriet whispered, but what could one expect? It was a good thing she wasn't a swooning sort of girl.

"It is a flattering offer, Lady Powlis," she said when she regained her composure. "But there will be plenty of people who'll think you're off your head for taking me as your companion."

Lady Powlis beamed as if she had just been afforded the highest compliment.

Charlotte's lips thinned. A lady didn't "go off her head." Her "faculties abandoned her," or some other such nonsense.

"We shall start with a period of trial employment to see if we suit," Lady Powlis said, clearly having missed her calling as a lawyer. "A pity my nephew cannot do the same with the lady he must marry."

And at that precise moment, the duke sauntered into the room, lithe, lean, and—startled when he realized he was not alone. He straightened his neckcloth, glancing around with a tight smile that hinted he knew something was in the air and that he might not want to be part of it. "I'm sorry. I must not—"

"Then you accept, dear," Lady Powlis said, lifting her hand to indicate that the duke remain silent until Harriet gave her reply.

Charlotte came to her feet. "You should sleep on it, Harriet. This is a grave decision."

"I require an answer now," Lady Powlis said ruthlessly. "Or I shall take my offer elsewhere."

The duke cast Harriet a half-pitying look. "I have no idea what she has offered you, but my instincts strongly suggest that you should refuse."

Charlotte slipped around him to the door. "Your aunt wants to take Miss Gardner on as her companion. You will excuse me a moment, won't you? If the girls have spotted your coach again, I shall never settle them down."

Harriet stared across the room. She couldn't bring herself to look at the duke after Charlotte's announcement. At the least he hadn't dropped in a shocked faint on the carpet. The very idea. Living under his roof. Bumping into each other on the stairs. Breathing the same air.

At length he sat down opposite his aunt. "Why don't you give Miss Gardner time alone to make up her mind?" he suggested in a neutral voice.

"I believe that she and I were on the verge of sealing our arrangement when you interrupted," she said crisply. "Weren't we, Harriet?"

"You can refuse," the duke said under his breath.

Harriet shook her head. "I can't just walk out of here without saying good-bye to everyone—"

"We'll be back and forth all the time to visit Edlyn," Lady Powlis said airily.

"But I don't have a decent frock—"

"I'll have a dressmaker fit you for a new wardrobe by the end of the week," Lady Powlis said, a Machiavellian gleam in her eye.

"But I—"

"Stop mumbling, dear. We shall worry about the particulars later. What do you need for the night? Whatever else can be sent for tomorrow."

"Where are you going to put her?" Griffin asked suddenly.

"She can have the sarcophagus suite," Lady Powlis replied.

Griffin sat forward. "The *what?*"

"It's the stranger's room, the one decorated *à la Égyptienne,* directly across from mine."

The duke regarded Harriet with a smile more unsettling than anything he could have said.

She could hear Miss Peppertree calling the girls to close their books. "You mean leave this minute, ma'am?" she asked slowly. "Right in the middle of a lesson on garden parties, and—"

"You don't have to agree," the duke said again, his eyes narrowing.

What *was* she agreeing to?

The academy had become her haven. She felt safe here. How safe would she be in a sarcophagus with a young virile duke wandering about the place? She had gotten used to the lumps in her bed—she had gotten used to a bed.

The Boscastles had educated and protected her. The duke was a Boscastle, too. Still, there had been nothing protective about the dark kisses he had coaxed from her on the staircase.

She could not turn her back on the school.

On the other hand, she could not stay here forever, watching Miss Peppertree grow bonier and afraid of every duke who crossed her path.

"Are you positive you have the spine for this position, Miss Gardner?" the duke asked from his chair. "I'm putting my head on the block as I say this, but you should know that every companion my aunt has employed left her position within a month."

"Fetch a bag, Miss Gardner," Lady Powlis ordered her.

Harriet would never admit it, but she looked up to Charlotte as the sister she had always wished for. Why hadn't Charlotte fought to keep her on, then? The Duchess of Scarfield ought to have a say in this, as well.

She could have cried.

She shook her head again. "I—"

"By this time next week," Lady Powlis said with remorseless pleasure, "you will be *attending* a garden party. Assuming that Griffin doesn't spoil the day by raising another of his storms."

Harriet bolted from the room.

Charlotte was standing right outside the door. They stared at each other in wordless concern, then turned to listen to the conversation between Griffin and his aunt.

"This is the worst idea you've had in ages," the duke said quietly. "Perhaps the worst one ever."

"Do you have something against my companion, Griffin?"

"Don't be silly. I do not even know her. Neither do you."

"But don't you like her?"

"What the devil difference does it make if I do? As I'm not hiring her to live with me, my feelings are not particularly relevant, are they?"

"Will she distract you?"

Charlotte put her hand over her eyes.

"Probably," the duke replied in a clipped tone, "although not as much as you or Edlyn have."

Charlotte groaned. Harriet patted her absent-mindedly on the arm.

Lady Powlis was quiet for a moment. "You have no particular wish to take me shopping for stockings and hats, do you?"

"Of course not," he said annoyedly. "But there are other ladies in our family, in London, who would probably enjoy spending such moments with you."

"Not ones who make me laugh."

Harriet swallowed, pulling Charlotte from the door. "What should I do?" she whispered.

"I don't know," Charlotte whispered back. "What do you want to do?"

"I want to stay with you—"

"Then fine—"

"—and I want to go."

She stared at the door.

With him.

Charlotte drew a sigh. "You can always come back. Unless something unpredictable comes to pass."

Harriet hugged her in gratitude. She understood the unspoken conditions of her release. She could return to her position unless she disgraced herself or so displeased Lady Powlis that no one would consider her for any decent employment again.

"Go and get your things," Charlotte said with a resigned smile. "At least if I am to lose you, it is to another Boscastle."

Chapter Ten

The Devil, I safely can aver,
Has neither hoof, nor tail, nor sting,
Nor is he, as some sages swear,
A spirit, neither here nor there,
In nothing—yet in everything.

PERCY BYSSHE SHELLEY
Peter Bell the Third

❧ ☙

Griffin's official London residence was a white-stone town house in Bedford Square that his father had visited only on the occasional summer. The Georgian front door opened onto a marble entryway lined with twelve ceiling-high columns, which stood like sentinels of a forgotten time. The rear garden was overgrown with weeds and boasted a quaint classical temple in its midst that had been taken over by pigeons.

Griffin would not have chosen to live in this fancy, unfriendly house in a hundred years. The looped damask curtains reeked of mildew and had not been opened since his mother's death twenty years ago. His brother had admired the Gothic design, which featured a pedimented urn or recessed caryatid every time one turned a bloody corner. The only cheerful room in this house was the library, and Griffin all but encamped there. He seemed to be unduly drawn to warmth since he had arrived in London.

It was only as Harriet tiptoed into the hall that he noticed the front door had a lacy ironwork fanlight and that her eyes glowed like a cat's in the dark.

"I told my nephew that there is little point in wasting money on renovations yet," Lady Powlis said, removing her pelisse. "Not when the future duchess will want to have a say in things. Her tastes will undoubtedly run counter to mine. The duke, I suspect, does not care one way or the other. He will never like this house. I am not particularly fond of it myself. Nor was my sweet sister-in-law."

Harriet stared up the yawning black staircase. "It wouldn't hurt to open the drapes here and there, would it?"

She turned, emitting an involuntary shriek as a stooped gray-haired butler appeared from one of the columns to take her cloak. Griffin grinned. He couldn't think of the old fellow's name at the moment, but he'd been sneaking up behind people, and giving them a scare ever since Griffin could remember.

He stared at Harriet. "Well, what do you think?"

"It's lonely." She shivered slightly. "And a bit eerie. No wonder Lady Powlis wanted company."

He bent his head to hers. "You're going to regret this."

"Am I?"

He stared down at her mouth, dropping his

voice. "You have no idea what you've gotten yourself into."

"Stop whispering in my companion's ear like that," his aunt said from the staircase. "You're going to give her the impression that you're as decadent as everyone says you are."

"Do you suppose," he asked Harriet very quietly, "that she and I may share you?"

Harriet lifted her brow, stepping carefully around his unmoving form. "It would be an honor to pick out your hankerchief in the morning and carry your reticule while we take brisk walks to build your stamina."

"There is nothing wrong with my stamina, I assure you."

"Well, maybe we can wear you out." She whirled. "A little exercise never hurt anyone."

He started to reach for her, a dangerous impulse, and then lowered his hand. What would he do if he caught her? His aunt had claimed her without a thought to the temptation she had put in his path. Not that he begrudged Primrose the right to seek such pleasant company. He had no desire to entertain the old lady every night.

And what he desired he would simply have to resist. If he could.

"Harriet!" his aunt shouted from the upstairs hall. "Is that rogue still keeping you down there in the dark?"

He saw Harriet pause on the landing to give him a fretful look before she vanished from his rueful scrutiny. He stared after her shapely figure with a smile. He might well be a rogue. He would have certainly kept his aunt's companion down here far longer if he could have gotten away with it.

But all of a sudden he wasn't alone in the dark.

In fact, he was standing directly in a circle of moonlight that had broken through the fanlight onto the floor.

And he swore that the light led directly up the stairs.

Harriet knew good fortune when it found her. From now on she wouldn't be banished to sleep in a garret or basement like an ordinary servant. Lady Powlis was giving her the *stranger's* suite, no less.

And a more strangely appointed room Harriet had never hoped to see. It was so hideous she could have run back down the stairs and—and thrown herself into the handsome duke's arms.

"Well," Lady Powlis said, biting her lip in pleasure as Harriet lit the taper on the bedstand. "What do you think? My sister, Glynnis, had it decorated several years ago after she returned from the Nile."

Harriet gazed unblinkingly around the main chamber. The bed had been constructed to resemble an Egyptian barge, its four gilt posts engraved with hieroglyphics and snake motifs that would be a rousing sight first thing in the morning. Smack in the middle of the headboard sat some winged bosomy Sphinx with a floating eyeball, which Harriet could swear was following her around the room. It was positively abnormal.

Lady Powlis dragged her into the dressing closet. "Wait until you see the size of the clothes chest."

Harriet gasped. *Ye gods, what a horror.* "So that's the sarc—It doesn't smell fusty in here by half. You're not going to tell me your sister's dead husband sleeps in that thing, are you? Because quite honestly, even I have certain standards."

Lady Powlis lifted the heavy lid and sniffed. "This odor can't be anything compared to a genuine sarcophagus. Imagine a coffin that could devour one's flesh in days."

Harriet swallowed. "What's it do to your clothes, I wonder?"

"Nothing a little camphor and lavender cannot fix."

Harriet retreated into the main suite. "I hope you'll forgive my unthinking comment about your sister's dearly departed."

Lady Powlis sighed, regarding her with a wistful smile. "I'll take you to meet my own late husband one day soon."

"I beg your pardon?"

"How odd, Harriet, that we should discuss him," she mused. "He will have been interred in the family vaults for exactly a decade this Friday. When we return to the castle, I shall introduce him to you."

"Return . . . but his grace will be bringing home a wife. I didn't think that we—that you and I— would have to leave London." Quitting the academy was one thing, but Harriet could not imagine herself gallivanting around the world. And would the duke accompany them?

"Who knows?" Lady Powlis said, as if reading Harriet's thoughts. "Perhaps we shall travel together to Egypt and have great adventures. Glynnis could be our guide. Would that not be delightful?"

"It sounds frightful," said a deep voice from the hall. Griffin popped his head around the door. "You aren't going to put her in that tomb with the last companion you had?"

"Some women say sleeping in a sarcophagus restores their youth," Lady Powlis said, closing the door to the closet.

Griffin leaned against the doorjamb, shaking his head. "I've never seen a more hideous room in my entire life."

Harriet sat down on a leopard-skin stool supported upon gilt palm-leaf legs and clawed feet. "You know, I might prefer a garret bedchamber, after all. It's warmer up there, and I don't need to take up all this room. A room this size should be reserved for proper company."

"But then you wouldn't be near me, dear," Lady Powlis reminded her. "And I shall want you available at all times."

Griffin abandoned Harriet to his aunt and her bedchamber of horrors. From the instant she stepped into his house tonight, the rules as he dimly understood them had changed. Suddenly he had been forced into the role of protector. Not one who claimed the rights that his male body clamored to assert, but one whose position was defined by an ancient code.

He sat on the edge of his bed, contemplating his boots.

His physical self knew nothing of chivalry. It generally disregarded rules and scorned discipline. It wanted, therefore it would have. His carnal nature craved soothing in the most fundamental of ways.

This arrangement would never work. It was unfair to him, but mostly to Harriet.

He decided that his aunt was the devil disguised in fine gray hair and fragile bones. Why else would she place temptation in his path?

When, in truth, had he ever been so tempted?

He wasn't the rakehell his older brother had been.

He wasn't much of a duke, either, for that matter.

He was rather lonely and at a loss as to what he was supposed to do with himself.

He already wanted another reason to see his aunt's companion.

Should he remind her that the sarcophagus was unsafe? Would anyone hear her cry for help if she fell inside the blessed contraption and couldn't get out? Why hadn't the servants noticed how damp that side of the house was at night? And why did he find it so easy to talk to her?

He glanced up from his feet to the door.

He really ought to ring to have the hearth in her room cleared of debris and lit. And while he was at it, he should warn her about the loose carpet at the top of the stairs that he had noticed only earlier that day. It wouldn't hurt to remind her he would not be far during the night, if the thought of mummies coming to life in her dressing closet kept her awake.

He got up. He had a responsibility to make everyone under his roof reasonably comfortable.

She couldn't have gone to bed yet. Perhaps she would be too unsettled by her surroundings to fall asleep.

He knocked at her door. It was neither a furtive knock nor one so insistent that Primrose would hear and demand to know what was going on.

Harriet opened the door in understandable hesitation. She was still dressed, not a button undone. He had no idea how she had managed it, but a small fire illuminated the room. Did she harbor a knack for pyromancy?

She had a book clasped in her hand. Her bright gold-bronze hair fell in a thick rope down her back.

"I'm sorry," he said, his voice suddenly hoarse. "I only wanted to make sure you'd be warm."

She blinked. "His grace jokes. It is like an oven in here."

"You won't sleep in that tomb thing, will you?"

"No." She gave him a strange look. "I thought I might use it to store my parasols and odd bits when they come tomorrow. Or perhaps I'll pretend it isn't there at all."

"That might be rather hard to do, considering its size." His eyes traveled over her. She appeared to be anything but a damsel in distress. "I know I can tease at times, but I have to ask again . . . are you sure you made the right choice?"

"No," she admitted, her eyes glinting. "I've never lived anywhere this quiet before."

"It won't be quiet tomorrow, I promise you." He was running out of excuses for being here. Her soft mouth curved in a knowing smile. He wasn't going to kiss her, no matter how sensual he imagined she would look lying across the bed behind her, or even how pleasant it would be to sit together in the firelight. He wasn't going to think of how much he had enjoyed dancing with her last night and how her presence had already brightened this house. And he certainly was *not* going to pace in his room the rest of the night, listening for any small sound she might make.

She cleared her throat. "Is that all you wanted?"

His gaze fell to the book she held against her. He exhaled, regaining mastery of his errant thoughts. "Has my aunt got you working for her already?"

She seemed reluctant to answer. Perhaps she had guessed he was only bargaining for time. He had not employed the most devious strategy in coming to her room.

"This is *my* book," she said, her fingers curling around the spine. "It's about a monster made up of dead body parts. He goes on a killing rage because the doctor who created him refuses to make him a wife."

"Another woman drawn to the dark and macabre," he mused. "Primrose would probably enjoy such a story. You should read it to her. No. You shouldn't. It might give her ideas."

She pushed her hand against the door. "Your aunt appears to be a dear lady devoted to her family. You ought to be ashamed of yourself for making fun of her all the time."

He sighed, duly caught out. "That's exactly what she keeps telling me. Just remember—she isn't at all as sweet as she appears."

Harriet smiled. "I know who I have to keep my eye on, thank you."

Chapter Eleven

No one can conceive
the variety of feelings which bore me onwards,
like a hurricane, in the first enthusiasm of success.

MARY SHELLEY
Frankenstein

❧ ❧

Lady Powlis did indeed put Harriet to work early the next morning, in the breakfast room, before the duke had a proper chance to sit down in private and enjoy his meal. It *was* quiet in the house, she thought. The girls at the academy would be bickering over who had gotten the last scone as they hurried to class. Harriet spent half her day intervening and demanding they apologize to one another.

The peace of this noble household was a true sign that she had moved up in the world. There were no offended feelings to soothe. No tears to mop up. Lady Powlis sat dictating an itinerary of all the functions that had been planned for the next fortnight.

It was so simple, so quiet—until Lady Powlis murmured, "And make a note to have the duke's tailor come tomorrow afternoon for his fitting."

Griffin looked up suspiciously from his paper. "Fitting for what?"

Lady Powlis shook her head in fond exasperation. "The wedding, Griff."

He frowned. "What wedding?"

Harriet put down her pen.

"The wedding," Lady Powlis said, in the quavery
voice that Harriet would soon realize disguised a
will of iron, "that we have been planning for almost a year. The wedding that all of Society is
dying to attend. The wedding that will release me
of *my* obligation to Glenmorgan's future."

He snorted. "There has to be an engagement
first, doesn't there?"

"The morning papers suggest you have taken
that step," his aunt said, with a meaningful glance
at the table.

"Good for the morning papers," he said.

Harriet rose hastily. "I'll leave you both alone to
sort this out. If you need—"

"Sit down at your desk, Harriet," Lady Powlis
snapped.

Harriet swallowed. "But I—"

"Sit down, girl. You'll be of no use to anyone if
the duke and I cannot speak frankly to each other
when you are in the room."

Griffin's eyes danced wickedly. "She's right. You
had better stay in case I need a witness to testify
that she forced me to marry against my will."

"Don't be such an idiot," his aunt said. "You are
going to turn Harriet against me, and I will never
forgive you."

"Why don't you join my side, Miss Gardner?" he said, grinning shamelessly.

She shook her head. "I have no idea what the pair of you are arguing about, and I'm sure it isn't any of my business." Which didn't mean she wasn't intently curious about the matter. Nor did it stop her from asking, after a long hesitation, "Has the duke proposed to this lady or not?"

Griffin's face darkened. "No. Never."

His aunt sputtered in denial. "His brother's factors pursued a match between them, and when Griffin inherited the dukedom, he inherited the promises and duties that go with it."

"I haven't even met her properly," Griffin said, folding his paper in half. "It is entirely possible that she will hate me on sight."

Harriet doubted that with all her heart. The duke might have a nasty reputation and he might make a forbidding first impression. But if any lady bothered to look past his portentous façade, she would find herself in the most pleasant sort of trouble, if not half in love.

She glanced up guiltily as she realized Lady Powlis was talking to her again.

"My nephew is behaving like a spoiled . . . rogue," her ladyship said with a deep sigh. "I can't understand what has come over him. Last night he made the biggest fuss in creation over a waltz—"

"Reel," Harriet murmured. "A Scotch reel."

"You made the fuss," Griffin pointed out, propping his legs up on the chair at the opposite side of

the table. "You embarrassed Miss Gardner to no
end. You didn't have to make a case of her in front
of everyone just because Edlyn disappeared for a
few moments. I could have found her by myself."

"Did I embarrass you, Miss Gardner?" Lady
Powlis asked with pursed lips.

"Nothing embarrasses me, ma'am."

"Just wait," Griffin said.

His aunt frowned at him. "Look at the way he's
sitting. *That* isn't embarrassing?"

Harriet blew out a quiet sigh and sank back into
her chair. This was fun. When would the fireworks
begin? Fortunately, the heated interlude gave her a
little extra time to finish her itinerary. Handwriting
had never come easily to Harriet. She labored twice
as long as anyone else in the academy at the task.

"Make up a list of eligible brides while you're at
it," Lady Powlis instructed her with a grim smile.
"If the duke does not think he and the lady chosen
for him will suit, then let him choose elsewhere."

Harriet shook her head. "Madam, I wouldn't
have any notion of where to begin. I am a mere—
well, until yesterday, I was an instructress. I
haven't—"

"There must be one or two academy graduates
who are still unwed," Lady Powlis said. "She
doesn't have to be perfect."

Griffin glanced at Harriet. "But it wouldn't
hurt."

She swallowed a laugh and reached for a fresh
piece of paper. She wrote down the name of the

butcher's daughter, who had a beefy hand when it came to dealing with unwanted customers. Then there was the Yorkshire graduate at the academy. Surely her parents wouldn't complain if their girl landed a duke instead of an earl. The third—she blinked, appalled to realize she'd started to write the name of her beloved fiend's inventor, *Frankenstein*. She crossed it out, immediately applying her pen to the paper to turn the *F* into a lumpy oval shape. The next thing she knew, the oval had a forked tail and cloven-soled boots.

Her breath froze as Griffin suddenly leapt up from his seat and leaned over her. "Auntie Primrose," he said with a low laugh, "your new companion is drawing something impolite."

Harriet gasped. She almost slapped the white-cuffed hand that reached down to confiscate her paper from the desk.

"Stop pestering the poor young woman," his aunt said sternly. "I can't remember when I have seen you behaving in such an off-putting fashion."

"Make her show it to you," he insisted. "She's drawn something with ears."

Harriet narrowed her gaze. "Those are petals, your grace. Forgive my lack of skill, but it was supposed to be a flower."

"A primrose?" Lady Powlis asked with a flattered smile.

The duke examined the sketch with a critical eye. "Only if primroses are grown with barbed lines through the stems."

"That would be one of the roots," Harriet said tightly.

Lady Powlis glanced up. "What kind of flower is it, Harriet?"

"A demonic variety by the look," Griffin answered, squinting one eye.

Harriet smiled, using her elbow to delicately dislodge the manly hand that had settled on the arm of her chair. The hand came right back. "It's a new breed from China," she said, adding tuberous roots to the rectangular forehead. "They're grown in hothouses all over England."

Griffin blinked. "That looks like me when I get up in the morning."

His aunt shook her head in despair. "This is why you aren't married."

"Not because insanity runs in the family?"

Lady Powlis gave Harriet a distressed look. "Do you understand now what I must live with? Go and fetch our cloaks, dear. If we have time, we will see about your new wardrobe. Perhaps we can find something prettier to entice Edlyn. She can't stay in mourning forever."

She rose. "Yes, madam."

"Oh, what I endure," her ladyship said with a moan, closing her eyes.

The duke made a face. "And what you inflict."

Harriet curtsied, slipping her scribbled paper into her pocket before she escaped the combative atmosphere. She had no intention of leaving behind evidence that would incriminate her. If the duke recognized himself in her drawing, he was more perceptive than she'd realized. And if he never found the perfect wife he deserved, she doubted it would be for lack of willing candidates.

Griffin stared at the closed door until his aunt's voice intruded on his silence. What kind of fiend had Primrose employed? What anarchy had he sanctioned under his authority? It was bad enough that Harriet's presence in the house virtually guaranteed he would never enjoy a good night's sleep again. But that she felt at liberty to mock him with a ridiculous drawing—well, it appeared he would have to put down his foot before she became the devil's apprentice.

"Do you find her attractive, Griff?"

He pivoted and gave her a blank stare.

"*Attractive*, Griff. I asked an ordinary enough question. Do you think my companion is appealing to the eye, with her vivid coloring and pretty face?"

"I do understand what attractive means, Aunt Encyclopedia of Unsolicited Knowledge."

"Dear me. I'm beginning to think you are the one who should become a student in the academy. Your manners have lapsed appallingly since . . . well, since you've assumed responsibility for your own life."

"Yes. Yes, I know. You remind me every chance you get, no matter where we are or who else might overhear."

"You will not forget that at the end of the week

we are taking your betrothed to the park? And that two nights later the marquess is hosting another ball in our honor? This is to be a more intimate affair."

He groaned.

"Or that Edlyn has been invited to a breakfast party, which naturally we shall chaperone?"

"Naturally." He edged toward the door.

"With my attractive companion."

"Am I too old to run away from home?" he asked under his breath.

"Dear Griff, I know I'm a bit of a bother, but please give London a chance."

And life, she might as well have said.

Chapter Twelve

What is this world's delight?
Lightning, that mocks the night.

PERCY BYSSHE SHELLEY
The Flower That Smiles Today

❧ ❧

Harriet would later look back upon her first day in Lady Powlis's employment as less of a trial period than as a sort of honeymoon. And a shorter-lived honeymoon no woman in English history had yet to endure, unless it had been her misfortune to marry Henry the Bride-Beheading King. For a few blissful hours, Harriet convinced herself that she had transcended this miserable world and gone directly to heaven. Was there a better position in London? Could anyone hope for a more benevolent employer?

Lady Powlis demanded so little of her that she felt guilty for accepting the generous wage she was given in advance. All the lonely old woman asked was that Harriet accompany her on a brisk drive in the duke's curricle to the dressmaker's and describe her experiences as a young actress. As her experiences treading the boards had been brief and marked with infamy, and her employer appeared in need of immediate entertainment, Harriet decided it would be a forgivable deceit to embellish what little of that time she could recall. Unfortunately, Lady Powlis sensed omissions in Harriet's tale and begged for more.

Only a fool gave everything away at the first offer.

"I will never divulge your secrets, Harriet."

"Of course you wouldn't."

"I will be patient, though."

Patient Lady Powlis might be. Unfortunately, by the end of that first day, Harriet had learned that her employer was also manipulative, tyrannical, and easily bored. No wonder the duke had warned her that she wouldn't last before he closed himself up in his library.

For the next four days, Harriet wore her feet off running up and down the stairs to answer the beldame's every request. Tea, milk, biscuits, magazines. Being of sound body, Harriet might not have bemoaned the exercise had, in between those random demands, the duke not emerged from his lair to frown at her in his forbidding way.

As if it were her fault that his aunt expected a companion to provide services as a circus entertainer, confidante, and fashion consultant at the same time. Not that Harriet knew a thing about the latest in French costumes and whether her employer should purchase French knickers or not.

"Must you thump about the house at all hours?" he finally demanded, dark and moody again, his cravat rakishly askew and his gaze following her every move.

She curtsied at his shadow. If he intended to act as though he'd never kissed her, well, so would she. He wouldn't know by her professional demeanor that she thought about it morning, noon, and especially at night, when she fell, bone-dead, into bed. He'd never guess by her impervious air that she yearned to feel that wicked mouth of his against hers again or that, even when he was in a mood, his melodious voice raised warm shivers on her skin. She knew what a man wanted from a woman in her position. Let him want. Let them both want. And let them pretend to completely ignore each other. It was much better this way. He stayed in his room. She stayed out of his way.

"Well?" he said, lifting his brow.

She bit her lip. "Your grace must forgive me. My mind was wandering. Did you ask me something?"

"Yes, I did," he said with a vexed scowl. "Why is it that every time I sit down at my desk, I am distracted by your banging up and down the stairs? I cannot write a letter, open an account book, or close my eyes for a moment without hearing you."

"Unless his grace knows of another way to placate her ladyship, I have no choice but to obey her."

He pushed off the wall. Harriet held her breath. All her senses went on the alert. What was he going to do? He had that intense expression on his face again, as if he were about to . . . whisper a secret in her ear. Or something else. She stood, immobilized, trapped in a delicious tension. *Touch me again. Wrap me in thunder.*

And then, like the voice of an enraged goddess roaring down from Olympus when another god was threatening her favorite mortal, Lady Powlis shouted, "Hurry up, Harriet! It looks to be a rainy day all of a sudden. We'll be soaked before we get in the carriage."

"She'll drive us both mad, I swear it," the duke said, his eyes burning into hers. "No companion has ever stayed for long."

Harriet sighed, her shoulders drooping. "I believe you."

He stared at her. "Do you?"

"Yes, but I cannot help wondering—"

"Go on."

She frowned, shaking off her fatigue. "No. It is not my place to wonder."

"But it is my place to make you finish what you started to say. In fact, you may *not* go upstairs until you do. And then she'll bellow at both of us."

"Fine." She lowered her voice, caught in his playful conspiracy. "I was just curious how you managed before. Was she this difficult in the castle?"

He leaned his head to hers. "She was worse."

"Then how—"

"—did we stand it? The aunts live in the east tower. We live in the west. The castle is quite large and has countless hiding places."

"No wonder she's in the habit of shouting." She

turned, resolving to escape before she asked anything else she ought not.

"Another fortnight, that's all you will last. I would bet on it."

And somehow Harriet suspected he wasn't referring as much to the challenges of her position as a companion as he was to the temptation she felt whenever she looked into his eyes.

Chapter Thirteen

I entreat you to hear me, before you give
vent to your hatred on my devoted head.

MARY SHELLEY
Frankenstein

❧ ❧

He wanted her gone. He wanted her here. If his
aunt did not seem happier since his brother's death,
she was at least diverted. And, obviously, so was
he, because he couldn't remember for the life of
him what he had promised to do that afternoon.
He knew he had an appointment. His valet had
brought him his new jacket and trousers from the
tailor. He thought there was supposed to be a
schedule of his activities on the desk. Or had Miss
Gardner confiscated it along with her horned ren-
dition of his head?

He was halfway back to the library when the butler intercepted him. "There is another lady visitor
here to see you, your grace," he said in an apolo-
getic voice. He had been guarding his master's door
like a bulldog against the stream of guests whose
calling cards had yet to be read, let alone acknowledged, this past week.

"If she isn't family, ask her to leave her card and . . . leave."

"I explained to the lady that one is not welcome without an express invitation."

"That was the proper thing to do."

"She insisted that your grace will forgive her presumptuous intrusion after she explains the urgent nature of her business."

"Tell her to put the presumptuous matter in writing and that the duke's secretary will respond as he deems proper," Lady Powlis said from the bottom of the stairs.

Griffin stared at her, cursing silently. Suddenly he remembered the appointment he had put from his mind. The park. An afternoon of stilted conversation with the woman the gossipmongers of London assumed he would marry. Primrose looked endearingly absurd in a striped green-and-cream carriage dress, her face hidden in the shadows of a plumed leghorn bonnet. She was leaning on her cane to descend one step at a time. It was difficult to believe she could drive a man to the edge of sanity.

Harriet came down the stairs behind her, her shawl and his aunt's gloves in hand. She was wearing a pale-mint muslin gown and a pair of flat-heeled slippers. She looked quite the demure companion. He might have believed she was exactly that, had her eyes not narrowed when they met his. She gave him a fleeting smile, then looked away.

The butler backed into the hall. "I shall have the

carriage brought to the door. By the way, your grace, your visitor asked me to mention that she is the owner of a certain academy in London."

Lady Powlis glanced at Griffin in alarm. "Do you think Edlyn has run away again?"

"Charlotte would have been pounding the door down if she had," he said, his face grim. Still, with Edlyn, the possibility of such a misadventure could not be ruled out. "Butler, bring the lady into my library."

The butler chuckled. "Yes, your grace."

Lady Powlis hastened to accompany him. "Harriet, please let the coachman know we might be late for our meeting and that he should send a footman to Lord Chatterton's house, as a courtesy to his daughter."

"I'm sure it's nothing," Griffin said, wondering if he could draw out the delay for the entire afternoon. He owed his brother favors yet unpaid, but courting a lady he had seen only once was surely not one of them.

A minute or so thereafter, the duke's visitor entered the drawing room and introduced herself to Griffin and Primrose as Lady Alice Clipstone, headmistress of a young ladies' finishing academy in London. From her plumed bonnet to her bright darting eyes, she reminded Griffin of a bird in search of a worm. He distrusted her on sight.

"Why are you here?" he inquired in unconcealed irritation.

"Your grace, please. I ask only that you hear me

out. I am not a person of happenstance behavior. In fact, I attended school myself with your esteemed cousin, the Duchess of Scarfield."

"Good for you," he said. "I trust that is not the urgent nature of your visit?"

She clasped her hands together. "I have information about a certain instructress at the duchess's school who will make your grace reconsider entrusting your niece to her care."

Harriet, he thought, his mood brightening.

"If this is common gossip about my companion," his aunt said, "the duke will banish you from this house immediately."

"Let's not be hasty," he said in a cordial tone. "Any matter that concerns Edlyn deserves to be heard."

Lady Clipstone took a breath. "It is not low gossip, your grace. What my conscience compels me to reveal is for the protection of young Miss Edlyn and your family."

He nodded encouragingly, ignoring the menacing scowl that settled on his aunt's face. "Low gossip," she mouthed at him. "You ought to be ashamed for listening."

Oddly, he did feel a little ashamed, but not enough to curb his curiosity. He motioned at Lady Clipstone. "Whatever you have to say, please do so quickly."

"I am sure that Miss Edlyn's future in Society is your primary concern."

She waited politely for Griffin to agree.

When he did not, she rushed on. "Of equal importance, as you know, is that she mingle with only the highest quality."

His aunt glared at her. "Which is why she is attending the finest academy in London."

Lady Clipstone lifted her chin with an air of triumph. "But does the finest academy hire a former thief and daughter of a wanted criminal to teach impressionable young ladies, and would you wish your niece's tender sensibilities exposed to a woman more experienced in vice than in the virtues those of the highest class embrace?"

She paused, as if overcome with emotion. Griffin glanced up at the ceiling, overcome with annoyance.

"Oh, get on with it," Lady Powlis said. "If you mean to slander Miss Gardner's reputation, I insist you prove your claims."

Lady Clipstone swallowed. "Her past is a matter of public record."

Primrose shot to her feet. "Are you going to toss this gabble-grinder out, Griff, or am I?"

He frowned as the woman rose and stared around the room in panic, as if searching for the closest exit. "I shall see myself out, thank you." Her heel caught on the Turkey carpet. "I shall be happy to take Miss Edlyn on as a pupil, by the way. And I promise that what she would learn under my tutelage would only enhance her social education."

For a full minute after her exit, Griffin and Primrose stood in silence at the window, watching her scramble into her small carriage and take flight.

"Fancy that," he said. "The schoolmistress has a few secrets."

Primrose sniffed. "You knew all along. And so did I. Charlotte told us as much."

"Yes," he said slowly. "But we didn't know everything."

"You don't know everything now," Harriet said quietly from behind them. "She didn't tell you the worst of what I've done. I promised the duchess I wouldn't speak of it, but I'm glad you found out. I'll pack now."

"You will not pack," Lady Powlis said. "We are going to the park."

Harriet shook her head, stepping back into the hall. "As you like, madam. I'll pack after we come home."

"We have a contract, Harriet," Lady Powlis called after her retreating figure. "I shall sue you if you leave."

Griffin broke into a grin.

"You needn't look so pleased," Primrose said, her cane lifted at an angle that his arse knew only too well. "Emma would never have taken Harriet under her wing had she not believed her to be worth redeeming."

"Pleased? How you wound me." He steadied her with his arm, keeping a safe distance from her cane. "She might prove to be a more dangerous woman than even you," he mused.

She shrugged off his arm with an indignant scowl. "Barring a gaol warden, she might also prove to be what this family desperately needs."

Chapter Fourteen

It moved towards the car, and took its seat
Beside the Daemon shape.

PERCY BYSSHE SHELLEY
The Daemon of the World

❧ ❧

They called for Edlyn at the academy.

Harriet doubted that the afternoon could hold a worse experience, until the duke's carriage stopped to collect Lady Constance Chatterton from her father's Mayfair residence. Nothing could alter history. Harriet could not undo what she had done. Nor could she disown her family, even though she had as little to do with them as possible. They'd been brave souls, the Boscastles, to give her another chance.

But brave or not, it wasn't right that they had to endure disgrace on her behalf. She'd never felt more humiliated in her life than when she'd heard Lady Clipstone reveal her past to the duke. What he actually thought of her after the crow's visit, or what she thought of him, remained unclear. It had crossed her mind to warn him that employing her would probably cause him more embarrassment in the future.

She just hadn't realized that it would happen twice in the same day.

Lady Powlis had squeezed her hand several times during the short drive, as if nothing had changed between them. Harriet was afraid to acknowledge her.

Could it be that simple? Another act of grace?

The duke made no attempt at all to reassure her. He sat, his broad-shouldered frame seemingly relaxed, his gaze impassive, even as his presence filled Harriet with unholy pleasure.

Then the carriage stopped. Lady Constance floated down the steps of her home in a lemon silk dress that paid court to her perfect white skin, her sable-brown hair, her guileless gray eyes. She moved with the confidence of a princess, each step dainty and as effortless as walking on air. Her jaunty fox-trimmed hat sat at just the perfect angle to enhance her aristocratic features. Envy poisoned Harriet's pleasure. She hoped Constance would get her slippers caught on the carriage steps and fall back into a pile of fresh horse droppings. She hoped Constance would stink of it and befoul the duke's next breath.

Petty, she admitted it. But so it went. Lady Constance's family claimed blue blood that harked back to a misty age when all it took to become royalty was to raise up an army of louts who would lop off the requisite number of heads and vanquish a country, allowing their leader to wed the daughter of the conquered king.

"Lady Powlis!" Constance exclaimed, in an elegantly pitched voice that made Harriet miserably aware of her own imperfect elocution. "How youthful you look! And Miss Edlyn, what a beautiful young woman you are! I shall glow with pride to introduce you around."

Her emotionless gray eyes dismissed Harriet in a glance.

Last, but for the longest time, she bestowed her attention upon the duke. Her eyes lowered at his polite if indifferent greeting. With a brief but ladylike hesitation, she sank into the space beside him, Edlyn scrunching up in obvious resentment to make room.

It was then that Lady Constance took over the world. In dulcet tones she told the duke that she marched for prison reform. She described the cast-off clothing that she generously donated to street whores. She counted off the charities she sponsored. She spoke of her stand against cesspools. She named the various orphanages she visited until Harriet crossed her eyes, picturing this pretty thing blowing kisses to the waifs who gazed up at her like a good fairy. As if a tossed-off kiss could rid their lives of hunger, abandon, and loneliness.

Lady Powlis fell asleep.

The duke muttered something.

Constance cocked her head. "You do remind me of Liam," she told him with a deep, sorrowful sigh. "My heart aches for what you have lost."

And Harriet's heart ached, too.

* * *

Women, Griffin thought in bemusement. They could torture and tease, provoke or please. Four of them, in varying moods, packed into a single carriage with an unwilling escort, did not an afternoon's pleasant alchemy create. Or perhaps he was suffering from a case of what his aunt called the blue devils. Lady Clipstone's unpleasant visit had cast a cloud over the day. Indeed, he felt the threat of rain in his bones.

He dared not look at Harriet again, in her garden-variety mint-green muslin gown with a bow knotted crookedly under the bodice. She had been shamed enough for one afternoon. Unadulterated anger coursed through him at the thought of it. Whatever doubts he harbored about her were his affair.

As one who lived under his protection—albeit not in the manner he might have privately wished—she would not again suffer insult in his presence. Did it matter that she had not been born a lady? She hadn't pretended otherwise. She wouldn't be working as a companion if she had greater expectations. He doubted his aunt would let her go at any price, however, even if it turned out Harriet was really a royal princess.

Which made him wonder suddenly why Primrose had been so eager to see him married off to the other woman in the carriage. The one his brother had expected to take as his wife along with the duchy.

Lady Constantly Chattering.

Poised, as full of herself as a champagne fountain. Beautiful. If one's taste ran to the cool and calculating. Her first glance had surveyed him as if he were a stud to be purchased for breeding purposes. Which, in an amusing sense, he supposed he would be. He had not felt the slightest spark of passion when their eyes met. He didn't care how well-bred or wealthy she was. Without passion, they might as well be two ceramic figures that graced a mantelpiece for display. The prospect of bedding her for the rest of his life appealed to him as much as did jumping into the Serpentine. And never coming up for air.

Lady Constance ignored the two footmen who stood waiting to assist her from the carriage. Griffin considered ignoring the slender gloved hand she waved in his direction. He was in fact more inclined to help the unfortunate Miss Gardner, who had ungracefully tumbled out the other side without benefit of footmen or folding steps. Fortunately, she sprang right back onto her feet, grinning up at the driver, who warned her not to slip.

"Shall we stroll?" Constance asked, glancing past him to the park.

Griffin watched his aunt abandon him, with her companion in tow. Edlyn wandered off alone. He glanced toward the path. A throng of well-heeled onlookers had collected against a row of curricles and phaetons as if to observe some momentous occasion.

"What are they waiting for?" he asked in amusement.

"Us," Constance said with a sigh, as if he should have known.

Us. "Any particular reason?"

"Your grace has lived in that medieval castle far too long." She tucked her hand into the crook of his arm. "Nod at them."

"Why should I? I have no particular fondness for strangers."

"It is expected of you. Do it." She smiled up at him, revealing an alarmingly sharp set of teeth. "You cannot disappoint the beau monde."

"You don't know me very well."

"Your grace takes his peerage too lightly, I'm afraid."

And he was rapidly deciding he'd like to keep it that way.

He looked down at the top of her high-brimmed hat and wondered whether she had hunted the animal herself. "May I be honest with you?"

"May honesty not wait until we have made our first public appearance?" When he refused to defer, she released another sigh. "Say what you must, then."

"I detest your hat."

"I detest your aunt's companion," she said without hesitation. "She will have to go."

He smiled then, but not at her or at their audience.

She gripped his forearm, her reticule banging

against his elbow. He couldn't imagine what she was carrying—the Crown jewels, perhaps—but whatever it was clunked between them like a ball and chain as they strolled toward the water.

"That is Lord Bermond in the caped coat," she said. "Invite him to go shooting. The woman holding the parasol is his mistress. Pretend she is invisible. And—" She frowned in displeasure. "Never mind. After we attend a soirée or two, you will forget your primeval village and let our civilized ways guide you onto a higher path."

"But I'm somewhat primeval myself."

"That is the unfortunate reputation that precedes you," she murmured.

His eyes darkened.

She would have been wise to take notice.

But she did not.

Harriet had no opportunity to venture an opinion of the graceful woman walking at the duke's side. It would have been improper to use the words that came to mind. Moreover, Lady Powlis conveyed their mutual disapproval in an eloquent if profane outburst that rendered Harriet's appraisal superfluous. She merely nodded at her ladyship's spate of insults. After all, she was paid to be an agreeable companion.

"Why do you not like her, madam?" she asked when she could slip a word in edgewise.

Lady Powlis swung her cane in the air like a master swordsman. "There is not a sincere bone in her body."

"But those bones *are* put together in a manner that his grace seems to find engrossing."

The sword swung toward Harriet. "Save the sauce for another goose. You know perfectly well that what I say is true."

"Quite so," Harriet said, trying to anticipate at which point of the compass the cane would next aim.

Lady Powlis's voice broke unexpectedly. "It's all wrong. And it is all my fault. I have pushed him into that conceited vixen's arms. I have used guilt and sorrow to encourage this match. I—" She paused, pale and out of breath.

Harriet glanced around the park in concern. She spotted Edlyn standing in the midst of what appeared to be a small assembly of governesses and their energetic charges. A cocker spaniel ran barking around a tree. "Shall we find a bench for you to rest?"

"I don't need rest. I need to find a wife who will care for him and Edlyn."

"And who cares for you, madam."

Lady Powlis suddenly looked deflated. "That is why I hired you, my girl."

Harriet shook her head. "Then, in all fairness, I will tell you again that the complaint lodged against me today is only the start of it. You would not be ill-advised to dismiss me."

"I pay you to agree with me, ill-advised or not."

"Yes, madam." Harriet's gaze drifted to the duke and the elegant lady guiding him toward a group of ladies and gentlemen who seemed eager to make his acquaintance. "She's beautiful."

"Beauty fades."

"She's an heiress."

"Wealth corrupts."

"His grace doesn't appear to mind whether she fades away or corrupts him."

She sighed as the duke broke away from the gathering. Lady Constance hesitated and then hurried after him. Suddenly Harriet resented the Boscastles for introducing her to a world in which she would always be an outsider, the design of a modern Prometheus who would meet a tragic fate only because she wanted a mate. She sighed in self-pity. She was really a little monster. Lady Constance had skin the color of moonlight. Harriet's blushed and went blotchy at every emotion. She could never float about with a fox on her head without looking like a court jester. She had never taken a stand against cesspits. She had, however, once pushed a boy who was chasing her into one.

Lady Powlis's voice broke into her thoughts. "I would do *anything* to stop this courtship, do you hear? I cannot bear another broken heart in my family. We must put an end to this no matter what it takes."

Harriet felt a breeze quiver through the air at the duke's approach. Lady Constance called back to one of the footmen to fetch her rabbit muff from the carriage. As the servant turned, a gray stillness enshrouded the park. The duke looked directly at Harriet. The unconcealed desire in his eyes tore through her like lightning.

She caught her breath. The clouds burst forth with such a sudden drenching rain that a malevolent wizard might have dumped a cauldron of bad wishes upon the gathering. Griffin glanced up with a deep laugh. The ladies around him shrieked, running for shelter, while the gentlemen complained about ruined attire and another afternoon better spent at the club.

"Look at her now," Lady Powlis whispered over Harriet's shoulder. "Her ringlets are dissolving in the rain."

"Perhaps she'll melt," Edlyn said, her lip curling.

Harriet turned in surprise, hard-pressed to constrain a laugh. "That isn't nice of you, Miss Edlyn. Ill thoughts against another are not to be spoken aloud."

Edlyn smiled wickedly. Harriet felt a rush of bittersweet satisfaction and smiled back. An unbreakable bond, an unexpected one, had been formed.

Lady Constance cast the duke a furious look and ran for the carriage. He watched her for a moment, then strode toward the three women huddled together in the rain. "Are you all mad, my little ducks? Must I gather you under my wing?"

Harriet started to laugh.

He pulled off his coat, threw it over Edlyn's head, offered one arm to Primrose, the other to Harriet.

There was grace, after all.

The four of them dashed for the carriage as one. The footmen met them halfway. Harriet laughed again, staring down at her muddy flat-heeled slippers.

She couldn't imagine anything more fun than this, not even a midnight ball. It made up for the misery that she had been dealt earlier in the day.

And then a cry of unadulterated terror immobilzed her, indeed, everyone within earshot, to the spot. She looked up through the rain as a scruffy young man darted from behind a tree. A knife glimmered in his hand and flashed up toward the woman standing in front of him. Lady Constance went a deathly shade of white. The servant who was holding an umbrella over her head backed away.

"Oh, no," Harriet whispered, swallowing hard. "Not again. Not now. Don't do it."

The young man was quick on his feet. Quicker than lightning. He ought to be. He had taught Harriet how to cut a purse. He shook his fist under Lady Constance's chin with one hand. The other efficiently severed the strings of her reticule from her limp grasp.

Quicker than lightning, Harriet thought, although not quicker than she or the duke. They broke into a run at the same instant and intersected when Griffin turned abruptly to impede her progress, throwing her a look of unhidden disgust.

"For the love of God, Harriet. What do you

think you are doing? You're only slowing me down. I'm more than capable of taking care of a little bastard like that."

"So am I," she said, rain washing down her neck in cold rivulets.

"You damned fool," he muttered. "I've lost him now because of you. What am I supposed to do?"

She stood before him with the calm acceptance of what could never be changed. "Go back to Lady Constance and comfort her. That was one of my half brothers who stole her bag. I'll get it back, don't you worry."

"Your brother, Harriet?" he said in disbelief.

"You know what I was. Now you know what I could have been. Frightening, isn't it?"

She walked around him.

"Where the hell do you think you're going?" he shouted at her.

"I'm going 'ome." She took off her slippers, one at a time, and tossed them at him over her shoulders. They didn't match her dress, anyway. "Take care of your family, duke. And yourself. You're not as bad as everyone thinks."

Chapter Fifteen

I had been struck senseless by his fiendish threats,
but now, for the first time,
the wickedness of my promise burst upon me.

MARY SHELLEY
Frankenstein

❧ ❧

The hackney driver who took Harriet to St. Giles
remembered her from the old days. He'd heard
how she had come up in the world. Everyone in the
streets from the dustmen to the bone pickers
boasted that they had once known Harriet Gardner. It was already common knowledge in the East
End that she was now employed in the household
of a duke. Last Christmas, she had sent the street
children sweets and cloaks discarded by the girls at
the academy. Still, she wasn't a saint like the lady
her half brother had just robbed. Pity. There wasn't
justice in the world.

"Don't forget," the driver said as he deposited
her on the corner of her old haunt. "Duke or not, if
'e don't do right by you, you always got yer friends,
'arry. We can take care of the nobs good and
proper."

Harriet shuddered, as much from the thought as
from the misty early evening air that evoked mem-

ories of her life in the slums. Her stockinged toes contracted as she walked across the cobbles. She was grateful the rain had stopped. She'd gone soft, in body and heart. That was the price one paid for living with the swells.

A low whistle rang from the pub on the corner. A long shadow fell into step at her right. A shorter one joined it at the left. Then another. Soon all the shadows marched alongside her, taunting in their singsong voices.

"Well, well, look wot the cat's dragged 'ome. Pretty, pretty."

"That ain't no mouse, you moron. That's the cat 'erself. 'ow's life treatin' you, love?"

"Better than you buggers ever did."

A gang of seven or so gathered—young men, if one could regard them as human at all, who had been mere boys two years ago. Her eyes narrowed as the eldest, Nicholas Rydell, took her by the hand. He'd always been the leader. "Do you wanna come out with me? We got a lay tonight down at the wharves."

She twisted her wrist, backhanded his chin, and continued walking briskly through the labyrinth of lanes. Guffaws of laughter at his indignant howl broke out behind her. She smiled. Ignorant bastards. Beggars. Poor hopeless sods.

She veered into a narrow alleyway. Pools of black water reflected what little moonlight penetrated between the tightly packed tenements. She opened the back door of the last house. No one heard her enter. For a moment, she wondered if she could bear facing her family again. Strangely, the place didn't stink of the boiled eels and cheap ale that had always turned her stomach.

She went into the kitchen. The stone floor had been swept. The sink looked clean. Her two half brothers, Luke and Rob, sat eating supper at what had once been a billiards table. Her temper erupted. She walked up to Rob—he with the insolent grin—snatched the spoon from his hand, and hit him over the head with it.

"You promised me after you assaulted the duchess that you would never, *ever* commit another crime upon the Boscastle family." Not that Lady Constance was a member of that esteemed clan yet.

He swore, ducking his head under the table. Luke stared up at Harriet in astonishment. "Them was your pals he rogered?" He kicked the cringing shape under the table in contempt. "You stole from your own sister?"

She stared at the hot coals burning in the hearth. Who in this house had the wits to tend a fire? Someone was missing. Someone was here. "He didn't steal from me. He robbed the duke's betrothed of her reticule. And I want it back."

Rob straightened. "All right. If it's that important to you, 'arry. Let me fetch it from upstairs."

"Be quiet about it," Luke said, his voice rough with impatience until he looked at Harriet again. "Bloody fool. 'e'll be next to go."

"That's it." Harriet nodded in certitude. Her father's absence explained everything. "Jack isn't here."

Luke stared down at his bowl of beef broth.

"Where is he?" she asked in resignation. "Not in gaol again. I can't afford to pay counsel every time he breaks the law. I'm putting out more for his defense than he steals."

"You don't know?" Luke raised his eyes with a look that turned her blood cold. "None of the Runners told you?"

"If he's done murder this time," she said, "he'll bloody well have to take what he deserves."

"Yeah." Luke gave a bitter laugh. "And so 'e did. Jack's dead. Ain't been seen in months."

She waited for him to burst into peals of laughter, to crow that he'd got her good this time. She waited for her drunken father to clump down the stairs like a beanstalk giant and try to cuff her ear, cursing when he missed. But the only sound was the heavy beat of her heart and—she turned—the gurgle of a baby in the cradle she hadn't even noticed.

"You should have told me," she said, glaring at Luke's downbent head. "A baby, and Jack is gone. I give you money every chance I get. You could have told me."

Luke's face softened as he looked over at the cradle. "I didn't think you cared. Jack was spittin' mad that you walked out on us. He said you was a traitor and we ought never talk to you again."

"I was arrested. I didn't have a choice."

"You didn't come back, though," he said. "He resented that. It don't matter now."

"He left you something." A young girl, clean and comely in blue sprigged muslin, slipped into the kitchen. "I've kept it for you. I'm Abigail, by the way. Where's your manners, Luke? Can't you admit to your own sister that you married me?"

He frowned as she passed a worn velvet pouch to Harriet. "Is it cash?"

" 'Tis none of your business," his wife said, going to the cradle in the corner. She lifted the tiny bundle and offered it to Harriet, who hesitated, then slipped the pouch into her bodice before holding out her arms.

Abigail smiled. "That boy's a demon when he don't get what he wants."

Weren't they all?

"I could have given Jack a decent burial," Harriet said, nuzzling the baby's head. "I hated him with all my heart, but I would have bought him a gravestone."

Luke shook his head. "Jack was always afraid the body snatchers or someone 'e'd soaked would disturb 'is bones. Someone told 'im about these doctors who took corpses apart to fashion monsters and—"

"Where did you put him, then?" Harriet asked impatiently.

"We rowed 'im out to sea in a whelk boat and tossed 'im overboard." Luke averted his gaze. "It's what Jack wanted, not to be a nuisance to his loved ones."

"Have you taken to smoking opium, Luke? He murdered someone." She covered the baby's ears with his blanket. Not that the little scrap hadn't heard worse in this house.

Luke shot her a dark scowl. " 'Twere in self-defense. He knocked off the friggin' barrister who bled us all dry. There was witnesses, too, but it don't matter. No magistrate'll ever believe wot one of us says. They lie easier than they breathe."

The baby gave a fussy cry and reached for Harriet's breast. "That's right," she laughed, handing him back to his mother. "Another blue-eyed demon breaking my heart and putting his hands where they don't be—"

A frantic shout interrupted her. "Trouble!" Rob came pelting into the kitchen, goblets and ropes of jewelry tucked under his arm. "Move it. Tea party's over." He tossed Lady Constance's reticule across the table. "Take it," he said to Harriet. "And give the screechin' bitch my regards."

"How many are there?" Luke asked, springing off his stool.

"I didn't bloody count 'em," Rob said. "There's a carriage coming down the street." He ran a hand through his flyaway red hair. "Wanna come with us, 'arry? We'll cut you in a bit."

She shook her head. "When are you going to learn? Get on, and if anything happens to that little baby—"

They were gone. All through the house, footsteps echoed, mattresses creaked, trapdoors opened and banged shut. Without giving it a second thought, she picked up Lady Constance's reticule, walked to the corner, and dropped it in the empty cradle.

"There's your christening gift from Auntie Harry, little precious, courtesy of someone who'll never miss it."

She walked from the kitchen and out into the night. The duke stood at the end of the alley, as dark and menacing as anyone a girl could meet on these streets. He was not going to let her past this time. Harriet forced herself not to run toward him. He'd shed his coat and cravat. His white lawn shirt needed a wash. He could use a good shave. She could have wept buckets at the sight of him.

"Did Lady Powlis send you here, duke?"

"Believe it or not," he said with a quiet sigh, "I do not do everything I'm told."

"Oh, I believe it."

He looked up at the stone-gray tenements. A figure wobbled on the rickety footbridge that arched midair from one upper window to the next. A glint of moonlight captured the strong angles of his face. She heard carriage wheels creak in the street. If he hadn't been the duke, Harriet might have mistaken him for a thoroughly disreputable person.

"So, what do you think of the place?" she asked softly, moving around him.

He shifted. His body stopped her progress. "Get inside the carriage, Harriet."

"What do you—"

He glanced at her. "It's a hovel."

"It's my home. Well, it was."

He blew out a breath. "Not exactly Mayfair."

"I ain't no May queen, neither." She paused. "I realize that this is an awkward time to ask, but I don't suppose you would give me references of character for another position?"

"Get into the carriage before I am forced to carry you."

She ventured a step back and smiled.

He took a step toward her. "You did not have my permission to leave the park. In fact, I forbade it."

"Please tell me your aunt is not waiting for me in the carriage."

"My aunt is not waiting for you in my carriage. However, I have promised her that you will not leave us again." And then, quicker than lightning, he advanced another step, locked one arm beneath her knees, the other around her shoulders, and, as Harriet would later describe it, bore her off into the night.

Chapter Sixteen

The Daemon leaning from the ethereal car
Gazed on the slumbering maid.

PERCY BYSSHE SHELLEY
The Daemon of the World

❧ ☙

The carriage had slowly rolled up behind them. A head popped up from one of several barrels that bordered the alley. A skeletal figure in a cape flashed a blade.

Griffin backed into the carriage steps. He could only hope that Harriet had neither noticed the pistol he had drawn from his waistband nor heard the bottle that one of the shadows had broken against the carriage wheel. Shattered glass, unfortunately, had a rather distinctive sound.

"Inside you go," he said cheerfully, pushing her safely against the squabs before he closed the door.

His coachman cocked his flintlock muskets.

He nodded grimly to the two footmen, who had dropped from the rear, both of them pale as chalk. "Do what you must. But please do not risk your necks in a fight."

The street gang surged toward him. He planted

his back against the carriage door and stood his guard.

The brawny leader of the shadows stared at him in silence, then raised his gaze. A subtle gentleness softened his scarred features. Griffin had no doubt that were he to turn around he would discover Harriet's face in the carriage window. Another male with blazing red hair barreled his way to the front of the group. Griffin blinked. He hadn't realized how closely the cutpurse in the park resembled Harriet.

It gave him pause. How could he possibly harm one who reminded him of the woman his aunt had sworn she could not live without and had made him promise on his mother's grave he would return safely to her side?

The cutpurse lifted his hand. He was a fool misguided by a false sense of power if ever Griffin had encountered one. He waited. It was a well-known fact in the family that many a Boscastle had claimed victory by simply outwaiting the opposition, be it a soldier on the field or a lady in a bedchamber.

The leader of the street gang clearly took offense at anyone who challenged his authority. The law of the underworld would be obeyed, or else. He shouldered Harriet's half brother aside and bowed mockingly in Griffin's shadow.

"Ladies and gentlemen, and those who are by nature neither, let us offer safe passage to these, our most esteemed guests, the Duke—and Duchess—of St. Giles."

The carriage door flew open and hit Griffin's shoulder. "Get in now, duke," Harriet said, "or I'll not be responsible for what happens next."

He complied. He would have hated to take down her brother when he looked so much like Harriet. The carriage set off undisturbed into the darkened street. Harriet settled beside him, not protesting when he drew her closer. The slippers she had thrown at him in the park sat on the opposite seat. He thought briefly of insisting she put them on. Instead, he reached down and caught one of her feet in his hand.

"You're as cold as a corpse," he exclaimed. "Give me your other foot so I can rub some blood back into your veins. You could catch your death walking about without shoes."

"What a fuss you make at times. I'm perfectly fine."

He should have taken her at her word. But of course once he touched her he couldn't bring himself to stop. He removed her garters and peeled off her ruined stockings, one at a time. The warm awareness of bare flesh lured him like a beggar to a banquet. It wasn't every day that a woman tossed her shoes at him and led him on a wild pursuit. Or that he had a legitimate excuse to knead her calf and inch his hand slowly toward her thigh.

He waited for her to protest, but when he glanced up he saw that she had closed her eyes. "Dear God, Harriet," he said with a laugh. "You do know how to turn a day in the park on its head.

Why didn't you tell me right off that was your brother? It would have been easier on us both."

She breathed out a sigh and smiled with a sultry regret that sent his thoughts in a thousand directions, all of them dark and tempting. "It happened too fast," she said. "And I lost my temper. I don't have red hair for nothing."

He shook his head. "Well, I think I've seen more of London this evening than I really wanted to."

She slid down deeper into the squabs. "I've never had anyone rub my feet before," she murmured, her voice languid, as if she was half asleep. "It felt nice. You have gentle hands."

He swallowed. "I have to admit that my hands are fighting temptation right now."

"Better than fighting a street gang, don't you think?"

He grunted. "I can't disagree with that."

She sighed deeply as his fingers drifted beneath her bent knee. "You needn't have worried, though," she said.

"Oh?"

"I wouldn't have let them hurt you."

He raised his eyebrows. "I don't think I would have enjoyed watching you take on a bunch of thugs to protect me."

"Somebody has to keep wayward young men in line."

"Forgive me if this sounds like an insult to your family, but I think those gentlemen are past the age of redemption."

"It's the only way they know to survive," she said, frowning up at him.

His hand tightened reflexively around her knee. "You learned a different way to live."

"Maybe," she said wistfully. "Who knows how long it'll last?"

"It had better last at least for the period for which my aunt has paid you. I wouldn't put it past her to come blazing here in a phaeton with pistols drawn. And even then I'd be the one who would get the blame for it."

She laughed. "I didn't get the purse," she said wistfully, then admitted, "No. That's a lie. I did. But I gave it to a little baby. I have a nephew no one thought to tell me about."

"Hang the purse." *And its owner,* he might have said. How could he possibly think about another woman when Harriet was letting him touch her like this? She hadn't made a single move to stop him. He hoped to God she wasn't relying on his willpower. Just because he wasn't a London rake didn't mean he was a saint. But, Lord, he couldn't help himself.

"She's beautiful," Harriet said out of the blue.

"Aunt Primrose?"

She bit her lower lip. "You know who I mean."

"Oh, her," he said absently, his hand stealing upward another inch. "I didn't notice." Her skin felt like raw silk. The texture of it sharpened his hunger.

"What *did* you notice?" she asked in curiosity.

"Her hat."

Her eyes grew wide.

"That's all?"

"Well, not exactly."

"Then—"

"She had really sharp teeth."

"You're awful," she whispered, laughter in her voice.

"She probably thinks so, too," he said with a grin.

"She might if she knew what you were doing right now," Harriet said, studying his face.

The thunder of his heart reverberated through his body. He leaned down, slipping one hand around her shoulders, the other into the vulnerable hollow between her thighs. "She *definitely* would if she knew what I was thinking."

His mouth grazed hers. He savored the sigh that escaped her. His fingers gently parted the folds of her sex and stroked. She stifled a cry against his cheek. He pitted every particle of his control against his instincts to keep himself from persuading her to give him more.

Harriet was, in fact, fighting a losing war against the sensations that coursed through her blood. Her breasts swelled inside her gown, as if all the little aches inside her body had joined to overpower her. The sight of Griffin standing alone in the alley, standing up to protect her, had pierced a chink in her defenses. She had let him carry her off without a word of protest. Indeed, now she wasn't making a fuss at all. She had not dreamed that she could be disarmed by the duke's knowing touch. She hadn't guessed that a man's gentleness could be his most potent weapon.

He seemed to understand, even if he was withholding his mercy. She moaned, her body begging, moving against his hand. She felt his fingers penetrate deeper to stretch her passage. She heard his breath, ragged in the silence, the roughness of it intensifying her own arousal. His face hovered above hers, one moment in shadow, the next revealed in the wavering carriage light behind the window.

He smiled with the allure of a fallen angel, so beautiful that her throat ached, and even when she closed her eyes, he was all she could see. "Harriet," he whispered, kissing her again, leading her deeper and deeper into swirling darkness. And just when she knew it couldn't get any darker, a storm broke inside her and enveloped her in black heat.

She lay for several moments afterward in wondrous contemplation. When at last he lifted himself from her prone form, she felt her heartbeat begin to slow. He stared at her in fierce silence, then kissed her softly on the mouth.

They sat apart for the duration of the drive. She did not ask him to explain how this would change her position in his life. She knew perfectly well that she had unleashed a force of nature, and now she would have to tame it or pay the price.

Chapter Seventeen

But I forget that I am moralizing
in the most interesting part of my tale,
and your looks remind me to proceed.

MARY SHELLEY
Frankenstein

❧ ❧

It was another unspoken rule in the Boscastle family that one discussed an unpleasantness only in private. In public one pretended these events had not occurred. If a Boscastle stopped to deny every accusation hurled his way, he would likely never make it from his front door to the pavement.

When Harriet arose the following morning and hastened to help Lady Powlis plan the afternoon, her ladyship made no reference to the previous day's disaster. She behaved in her usual grumpy manner, while two chambermaids tended the fire and hunted for the bonnet that Primrose insisted had been stolen, until Harriet reminded her she had sent it back to the milliner's to be replumed.

The minute Lady Powlis dismissed the chambermaids, she jumped from her armchair, as spry as an elf, and closed the door. "I demand a full accounting, every detail."

And so Harriet gave her an accounting, naturally

leaving out the details of the carriage ride, which she herself had reviewed countless times. If her ladyship once again suspected certain omissions, the grim depiction of her visit to St. Giles seemed enough to occupy her mind.

"By the by, I am delighted to death that you dropped Lady Constipation's bag in the cradle."

"Lady—" Harriet shook her head. "Oh, madam, how looks deceive. And here I've always thought that a lady could never slip into low talk. How I admire you for breaking that rule with such aplomb."

"I shall slip into something much lower if my nephew marries that piece of work."

Harriet smiled. She knew a powerful ally when she found one. The duke had to be mad if he thought Primrose would drive her away. "Let me ring for some tea and cake. It's hours before the breakfast party. I should not want all this distress to weaken your ladyship."

"What comfort you are, dear." Her voice dropped to a conspiratorial tone. "You didn't tell me *everything* about yesterday, did you?"

"Madam, my life is an open book."

"I shall dismiss you, Harriet, if I discover that you are fibbing."

Harriet nodded demurely. "Yes, and so you should."

But Harriet kept her thoughts to herself for the rest of the day. The duke escorted her, his aunt, and Edlyn to a breakfast party at the Mayfair mansion of a viscount whose title escaped Harriet's notice. She had enough to worry about, what with keeping an eye on Miss Edlyn, *not* stealing looks at the duke, and placating Lady Powlis, who ate half a mutton pie and complained about her bunions and the bonnet that was taking forever to replume.

It was an enjoyable party, if only because the duke spent most of his time with his handsome cousins and not with Lady Constance, who was said to be recovering from the insult inflicted upon her person by the cutpurse in the park. Harriet overheard several ladies at the party discussing the incident. One ventured to guess that Constance might not make another public appearance until the perpetrator was caught. Her friend whispered that Constance's doctor had suggested the young lady spend the rest of the Season taking the waters. Harriet was afraid that Lady Constance was made of sterner stuff.

"Harriet." Lady Powlis poked her gently with her cane. "Where has Edlyn gone now?"

Harriet glanced up. "She was watching the archery contest a minute ago."

"Well, I cannot see her through the featherbrains dancing about the place. Be an angel and make sure that she has not been lured off by some handsome fortune hunter. And take a bite of this pie. I think the meat is off."

"Do you wish me to taste it before or after I find Miss Edlyn, madam?"

"I wish you to stop answering me in that impertinent manner. And I forbid you to taste the pie. No point in both of us taking ill."

Harriet set off through the park, leaving Lady Powlis at the trestle tables that had been arranged around a drooping fig tree. Miss Edlyn was not watching the archery contest. The duke, however, had removed his frock coat and was sauntering across the green to compete. Harriet would have given a month's wages to watch. An ornamental bridge that crossed a pond was crowded with ladies who gathered to cheer him on. His black hair shone like a raven's wing in the dappled light. He paused, looking around as if he was waiting for someone to join him.

It was then that Harriet spotted Edlyn hurrying up the steps of the ivy-draped rotunda. Harriet glanced back wistfully at the duke. He had raised his bow to take aim at the target. She turned for a fraction of a second to witness Edlyn emerge from the other side of the edifice, appearing considerably brighter than she had been in days. She appeared to be by herself. A lady in a bonnet was walking in the other direction.

And there wasn't a rake in view, disregarding the duke, whose arrow had struck the target dead center, to the delight of his female audience. The cheers and claps of his devoted supporters echoed in the park, a chorus that Harriet could not escape. She would have applauded him herself, had a companion been allowed to express her enthusiasm in public.

All in all, however, discounting her ladyship's indigestion, Harriet decided it had been a pleasant day. An uncommon one, indeed, without a single drop of rain to ruin the party.

The same could not be said of the following night's entertainment.

"Grayson has promised that this will be an intimate affair," Lady Powlis reassured the duke, when he complained that he would rather not go. "I don't see why you're being so unsociable, Griff. The marquess is family, after all. One does not travel to London to sit brooding in a library."

"But we just attended one of his balls."

"This is meant to be a quiet party," she insisted. "I don't imagine there will be a crush."

Yet even Harriet knew that what the Marquess of Sedgecroft considered to be a private supper could include a hundred or so guests. Most of them would be titled or well connected at court, although the marquess was probably best known in the ton for allowing love affairs to take place during his soirées. The mansion provided many private chambers suitable for this purpose and, for family only, an Italian gallery where acts of amour could unfold without a chance of interruption. If Miss Edlyn or any of the academy's graduating ladies were invited, it would fall to Harriet or Charlotte Boscastle to make certain some scoundrel did not compromise their good names. Although Harriet was no longer employed at the elite school, she had formed a surprising bond with those girls who struggled alongside her for acceptance.

Chapter Eighteen

I pursued a maiden and clasped a reed.
Gods and men, we are all deluded thus!

PERCY BYSSHE SHELLEY
Song of Pan

❧ ❧

Griffin danced the first dance with his cousin Charlotte, whose gaze, he noted, moved about the ballroom as if she were a master spy intent on thwarting an act of sabotage that threatened the security of England. In a way he supposed that an impromptu tryst might indeed be interpreted as such. For example, a duke's ward could be caught alone with a rogue. The rogue, finding three or four Boscastle men breathing down his neck, would have no choice but to offer marriage. The prospect of the sullied maiden making a stronger alliance would be dashed.

And it was in the course of coming to this conclusion that he realized it was not Edlyn's virtue that appeared to be at risk.

It was Harriet's.

His niece was sitting sullenly with Primrose and the elite circle of ladies who had been invited to the party. One or two respectable young lords stood flirting with . . . well, it was hard to identify their quarry at this distance. He hoped to heaven it was not his aunt.

But the dashing gentleman who was leading Harriet around the floor had an infatuated look if ever Griffin had seen one. To be frighteningly honest, it might be what Griffin looked like during the unguarded moments he had spent in her company.

"Do you think," he asked Charlotte, "that it is proper for a companion to dance in front of girls who are meant to emulate her?"

Charlotte clearly perceived this to be an odd question by her startled look. "But I saw you dance with Harriet the other night."

"That was different. I am not obligated to abide by any rules of etiquette. Am I?"

Charlotte lifted her brow. "I was led to believe that Primrose finds her to be the perfect companion."

So did he.

"I shall tell you a secret," he said. "Primrose is very possessive of that young woman."

"Well, so was I," Charlotte confessed. "And your aunt stole her away from me."

His gaze cut straight again to Harriet. She was laughing, out of pace with the line of other dancers but determined in her unpretentious way to keep up. She drifted past him as the dance ended. Her face was upturned to her partner, until she noticed

Griffin watching her. She gave him a distracted smile, which he did not return.

He shook his head.

"Griff?" Charlotte said softly.

He led her back to the circle of chairs where his aunt sat with the marchioness and several other close family friends. The flame-haired figure in silver silk was whirled back into another dance. By the same man.

His aunt glanced up at him. "If he asks her to dance one more time, it will be your duty to object."

Lady Jane seemed to hesitate, then glanced up at Griffin, her green eyes sparkling. "It's all right. If it makes you uncomfortable to spoil Miss Gardner's romance, we shall have Grayson, or even Weed, solve the problem."

"It doesn't make me uncomfortable," he said in a dismissive voice. "I simply don't think that it's my place to enforce—does she *know* the gentleman?"

Lady Jane shrugged, darting him a shrewd glance. "She might. He's the son of one of Grayson's bankers, and he's always invited. Strange. I never paid attention until now, but he doesn't dance with anyone else." She drew a breath, her gaze moving past Griffin. "Well, speaking of romance, *yours* appears to have just arrived. Aren't we fashionably late and looking none the worse for our horrid experience in the park?"

"*My* romance?" Griffin said bleakly.

His aunt made a rude noise in her throat.

He glanced around and saw Constance standing in a gown of sea-foam satin, male admirers flocking her at either side. His heart sank. Was he meant to do something? Had this been staged? He glanced down accusingly at his aunt.

"I didn't know," she whispered, shaking her head. "I hadn't a clue that she was on the guest list."

"What about that other list?" he asked in suspicion.

"The one Harriet was working on?"

He nodded tersely. "I hope you're not going to tell me there were others."

"I never even saw that one," Primrose said with an indignant sniff. "In fact, I never saw any evidence of that demoniacal drawing you went on about at all."

"Well, I didn't make it up."

"I hope you aren't trying to get my companion in trouble again, Griff. It shows a really unsavory side of your character that I never dreamt existed."

Jane studied him with a cautious smile. "Forgive me if it's too soon to inquire, but are the nuptials to be held here in Grayson's private chapel?"

"It's too soon," Griffin and Primrose said at the same instant.

"Oh." Jane pursed her lips, allowing a moment to pass. "Then you probably won't want a tour of the chapel tonight, after everyone but family goes home."

"Probably not," Primrose answered before Griff even opened his mouth again.

He looked up reluctantly.

Constance sent him a beseeching smile, as if to say, *Save me from these scoundrels. My beauty is so overwhelming that I cannot defend myself for another moment.*

His aunt touched his wrist. "Do what is polite. Nothing more."

He bent over her. "Primrose?"

"Yes, Griffin?"

"Stop telling me what to do every five minutes."

She cast her gaze down in apology. "I am an old bother," she said ruefully. "But it's only because I care so deeply about you."

"I know." He straightened, motioning for a footman to take his empty glass.

"One more thing," she said before he could escape.

He turned his head.

"Miss Gardner just went through the French doors with that attentive gentleman. Please fetch her for me."

"I shall send one of the footmen."

"You will not. If anybody is to catch Harriet in an indiscretion, it shall be one of us. I don't want her forced into marrying a banker's son and abandoning me."

"The devil," he said, and stared at the doors that stood invitingly open to the night. It was terrifying how at times he and his aunt thought alike. "You do understand that Lady Constance will take this as a deliberate slight on my part?"

Jane smiled. "By the look of things, she will be well amused for a minute or two. If not, I have my own ways of providing a distraction."

Chapter Nineteen

How can I see so noble a creature
destroyed by misery,
without feeling the most poignant grief?

MARY SHELLEY
Frankenstein

જ્ર ભ્ર

Harriet had succeeded in eluding her persistent suitor by sending him off twice to fetch her champagne, which she covertly emptied into a potted fern. If she had her way, he'd be toasting himself in the dark and not even realize she wanted to escape him. He was a sweet boy and an utter bore. She would have to sneak back to Lady Powlis through one of the rooms off the garden. She stifled a yawn. She hoped her employer would sleep late tomorrow morning. Her feet hurt from dancing. She had taken but a few bites at supper, and she needed nourishment to keep up with the Boscastles. She fled down the torchlit terrace steps and onto a small path.

As she approached the statue of a beheaded Hermes that was her guidepost, she heard laughter and low whispers drifting from the garden depths. She paused, narrowing her eyes in concentration. Other than Edlyn, only three students from the academy had been invited to tonight's affair, and they were all on their best behavior.

She drew behind the headless statue as the voices grew nearer. She knew instinctively that this was a conversation she should not interrupt.

Even if she would learn a few love secrets by listening, a love that could be revealed only in stolen moments was not what Harriet desired. Passion, yes. But only with a promise of forever. The gutter girl had her morals.

"I don't care if he does see us together," a woman said, and not quietly, either.

The gentleman escorting her replied, "But you will care if you lose your chance to become a duchess. There are few dukes for an ambitious lady to marry in England. Fewer yet are those in their prime."

"I know."

"Perhaps he is not worth the sacrifice," her escort mused. "If he was capable of murdering his own brother, imagine what might happen to his wife."

Harriet stared up at the moonless sky, wondering why the failings of human nature never ceased to surprise her. She should have developed a tougher hide by now. She didn't move. She could have jumped out, grabbed Constance by her pretty curls, and shoved her, heels over arse, into the dirt where she belonged. But ladies did not engage in fisticuffs. It was common. Gentlewomen vented their spleen with veiled insults and whispered hurtful things behind one another's backs. Harriet would have to learn the proper protocol for vanquishing a rival.

"He doesn't have any brothers for you to marry, does he?" the man asked thoughtfully.

"None that will become duke, unless he dies."

"Well, he looked damned healthy to me."

"He is uncouth," Constance said, her voice rising. "He has ignored me yet again tonight. And he stares at that little companion of his aunt's with such obvious desire that I shall have her drowned like a cat in a well should I marry him."

Harriet unfolded her arms. Protocol and fisticuffs be damned. This called for pistols at dawn. Of course, she could hardly run back to the duke with what she'd overheard. Lady Constance would deny everything and accuse Harriet of malicious mischief. His aunt was another matter.

The voices receded.

She edged around the statue and proceeded in silence through the garden to a service door where a bored-looking footman stood guard.

"Miss Harriet," he said, perking up at the sight of her. "Protecting a lost lamb, are you? Guard yourself while you're at it."

Protecting a lost beast was more apt, she reflected. She slipped by the footman with a grateful smile and stole through a dark antechamber. She made a quick survey of the hallways and alcoves where an unseen guest might hide. It would be too ironic if she caught the duke in the midst of his own indiscretion. She must never tell him. It would make her look spiteful. She put her hand to her eyes. Yes, she must, but not in the middle of a party.

"Harriet," a stern voice said from the end of the hall. "Is anything wrong—you aren't crying, are you?"

The duke strode toward her, black and white, sin and wicked sweetness. She lowered her hand and stood watching him as if she, like the statue in the garden, had been turned to stone and lost her poor head besides.

"Were you just out on the terrace?" he demanded.

She nodded, looking up slowly into his eyes. How could anyone believe he had murdered his brother? Yes, that hard face of his would not lay any suspicions to rest, and he was a frustrating man to understand. But Harriet thought he liked it that way.

His dark gaze searched the shadows behind her. "You've been all this time by yourself?"

"Yes."

"And the other gentleman?" he asked, his brow furrowing.

She hesitated. The other gentleman. "You mean the one I danced with?"

He regarded her in a long unsmiling silence. "Where is he?"

"I don't know. Drinking champagne, I think. I'm not his keeper."

"Alone?" he asked dubiously. "He left you alone while he went off to drink? Why?"

She swallowed. If he kept interrogating her and staring at her with his irresistible blue eyes, she'd be tempted to blurt out the truth. She would have to tell him exactly what she had overheard in the garden. And while she would dearly love to show Lady Constance in a bad light, she reminded herself that this wasn't the proper time or place to test his temper.

"I don't know why he left me," she said again. "Maybe my dancing drove him to drink. Maybe he saw you staring at us like some big ogre. I hope you don't take offense, but you do have a scowl that goes right through a body."

"I thought I was being very subtle."

She snorted. "You can't be serious. My poor dance partner was shaking in his buckled shoes."

He smiled, not making any effort at denial.

She waited a few moments, and when he said nothing more, she made a quick attempt to slip around him.

He caught her by the elbow, pulling her to his side. "Something happened to you." He studied her closely, lifting her face in his hand.

She let him look. She'd learned a long time ago that a guileless stare could cover a guilty conscience. Not that she'd done anything wrong. But, dear heaven, you wouldn't know it by how fast her heart was beating.

His eyes traveled from her face down the front of

her silvery gown to the tips of her dancing pumps. "I was on the terrace a few minutes ago myself," he said, walking her into the wall. "I didn't notice you."

"I didn't see your grace, either. But then, perhaps you missed me as I left the garden. It's easy to get lost in this place."

He frowned. "I walked through the garden, too."

She shouldn't ask. "Did your grace find anything of interest there?"

He lifted his brow. "Not as interesting as what I have found in the hall."

"The marquess collects many priceless works of art."

"I have heard," he murmured, "that some of the rooms in this house have been designed with seduction in mind."

"So the rumors go."

His thumb stroked from her ear to her chin. "The family has been invited to stay for a private supper after everyone else leaves."

She disregarded the inner voice that warned her of impending pleasure. "Then you're obliged to stay."

"I won't stay unless you stay with me," he said stubbornly.

"How old are you, your grace?"

He sketched his thumb along the bumpy lace that bordered the tops of her breasts. "What difference does it make?"

She had to smile. "Not much to a person who's accustomed to having everything go his way. Why did you come to London if all you wanted was to be alone?"

"I never said I wanted to be alone," he said with a cool smile. "I only ask to be able to choose my company."

"Some of us aren't allowed even that."

"Then you should never have let me touch you, Harriet. I cannot look at you now and not ache."

"That's life in London."

His mouth hardened. "Don't you know what happens to young women who wander off in the dark?"

Her laugh was bittersweet. "Better than you ever will."

He swallowed hard. "I don't want to imagine that part of your life."

She laid her head back against the wall. A relentless hunger slowly pervaded her body. A craving he had awakened and only he could appease. "Aren't you afraid to be alone with a man who might have murdered his brother?" he asked in a low, lilting voice.

"Are you making a confession, duke?"

His mouth curled in a smile. He took a step, and suddenly his free hand locked around her waist. A wave of faintness washed over her. Before she could draw another breath, he had trapped her between his hard body and the wall.

She felt the steel length of his phallus pressing

through her thin dress and petticoat to her belly. Her woman's place moistened at his unabashed sexuality. She had a notion what it meant. A prelude to a more intimate act. "I would very much like to be alone with you," he whispered in her hair.

She wanted it to happen, here, now. The desire that flooded her veins silenced all her common sense. She wanted him more than air or dignity. His blue eyes flickered to her face. His nostrils flared. He knew.

He drew his hand up slowly between their bodies and unlaced the front of her gown before she could take another breath. A rush of bracing air stung her breasts as he caught a fistful of silk and tugged. His dark head lowered. She felt her will dissolve. His tongue teased back and forth at the tips of her breasts until she was shaking with the sharpest need she had ever known. If he didn't stop, she would slide to the floor.

"Harriet," he whispered, looking up into her face. "*Harriet,* please, I need you."

She stared down into his eyes, falling into a darkness so endless she could barely hear his voice. "No," she said, her voice clear and distinct. "Not this time. Have a temper if you like."

He took a long breath. Still in a haze, she watched as he pulled her bodice back over her swollen breasts, relacing the ribbons with a look of burning regret. Then he lowered his head once again and branded her mouth with a kiss.

"If your door is ever left unlocked at night, I shall assume it is an invitation."

She smoothed down her skirt. He backed away. They returned via separate doors to the ballroom. Her mind took forever to recover. In fact, it wasn't until after the marquess's private supper party began that she realized there was no lock upon her bedchamber door to discourage the duke's advances.

Chapter Twenty

The wise want love,
and those who love want wisdom.

PERCY BYSSHE SHELLEY
Prometheus Unbound

❧ ❧

He danced the last dance of the evening with Constance, his sole intention to throw the scandal-mongers off his true scent. He realized too late that he and Harriet could have made a more discreet return to the ballroom and that certain conclusions would be drawn. Did the duke find his aunt's abigail more desirable than one of Society's own? Such speculation amused the ton.

Constance found nothing amusing in his behavior and did not hesitate to say so. "This was meant to be our night."

"Was it?" he asked in surprise.

"I thought our engagement might be announced."

"Did you?" He noticed Harriet standing behind his aunt, their expressions of mutual disapproval rather delightful.

"My father has already had papers drawn for the wedding."

"To my late brother, perhaps. But not to me."

She smiled thinly, walking the steps of the last set as if they were opponents on a dueling field, not on a dance floor. "Your grace is too honest."

He bowed in relief as the dance ended. "And, you, my lady, are only so in the moonlight."

For a moment she appeared not to understand what he meant. But then she gave a slight nod, not bothering to lie. "At least I do not engage in affairs with those beneath my station. Lord Hargrave is merely a friend."

He walked beside her to the supper room, Constance calling back farewells to the other guests who had not been invited to stay. Her dark hair lay tightly coiled upon the whitest skin, aside from Edlyn's, that he had ever seen. Her eyes shone like cold, distant stars.

She paused without warning, people crowding all around them. "You may kiss me now."

"But everyone is watching."

"I know. Just kiss me and be done with it."

The thought held as much appeal as did a wasp sting. But since when did a Boscastle male refuse an offer to indulge a lady?

She tilted her face. "On the cheek. Lips closed."

He stared down at her. She looked for all the world as if she were awaiting a guillotine to drop. "Why don't we just shake hands and go from there?"

"If his grace does not pay me court tonight, the

papers will report that we have become estranged."

"Estranged? Before we are even properly engaged?" He laughed. "What a complicated world is London's Society. I admit it does not interest me at all."

"Your brother had an instinctive respect for the roles one must play. Your instincts, I fear, are far less refined."

"And that is why you fear them?" he asked curiously.

"What I fear is that you shall make fools of both of us, your grace."

"And if I do not care?"

She regarded him with contempt. "Ours is to be an arranged marriage. Whether you care or not is irrelevant."

If Griffin had ever felt the slightest interest in pursuing a match between them, even for the purpose of breeding heirs, it dissipated. Disregarding the fact that his male parts did not exactly dance in her presence, he was repulsed by the unfeeling ease with which she was as willing to share his bed, his life, as she had been his late brother's.

It was a well-known fact that a Boscastle could not survive without passion. Perhaps if Griffin had never come to London, he would have lived the rest of his days denying what his ancestry had ordained.

Perhaps he would never have met a woman with hair the color of a pagan bonfire and a spirit disciplined enough to becalm the beast he was afraid he had become.

Harriet slept late and not well, dreaming of a young duke who abducted her from her warm bed in a flying chariot and carried her into darkness. Her teeth chattered like a skeleton's. It was perishing cold up in the clouds, despite what the poets might claim, and the duke had turned a deaf ear to her objections. Harriet's dream counterpart was less impressed with romantic gestures than she was with practical matters.

She reached through the mist for his cloak, pulling it off the duke's broad shoulders with a cry of shock. He was nude beneath, his chest and torso as hard and beautifully sculpted as the statues in the marquess's garden. *A work of art,* Lady Hermia Dalrymple would announce when the girls at the academy took out their sketchbooks. The human body should reflect the hallowed perfection that its creator had intended.

In Harriet's dream, as in her worldly experiences, not even a duke was hallowed. Nor did he seem to be entirely human. "I can't find my heart," he said, as she huddled deeper into his cloak and they ascended into his dark abode. "Do you happen to have a chisel on you, Harriet? I know they come in handy for housebreaking . . ."

She sat up in bed, the callused hand that shook her arm bringing her crashing straight back to earth. "His grace wishes to see you in the library, miss," the chambermaid, Charity, hissed in her ear.

Harriet was quick. She'd woken to worse. She had grabbed her dead-drunk father by the ears and shoved him to his feet, the pair of them pounding through hidden alleys with the peelers at their heels. But she was properly employed now, if subject to the demands of a duke. She stretched her arms and legs, wiggling her toes under the bedcovers. Who did he think he was to order a body half dressed out of bed at this hour of the day? "I haven't done my hair or had tea. What's the hurry?"

Charity shook her harder. "He said *now*. And he's in one of those moods, if you know what I mean."

"Is he?"

The last Harriet had seen of him, he was studying Lady Constance in complete absorption. Well, he could wait. She donned her morning frock, washed her face, and rinsed her mouth with rosemary water. But her hair—dear God. What a monstrous fright the looking glass reflected. Tangles of blazing red hair that took a good hour or so to tame before she could appear in polite company. Most of the time she braided it before bed. But last night she hadn't bothered. The duke had half seduced her in the hall and then danced the last dance, right afterward, with the woman the ton expected him to marry.

Let him see her looking as though she'd been struck by lightning. Harriet took grim pleasure in the thought.

"Come on," Charity urged, hauling her to the door. "Never mind your hair."

"It looks that bad?"

"I've never seen the likes of it. But at least you still got your head and we still got jobs."

Harriet lifted her chin. "I work for Lady Powlis."

Charity pushed her through the door. "And who's to say he won't put that fussy old thing out to pasture once he takes a wife?"

He sat, unspeaking, as she entered the library and stood before him. Harriet knew the trick. She'd waited often enough before the magistrates to glean that when silence built, the person who wielded the least power—usually her—would break down. In this case, she was too annoyed to give him the satisfaction. She might have forgotten in time that he had danced with another woman last night. But she would never forgive him for insisting she appear before him with her hair as unruly as a gorse bush.

He drummed his fingers on the desk. "You took an inordinate amount of time responding to my call."

"Sorry if your grace had to wait," she said, breathless and annoyed. "I—"

A knock at the door saved further explanation. The duke snapped, "Enter," and a footman wheeled in a tray that bore a porcelain teapot with steam rising from its spout, a single cup, a single plate, and three covered silver serving dishes. The savory aroma of fried bacon and hot buttered toast wafted in the air.

Harriet's stomach gave a loud rumble in the silence. Was the self-indulgent so-and-so going to stuff his handsome face while she stood here, half fainting from lack of nourishment and the aftereffects of the previous evening's impropriety?

He leaned back in his chair. "What happened to your hair?"

She counted to ten. Then to twenty. She clasped her hands before her and thought of her former life. She thought of her newborn nephew and her half brothers, trapped by their own ignorance in the squalor of St. Giles. She resurrected long-buried images of intimidation, abuse, of hunger, and shame. But even after all that mental palaver, she was hard-pressed not to fly across the duke's cluttered desk and smack him a good one.

Instead, she bobbed an insolent curtsy and backed like a sleepwalker to the door. A voice—it sounded more like a toad croaking his last than her own—quoted the etiquette manual's advice on how one properly disengaged from a perilous situation.

"Excuse me for such a discourteous departure, your grace. But I feel a sudden spell of giddiness calling me to the chaise—"

He stood abruptly.

She groped behind her for the doorknob, her other hand fluttering to her eyes. "If you are going to apologize for last night—"

"Apologize?"

She peeked at him through her fingers.

What *had* she been thinking? The fiend looked anything but sorry. Perhaps she was still dreaming. Had William the Conqueror, another famous duke who had been known to be a bastard, apologized for invading England? She wrenched open the door. He reached around her and closed it again.

"Just what are you doing?" she asked indignantly.

He caught her beneath her knees, lifting her into the air with a look of mock alarm. "I cannot allow you to go fainting in the hall, or I shall be blamed for it. There is a perfectly good sofa behind us that you may swoon upon to your heart's content."

"How convenient."

"Isn't it?" he muttered, hefting her up a little higher to navigate his way across the room.

She locked her hands reflexively around his neck. It was either that or hit her head against the furniture. He bore her toward the sofa like a barbarian, apparently unconcerned that she might have a word or two to say about the matter.

"There." He deposited her ungently on the burgundy damask sofa that sat between two sash windows. "I will give you three minutes to recover before I call a physician to the house. While you're at it, I suggest you do something about your hair."

"*That*," she said, sitting up, "is the last insult I shall endure. I do not care if you are a duke and live in a castle made of diamonds. I do not care if every woman in the entire world dreams of becoming your wife. I—"

He sat down beside her, his expression encouraging her to continue. Harriet lost her train of thought. She had never noticed how the daylight brought out the singular beauty of his face. "I—I forgot what I was saying."

He stretched his arm across the back of the sofa. "Something about diamonds, a wife, and—ah, the last insult. Which, oddly enough, leads me to the reason I summoned you with such urgency that you . . . you obviously had no time to prepare."

Harriet compressed her lips. He was going to dismiss her, and she hated him. She hated him not only because he was a duke but because he smelled divine and his sultry eyes sent little shocks into her deepest regions. She hated herself for not moving when his carved mouth suddenly hovered a mere breath from hers. And she might actually have fainted if all the gin in her father's blood hadn't made her as strong as a cart horse.

"If you are going to let me go, your grace, then have the decency to do so before dark."

He frowned. "Certainly not before breakfast."

His shoulder pressed her deeper into the sofa. The ebony buttons of his cutaway black jacket brushed against her unadorned muslin bodice.

"Do you still feel faint?" he asked, lifting a strand of her hair to the light. "If so, I think you'd better have a cup of tea and a bite to eat before I explain why I needed to see you. A hearty breakfast might settle your nerves."

She combed her fingers through her hair, reclaiming the strand he was studying in fascination. Settle her nerves. Of all the gall. He'd done more to tangle up her inners than the month she'd shared a gaol cell with a murderess. But—she *was* hungry.

"You had that breakfast ordered for me?" she asked, halfway to the table before he could answer.

"I ate earlier," he said. "Please, serve yourself."

She touched her palm to the pot. Still piping hot. The bacon and toast tempted her. It seemed a pity to let a decent meal go to waste, especially when she knew how hard the servants worked to please the young duke, in the hope he would keep them on.

She seated herself in the chair at the table, folding her limbs as gracefully as the sticks of a fan, as she had been taught at the academy. In the old days she'd have attacked her plate like a farmhand. But now she forced herself to take delicate nibbles here and there.

He turned to the window with a troubled frown. Harriet placed her toast back on the plate. She glanced at his desk, suddenly noticing the papers scattered everywhere, some even strewn across the floor, as if he'd thrown them in a temper.

"I think you had better tell me what the matter is," she said, biting her lip.

He shook his head. "Finish that toast. I haven't

seen a lady eat a decent meal since I arrived in London. Perhaps I scare their appetites away."

Entirely possible.

She took a delicate sip of tea, sighing in pleasure. There was nothing like a strong brew to start the day.

Except for a duke's kiss.

"What happened to your desk, or shouldn't I ask?"

He pivoted. "My secretary quit last night."

"I wonder why," she said without thinking. "But you don't—you don't expect *me* to—"

"—take his place? Absolutely not. My aunt would never share you. I'm surprised she hasn't shouted the roof down to find you."

"We went to bed late last night," she reminded him. "It was light when I fell asleep."

"Well, while we slept, the devil's printshops were hard at work. You have not read the morning papers?"

"I didn't even have time to do my hair."

He gave her a rueful smile. "I should have ordered a brush and ribbon to go with breakfast."

She vented a sigh. "You aren't going to dismiss me?"

"Why should I?"

"Last night . . . well . . ."

"Do you think that was your fault?" His frown deepened. "As to dismissing you, I would not risk my aunt's wrath. You may, however, wish to leave of your own volition after I explain what is being said about me." He paused. "About us."

Silence fell. Harriet felt a little ashamed she'd been so preoccupied with her own assumptions that she hadn't considered he might have had a good reason to summon her.

"I know what has been said of you, your grace. I've been accused of worse."

"Do you know what is being said now?"

She shook her head. He sounded so grim she decided she might be better left in the dark.

"We have been accused of conducting a liaison."

"Oh." She almost laughed in relief. "Is that all?"

He looked at her in frustration. "It would be appropriate on your part to burst into tears and accuse me of damaging whatever good reputation you have worked to achieve."

"Lady Powlis will murder me," she said suddenly.

"No," he corrected. "She will murder *me*."

"But it's all absurd," she said, shaking her head. "It's a lie; you and I—"

She didn't finish. The dark glance he sent her seemed to be fraught with a message she was afraid to interpret.

"Is it really that absurd?" he asked.

She came slowly to her feet. "It is, unless you're offering me a position as your mistress."

He gave her a fierce look. "I'm offering you the chance to escape before it comes to that." He half turned. "Your door does not have a lock."

"How did you—" She saw the faint smile that tightened his face. "What if her ladyship reads the scandal sheets?"

"Undoubtedly she will."

Harriet stared absently at the letters scattered around his desk. "Will she believe them?"

"She did not believe I murdered Liam when the court of public opinion accused me. This, however, is another matter. There is an element of truth to it."

"Then I must be as guilty as you are," she said under her breath.

His head lifted.

"Go," he said in a controlled voice. "And do not give any person who questions you about this scandal the satisfaction of a reply."

"Yes, your grace."

She turned in hesitation, torn between what he ordered her to do and what her heart told her he really meant. "May I say one more thing?" she asked, hurrying on before he answered. "Words can't hurt you unless you let them. I'd have shriveled up into dust years ago if I had believed what my own father said about me."

He shook his head. "I don't give a damn what I am accused of being. I'm perfectly able to defend myself. But when my name is used as a weapon against those I care for, it is a different thing altogether."

"I think I understand." She stepped back, resisting the temptation to tidy the room before she left.

It was unsettling to leave him in such a mess, even if it was of his own doing.

"Harriet . . ."

"Your grace?"

"For the love of God, do something about your hair."

Her hair. Griffin released his breath as she left the room. No other lady's companion could have brought the fortune Harriet would command on the market as a courtesan. She looked for all the world like the Irish Princess Isolde of the pure healing hands and secret passions. Would she heed his warning? Had he given her fair notice of his intentions? He believed he had. He'd done his best to explain himself. She claimed to understand, but if she understood the strength of his desires, she would not be so brave in his presence.

He glanced around the room, smiling unwillingly at the image of Harriet feigning an attack of the vapors. She'd had him half convinced as he lowered her to the sofa that he had sent her into a swoon.

She might indeed have been a duchess for how well she pretended indisposition. Only the mischief in her eyes had betrayed her.

His gaze lit upon the drawstring pouch that sat amid the disarranged papers on the desk. He had discovered it on the carriage floor the night he had brought her home from St. Giles. He'd meant to give it to her, although the strand of false pearls within seemed hardly worth the bother. Perhaps the necklace held some personal value, a gift from an early admirer. The cheap paste used to coat the glass beads had crumbled off in his fingers. In truth, he had felt so insulted on her behalf that he remained uncertain whether he would return the tawdry bauble to her at all or replace it with something more befitting her importance in his life.

Chapter Twenty-one

What his feelings were whom I pursued
I cannot know.

MARY SHELLEY
Frankenstein

❧ ❧

Lady Powlis had read the morning papers and was not pleased. Whether she blamed Harriet or her nephew or the gossip reporters for the rumors of their liaison, she did not immediately articulate. She did manage, however, to exile to the basement every servant who crossed her path, for some imagined misdeed.

By late afternoon she had dismissed her companion so many times that Harriet finally threw up her hands and said, "Don't trouble yourself. I'm already leaving."

"You shall not leave this house, Miss Gardner."

"I wouldn't stay for all the tea in China."

She wheeled, snatching her cloak from the hallstand, and walked into the tall figure coming through the front door. Wisely, the duke had been gone all day, leaving Harriet to bear the brunt of his aunt's distress. His black hair was ruffled from what must have been a hard ride.

"I've been knocking for ages. Where is Butler? The footmen? What has happened now?"

"Ask her ladyship," Harriet said, flinging her cloak around her shoulders.

Lady Powlis scowled up at him. "Miss Gardner is threatening to leave me. What do you have to say about that?"

"I say it's a blessed miracle she has lasted this long."

"I'd dismiss you, too, if I could," his aunt fired back at him.

"Go ahead," he said, tossing his gloves at her feet like a gauntlet. "I'm fed up with you bellowing like a sailor night and day."

"How dare you, you . . . wicked duke."

He folded his arms in disgust. "You aren't telling me you actually *believe* what you read?"

Harriet glanced from the duke to Lady Powlis in consternation. They looked as though they would face off like a pair of street brawlers at any moment. Over her. "Madam," she said, positioning herself between the pair of them, "it is clear that my presence in this house is a disruption to his grace and—"

"Nonsense. Everything is a disruption to the duke. Where are you going with that cloak, Miss Gardner?"

"I'm leaving before I cause any more consternation."

"You cannot leave," Lady Powlis said. "I have

paid you in advance. You accepted your wages, and I insist you work out what you owe me."

Griffin bent to pick up his gloves, muttering under his breath, "I shall turn and walk out of this house forever, Primrose, if you confess that you actually believe what has been said of me."

"And me," Harriet said, suddenly tempted to sneak out to buy one of the papers that the servants had been ordered to destroy.

Lady Powlis shook her head as if she were waking up from a long nap. "Of course I don't believe it," she said in a rather unconvincing voice. "However, others will. And I cannot help but think that where there is smoke—"

"—there is usually a Boscastle in the vicinity," Griffin concluded with a wry smile. "You're the one who filled me in on the family's notorious history."

Her mouth pinched. "Yes. But even I did not expect history to repeat itself quite this quickly." She regarded him with an unflinching stare. "You will find your every action closely scrutinized from now on."

"I don't plan to attend another social event in my life," he retorted. "The scandalmongers will have a hard time keeping an eye on me if I hide inside the house."

"That will only serve to heighten their curiosity. Furthermore, *I* shall be keeping an eye on you."

He unfastened his riding coat, reaching over Harriet's head to place his gloves on the hallstand. Harriet hazarded a glance at him, surprised to see a thick bundle of papers tucked inside the waistband of his trousers. Had he been buying up the gossip rags as fast as they were printed? Wicked of her, Harriet knew, but she had to smile at the thought.

Lady Powlis had calmed down considerably by the time a light dinner was served. She apologized profusely to the household staff, and to Harriet, for her bad temper. When Griffin inquired whether he was to be included in this act of grace, she scowled at him for several moments, then grazed his cheek with a grudging kiss. It did not take Harriet long to understand the reason for her employer's lighter mood.

Miss Edlyn had come to spend the evening with them, apparently of her own volition. She was wearing yet another of her somber gray frocks. She still reminded Harriet of a lost wraith looking for a kindred spirit in a graveyard. But Edlyn took Harriet by complete surprise when, upon entering the house, she embraced not only Lady Powlis and Griffin but Harriet herself.

Lady Powlis's eyes grew misty with emotion. "I think your brief stay at the academy has done you a world of good, my girl. We have missed you, though, I admit."

They retired to the duke's library after a dessert of raspberry trifle. His grace sat at his desk, sifting through his correspondences. Edlyn, dealing yet another welcome surprise, curled up on the sofa with her head resting upon Lady Powlis's shoulder as they perused a stack of fashion magazines.

Harriet took out her beloved novel. A cozy fire burned in the grate. The duke brought a bottle of his best French brandy, pouring four glasses to offer around the intimate gathering. Harriet refused at first. As the daughter of an abusive drunk, she harbored a fear of falling prey to the lure of strong spirits. Her father became a right demon when he was soused. Still, she took a deep swallow to appear convivial and to join the duke's toast to her ladyship's health.

Her eyes watered as the brandy went down. Her throat burned like the blazes, and it was all she could do to catch her breath when she glanced up to discover the three others in the room watching her in mirthful expectation. Then Edlyn burst into giggles, and Harriet sputtered and started to cough, rising from her chair with her hand pressed to her throat.

"Help her, Griffin," his aunt said, passing her glass to Edlyn.

"What do you want me to do?" he asked, approaching Harriet with a grin that did little to ease her breathless embarrassment.

"Thump her on the back," Lady Powlis insisted. But when he gave her a strong whack, Harriet only coughed all the harder and waved him away with the piece of paper she'd snatched off his desk.

A deathly hush descended upon the room. The duke—in fact, all four of them—stared down in horror at the sheet she had plucked at random from the disordered correspondence on his blotter. She could not have snatched up just any inconsequential paper. This, she soon perceived, was neither an invitation to another party nor a benign business letter from one of the solicitors who handled Griffin's London affairs. To her shock, she appeared to have picked out one of the scandal sheets he had gathered from the streets and intended to destroy. Harriet doubted he had meant to keep it for his personal titillation. And yet, if she had not been in polite company, she might have been tempted to study the salacious print herself. Something indeed drew the eye to the illustration of an amorous couple engaged in—well, the vulgar position of their unclad forms spoke for itself. As did the caption emblazoned beneath, which read: *The Wicked Duke Takes a Wife from the Gutters of St. Giles!*

"I should burn this," she said to herself, looking up inadvertently at the duke. "In fact, I shall do so right now."

His eyes widened in warning. "I forbid you to set another room on fire, Miss Gardner. Give it back to me, if you would."

She nodded, pretending not to notice that he carefully slipped the print into the top drawer of his desk. She wondered again if he intended to dispose of the thing or examine it during his private hours. Harriet found herself inexplicably flustered that he might derive pleasure from a depiction of their coupling. She felt, in fact, as though she could finish the rest of her brandy and not suffer any ill effects at all.

Again, oddly enough, it was Edlyn who sought to calm the storm of emotions that threatened to spoil the evening's peace. With a tactfulness that Harriet could only attribute to the academy's influence, Edlyn rose from the sofa and retrieved the book that had fallen from Harriet's lap. "Is *this* the sort of novel that entertains you, Harriet?"

The duke looked up from his desk. "She is apparently attracted to the dark and horrible."

"I enjoy a good fright now and then," she admitted. "Would you like to read the book, your grace?"

"Not yet." He paused as Edlyn returned to the sofa, leafing thoughtfully through the well-worn pages. "Perhaps I may borrow it after my niece has had the pleasure."

"It might keep you up at night," Harriet murmured. "And it's more than a little morbid."

"Does it have a happy ending?" Lady Powlis asked, attempting to look over Edlyn's shoulder.

Harriet sighed. "Let us just say that I am still hoping for a sequel."

Chapter Twenty-two

Whose is the love that, gleaming through the world,
Wards off the poisonous arrow of its scorn?
Whose is the warm and partial praise,
Virtue's most sweet reward?

PERCY BYSSHE SHELLEY
"To Harriet" from *Queen Mab*

❧ ❧

At ten o'clock that evening, Griffin and his aunt escorted Edlyn back to the academy. Lady Powlis chattered benignly for the first minute or so of the drive. Buoyed up on a crest of hope for Edlyn's future, she seemed to have forgotten that earlier in the day she had denounced Griffin as a demon and threatened to excommunicate him, bell, book, and candle, from the body of the Boscastle clan until he repented of his sins.

For the life of him, he didn't understand why he continued to put up with her nonsense. He was past the age of embarrassment. She was past the age of doing him a serious injury with her cane. But somehow the thought of a future without Primrose or Edlyn seemed too empty to contemplate.

As did a life without his aunt's companion. It was tempting to attribute his attraction to Harriet to basic instinct. But it wasn't physical desire alone that had turned a quiet evening by the fire into one of the most contented he could remember. And it wasn't sexual need that had provoked him to laugh when Harriet had found the print of him swiving her to a fare-thee-well. Not that he hadn't imagined engaging in the act those lewd pictures revealed. He'd given himself away, keeping the print right in the drawer where he kept his most important papers, property deeds, marriage contracts, his brother's journal. Furthermore, he would probably take it out again later tonight and study it when he was by himself.

It might keep him from her door tonight.

Then again, it might just send him there on winged feet.

"I hope you have learned a lesson," his aunt murmured as the carriage neared Bedford Square.

"What lesson was I meant to learn?" he inquired, girding his loins for his next trial.

"That one can always be improved."

He blew out a sigh. "Do you wish to turn around and drop me off at the academy, too?"

"Don't be silly, Griff. I meant that you should look upon Harriet as a source of inspiration, not as a, well, as a young woman to dally with."

He frowned. "I don't believe I have ever dallied with anyone in my life."

"Then you are *trifling* with her affections."

"You're the one who put away all that trifle at dinner."

She leaned back, shoulders straight, and knocked

him on the ankle with her cane. "Don't you know the proper way to address me by now?"

He bent to rub his foot, muttering, "Why? Are you an envelope?"

"The ladies accepted to that academy attend for one purpose, Griffin."

"To learn to hurt people with canes when they're older?"

"For marriage. Harriet Gardner will either find herself a decent husband and enter a state of holy matrimony, or she will stay on as my companion—"

"—in a state of holy misery?" He drew his feet in quickly. "Sorry. Only a joke. No need for corporal punishment."

"She will never make a good marriage or establish a reputation for service if this scandal continues. In effect, what I am saying is that *your* actions can ruin any chance of happiness she has worked for." She paused, her wrinkled face concerned. "Are you listening to me?"

"Indeed, madam. Every word you have uttered is embedded into my skull like a nail."

"There is no need for rudeness. If you do not take immediate action to remedy this situation, I shall insist Miss Gardner return to the sanctuary of her academy. Yes, Griffin. Sanctuary. That is what I meant."

"I know what—"

"A consecrated place of refuge, where she will be protected from unscrupulous inclinations on your part that shall not be mentioned. And if I have to lose her because you refuse to behave, well, it will be the end of me. And of you."

He turned his face to the carriage window, hiding a smile. "I understand."

Harriet had decided to tidy up the duke's library. She'd been about to call in one of the maids for company, but then she discovered another print hidden under his blotter, this one so graphic she actually sat down in his chair, her mouth open, to stare. She was still staring when she heard hoofbeats in the street and coach wheels grinding to a bumpy halt.

She flew about the library, smoothing the cushions, setting the brandy glasses on a tray, picking up the book Miss Edlyn had leafed through and left on the sofa, a small piece of paper marking her place.

There. Now she could sit in her chair by the fire, innocent-as-you-like, reading her book. The duke would never dream by looking at her that she'd had a good gander at those prints.

But then a woman's voice at the door—and Butler gently rebuffing—pulled Harriet right back to her feet. She knew who the caller was. She darted across the room and slipped into the armchair at the duke's desk.

When Lady Constance entered the room a moment later, the butler shaking his head at Harriet in apprehension, Harriet appeared to be busy answering invitations. "His grace is not home tonight," she said, dipping her pen into the inkpot. "Was he expecting you at this late hour?"

"No, he wasn't," Constance snapped. "And I didn't come to see him. I wanted to talk to you."

Harriet raised her chin. "About?" she asked haughtily.

"You know perfectly well. It is the talk of London."

Harriet lowered her quill. "Oh, *that*. You mean Lady Powlis buying all those French knickers from Madame Devine's shop. Isn't she a scandal?"

"I don't know anything about her knickers, you little witch. Only fast French girls actually wear them. A lady would not be caught dead in the vulgar things."

"Is it considered more ladylike to be caught dead in the buff?"

Constance reached into her white fur muff and threw several crumpled broadsheets across the desk. "Do not pretend that you or the duke know anything about propriety. There is nothing proper about these, is there?"

Harriet felt sick as she looked down at the satirical drawing of a gentleman feeding a riderless horse an apple. There was no question that the horseman rewarding his mount was the duke. The body that lay at his feet like a broken puppet could only be his brother.

The Duke's Heir Feeds the Apple of Evil to His Apprentice.

"It was an accident," Harriet said between her teeth. "There were witnesses to what happened."

"The groom who works for him?" Constance asked with a laugh.

Harriet wanted to crumple up the paper and pelt her with it. "You knew this before."

"Yes, I knew," Constance said. "But it wasn't until after I met him that I realized he might actually be capable of murder."

And so might Harriet.

"Has he tried to hurt *you*?" she asked, suddenly curious.

"Of course not," Constance retorted. "It's just that whenever I see him, there is—" She shook her head as if unable to describe the duke's impact on the female heart.

"Thunder and lightning?" Harriet offered helpfully.

"Yes." Constance shuddered. "With a pinch of brimstone thrown in."

As much as she was enjoying this little chat, Harriet decided it would be a disloyalty on her part to continue. "Well, for what it's worth, I have not witnessed him murder anyone since I have been in this house."

"I'm not talking about murder," Constance said, swinging around the desk. "It's this other rumor." She stabbed a gloved finger at the print beneath. "Read *this*," she ordered, looking more like a dragon than a china doll.

"Why should I? It's all rubbish."

Constance made a face. "Can you even read?"

Harriet scratched the top of her head. "I know me letters sommat. If I sees 'em slow and big like."

"Has he slept with you?"

Harriet looked up slowly. "What did you say?"

Constance lowered her voice. "I asked if he has slept with you."

"Ask him yourself."

"I'm asking you." Constance sifted through the broadsheets, holding one to Harriet's face as if she had taken it from a rubbish heap. "Even if you cannot read, I assume you can decipher a cartoon."

Harriet glanced in reluctant interest at the drawing. Some filthy-minded sod had depicted the duke, blade-nosed and in a billowing black cloak, bent over a woman sprawled in the gutter. If the crudity of the cartoon weren't insult enough, the artist had portrayed Harriet's thighs to be five times their natural size, like enormous satin bolsters. And, good grief, either she needed spectacles, or there were three of them.

"Do you have any idea how humiliating this is?" Constance said coldly. "Fortunately, most people with an ounce of intelligence ignore these outrageous fabrications. There are, however, those in the fashionable world who take gossip as gospel."

Harriet drummed her fingers against her upper arm, her eyes fixed in a vacant stare at the window. Another carriage had stopped in the street. She heard the petulant voice that had become familiar.

And those boots thundering up the steps. They had become welcome sounds.

"Do you understand what this means?" Constance asked in an urgent whisper. "The duke and I will live primarily in London. I will not be mocked by sly rumors that my husband is a ravaging beast when in truth he has been seduced by a common strumpet."

"I see."

"Do you? Then you must decry these rumors in public, accept your guilt, and go away." Constance gathered up her papers and produced a small purse from her reticule. "I suggest country employment. Perhaps it is overly kind to do so, but I shall have letters of character written for you to take."

She shook the purse as if the jingle of coins would rouse Harriet from the trance that had befallen her.

"All you have to do is admit the truth."

"All I have to do is admit the truth."

"And go away."

"And go away."

"Must you repeat everything I say? Oh, never mind. Just do as I tell you." Constance stuffed the papers back into her rabbit muff. "If anyone asks, and they will, you will deny that the duke ravished you like a beast. You will admit that *you* seduced his grace."

"I did what?"

Constance cast a nervous glance under the table as if to assure herself she'd left no other papers behind. "This has taken me longer than I thought.

My driver is waiting across from the carriage house. Should I be spotted leaving at this late hour, you are to say that I called on Lady Powlis to ask after her health. These papers must have upset her, too."

"Oh, they did," Harriet said, rising from the chair.

Constance tucked the coin purse into Harriet's bodice. "There. Remember what to say."

The gesture would have been offensive enough if it had been made by a man, although in that event a measure of dubious flattery at one's desirability might have eased the sting. But at Constance's hand it became a vile insult. Harriet considered flinging the purse back in her face. But money was money, and she had a nephew now who could use a little gent's wardrobe, if not a few warm blankets.

Constance spun on her heel, her scheme apparently executed to her satisfaction. Harriet waited until she reached the door before calling her back.

"There is only one problem," Harriet said with an abashed smile.

Constance flashed her an impatient look. "Which is?"

"The truth. About the duke. And the darkness he cannot conquer."

The color slowly faded from Lady Constance's cheeks, and in that moment Harriet knew that the true monster in her nature had cast off its feeble grasp on gentility. "The rumors about the duke are true," she said, her voice clear and articulate. "Every one of them."

The fur muff drooped from Constance's grasp. "He murdered his brother?"

Harriet waved her hand. "Probably. But that's neither here nor there."

"Then—"

Having chosen to take the low road, Harriet hurtled down it with wholehearted enthusiasm. "I meant the part about him ravishing me like a beast."

The muff slid to the floor. Constance looked ill. "He . . . ravaged you?"

"Ravished, ravaged, pillaged, plundered. I might have been a tender rosebud bruised by a great storm, plucked from my virtuous—"

"He . . ." Constance wrinkled her perfect nose. "In the gutter?"

"Of course not. It's bleedin' cold on the cobbles, and there are rats, besides. I do have some pride."

Constance drew a breath of distress. Clearly Harriet's description implied a sacrifice on the altar of carnal affairs at which Constance would not kneel, even for a duchy.

"Would you care for a vinaigrette?" Harriet inquired solicitously. "I think the duke might still have one in the brandy cabinet from when he sent me into a swoon yesterday."

Constance shook her head, opening the door and disappearing down the columned hallway as if the fiends of hell were nipping at her little behind.

"What about your money?" Harriet shouted, running after her.

"Oh—oh. Keep it!"

"Thank you." Harriet grinned up at the chambermaids hanging slack-jawed over the stair rails. "I'll buy you a pair of knickers if I've got anything left over."

Well, she had done it again. She knew full well that she would have to admit to Lady Powlis what had happened and that she would have to pay for her sins. She had defamed the duke's character, and she must be in shock over it, because she didn't feel the slightest bit guilty. It was this lack of remorse that a magistrate had once warned her was the mark of the true criminal.

Wait. She thought she might be starting to feel a twinge of regret.

No, she wasn't.

She'd do exactly the same thing if the nasty woman provoked her again. She dashed through the front hall and back toward the library. She might as well wring every drop of sweetness from her revenge. The only thing that could have made it better was if the fleeing damsel had run smack into the duke and popped him proper for being such a wicked defiler of paid companions.

And the only thing that could have made it worse was when his diabolical figure appeared from one of the columns behind her. Almost as if he had been lurking in the hall for quite some time. Perhaps even long enough to have overheard the inflammatory confession his aunt's companion had made.

Chapter Twenty-three

What then became of me?
I know not; I lost sensation,
and chains and darkness
were the only objects that pressed upon me.

MARY SHELLEY
Frankenstein

❧ ❧

She edged toward the door. "You're—"

"—a ravaging beast?"

Heaven help her, he looked it, too, in the dark, speaking in the deep voice that seemed to enwrap her in heat. "I didn't know your grace had returned."

As he advanced on her, Harriet wove in and out of the marble columns until she stood, trapped, behind the middle pillar in the hall. "Do you know what you've done?" he asked quietly.

"I've . . . slandered you," she whispered.

"And mortified Lady Constance right down to the hairs of her little white muff." He circled the column, each step forcing her farther and farther down the hall. "You have cost me the wife I was supposed to bring home."

She frowned. "You're better off without her. Lady Powlis thinks so, too."

"And when is it that I become this ravaging

beast?" he mused. "At the stroke of midnight? Once a month, when the moon is full? Or do I merely need to throw off my cloak to make you tremble in terror?"

She stepped away from him. He followed, his eyes smoldering with dark intent. Her heart was pounding in her breast. She bumped up against the library door. He raised his hand. His leather-encased fingers traced the contours of her jaw.

"What sort of beast do you suppose I am at heart?" he inquired softly. "A Caligula? A Blue-beard who murdered his wives? If you continue to spread these rumors of my bestial desires, there will be no one left in London for me to ravish."

Sweet mercy. His voice awakened the most ancient of all desires. She felt her body, her whole being, tense in expectation; whether she led or followed him into the library, she was unsure.

She only knew that once the door closed, he began to undress her, button by button, hook by hook, in the room where an hour or so ago she had sat in warm gratitude with his family.

"What if someone comes in?" she whispered, staring into the fire as he kissed her bare shoulder, then her breasts and her back, until she sank down upon the sofa, holding up what she could of her unhooked dress, shift, and simple corset.

"I have a lock on all my doors," he answered with a hesitant smile.

"Your grace has the advantage," she whispered.

"I don't think so."

"And do you think a locked door will allay her ladyship's suspicions?"

"Indeed," he said calmly, undoing his coat and then cravat, "it will not."

"Then?"

He raised his brow. "I spent an entire afternoon collecting broadsheets and newspapers to protect your reputation."

"Only to ruin me a few hours later?"

He smiled again. "I hoped that you could save me."

She settled into the farthest corner of the sofa. The fire felt pleasant on her bare arms and breasts, although there was enough heat in his gaze to keep her warm for the rest of the night.

He sat down beside her, leaning forward to kiss her before she could catch her breath. Her throat closed. It felt natural to surrender, to stop fighting the temptation that tingled through her veins.

"I need you," he whispered as his lips teased hers. "I need your comfort so very desperately. Don't deny me, Harriet. I don't want another woman. I think you know that. Maybe meeting you was the only reason I had to come to London."

She stared up into his starkly beautiful face. "His grace has taken leave of his senses," she said softly.

"No, he hasn't. He's being sensible for once."

He stroked his hand over the curve of her shoulder, and Harriet let herself drift into a shimmering darkness. Her heart quickened in expectation, and a pleasant warmth weighed down her body. The next thing she knew he was cupping her breasts in his palms, trapping the hard tips between his fingers.

She drew a breath, her inner muscles tightening in anticipation. She stirred. It seemed an effort to even speak, and then her voice came out slurred.

"Men want women like me all the time. It doesn't mean anything."

"But I'm not like the others. I thought you knew that, too."

"Perhaps I did."

She closed her eyes as his body, large and breathtakingly male, overshadowed hers. His hand dipped in subtle degrees into the delta of her sex, and she whimpered, forgetting to breathe as his fingers parted her folds. She shivered, remembering how he had caressed her the night he brought her home. He had shown restraint in the carriage. But now he needed her. And she did him. His touch had promised secret pleasures. Her body moistened and ached to offer itself to him in return.

"I've never trusted anyone like this," she whispered.

"Trust that whatever happens between us, you will not suffer for it."

"So promises the demon of the world."

"Am I a demon because I need you?" he whispered in a low voice. "Am I at fault because I look at you and cannot think?" He lowered his head to her breasts, his mouth seducing her will. "Too much or more?"

She sifted her fingers through his silky hair. "More."

He exhaled, repositioning his lower body.

His erection throbbed inside his trousers. He could find his soul in her tonight. He could pet and tease her into a hundred little deaths. But even then he would be at her mercy.

"You're still a virgin?"

She nodded, lifting her arm to shield her eyes. "It wouldn't matter," he said quickly. "Harriet, whatever you are or have been is all that I desire."

"The same old story," she murmured in rue, "but so prettily told."

He could reassure her otherwise. He could offer an oath to bind his word. But for this moment her delicately sculpted body invited seduction. His proof would come in due time.

Now. Now.

He groaned as she pressed against his hand in a slow, instinctual rhythm. That was it. He would tempt her beyond what either of them could endure. "Not too much at once," he said thickly, working her faster, harder now.

She moaned, her body vulnerable as she neared her peak, her nipples dark and prominent. He clenched his teeth. Blood rushed to his groin at the thought of burying himself in her pulsing sweetness. Suddenly she gripped his wrist. Her spine arched. He had her now. He nudged her knees farther apart and dropped his head, fastening his mouth on her taut bud at the moment he sensed she would break. Her body convulsed.

He gave her no time to recover before he stood and unbuttoned his trousers. "I can't wait," he whispered, gently pushing her breasts together to form a cleft for his cock. "Hold yourself for me like this."

She lifted her luminous eyes to his. Her gaze smoldered with acceptance, a willingness to please. Slowly, he slid his shaft between the pocket of her plump breasts, his shoulders flexing in anticipation. His hips pumped up and down in a mimicry of what he truly wanted. For now her warm flesh welcomed him, and he would find relief or never know a moment's rest again.

His mind wandered into blackness. He heard light rain pattering against the windows. He bore the scent of her on his mouth. He stared down at her, his breathing suspended. Soon. She looked so beautiful. His body could not last another minute. Close. He felt the end approach, elude him. Another thrust. She whispered his name. Closer. Not inside her. He had spared her violation. Enough for now.

His body jerked. The force of his climax surprised him, a pulsing heat and energy that he could not control. He groaned. In blind instinct he brought his discarded cravat to her throat, then to her breasts and her hands, wiping away the evidence of his spent desire from her skin.

"Harriet." Sanity returned one breath at a time.

He sat beside her and stared into the dying fire. She rose to dress. He pulled her back, his hand tightening over hers. Even now his body could not be trusted. Even now he felt both a hunger and deep contentment in her company.

"Oh, duke," she whispered in a wistful voice. "I never knew . . . well."

From the corner of his eye he saw her tuck away a few tendrils of her hair and glance about the room, as if to reassure herself all was in order.

"What sort of wife," he asked carefully, refastening his cuffs, "do you advise a man like me to marry?"

He dared not look up. He felt her temper flare halfway across the room.

"Perhaps one," she replied, "who doesn't mind your devilish moods or meeting your private needs while discussing the woman of your dreams."

He smiled. "Go to bed, Harriet. Sleep well tonight. And"—he sighed—"thank you for keeping me company."

For a time after she left, he stood in the firelight and reflected upon what he would have to do. As he turned toward his desk, he noticed the purse of coins Harriet had dropped on the carpet and the book that she had encouraged him to read. He picked up the well-worn volume and placed it on the bookshelf behind his desk. He wondered what in such a macabre story held fascination for Harriet. Perhaps if he studied it, he would learn why she was not afraid of him.

Chapter Twenty-four

Beneath whose looks did my reviving soul
Riper in truth and virtuous daring grow?

PERCY BYSSHE SHELLEY
To Harriet

꙳ ꙳

The sunlight stung her eyes. She lifted her arm to her face and thought of Griffin, surprised she hadn't dreamed of him again during the night. She rolled over, wondering how she would be able to look at him without thinking of what they had done. And where she had left the purse that had been so rudely given her last night.

An irate voice from outside the door blasted her right out of bed. "Are you still asleep, Harriet? I've been calling you for ages. We are supposed to spend the day shopping with Lady Dalrymple, and I cannot find my hat."

"Coming," she muttered. "Hold on to your garters, madam."

She dressed and left her room at the precise moment the duke emerged from his. She nodded uncertainly, examining his elegant serge-lined cape and buff trousers with a suspicious eye. And just when he appeared to be on the verge of breaking the silence between them, a maidservant came clumping up the stairs with her ladyship's morning tea.

"Good luck to you on your shopping expedition," he murmured as he hastened to escape.

"And the same—" No. She would not wish him luck searching for a wife. "Will his grace be home in time for supper?" she called after him in a piqued voice.

He glanced back with a wry grin. "I think I might."

She bit her lip. She shouldn't give him any further encouragement. It was clear that he would break her heart. She ran impulsively to the top of the stairs, wanting to hail curses on whatever courtship he might enter in the course of the afternoon. But it wasn't her place.

Lady Powlis, recognizing no such limitations, stuck her head out of her door. "Remind my nephew that he has promised to play noughts and crosses with me tonight."

"Her ladyship—"

He paused at the front door, so indecently handsome that it grieved her to look at him. "I heard quite clearly."

"Fine, then," Harriet said, suddenly infuriated with herself. "We shall expect you home at—a decent hour."

It rained for three days straight. The duke spent long hours in his library, and while Harriet sensed that he was up to something, she could not feel regret for the night he had tutored her in pleasure. She wondered what he'd been like before his brother's death. From what Lady Powlis had revealed, he had not always been the man who fascinated and frustrated Harriet in equal measures. But she was pleased that he never mentioned another woman when he came home in the afternoon for tea or again at night when he sat with her and his aunt for the obligatory hour.

And then one evening over her nightly brandy, while Harriet was pretending to read, Lady Powlis said quite out of the blue, "You will never get married at this rate, Griffin. And I am longing to go home."

He looked up unexpectedly at Harriet, with an intensity that gripped her in both horror and hope.

That night she was so restless that she left her bed and wandered about the house. In the old days she could steal like air through a room. She could see like a cat in the dark and sense when a person was about to wake up and wonder whether the servants had remembered to lock all the doors.

She'd once stuffed an entire silver service into her gown and walked from Grosvenor Square back to St. Giles like a knight in stolen armor. Fortunately she hadn't been forced to run from the peelers or fend off a street predator with a knife or fork before she reached home.

She had depended on her instincts in those days.

But life had been uncomplicated when only survival counted. She hadn't cared what anyone thought of her. And she had never walked into a man's library alone and stood before him in a thin muslin nightrail that offered no protection at all from the desire in his eyes.

"Is something the matter?" he asked, rising from his desk.

"I can't sleep."

"Then—"

"And I can't eat."

"Or read," he said in resignation.

"Or pay attention to anything your aunt tells me."

"Or to the hand of cards you are dealt at the club."

"Furthermore," she said, "you, if not the entire Boscastle family, are to blame. I don't belong here at all. And—"

Her voice broke. He stepped around the desk, nodding as if anything she'd said made the least bit of sense.

"And furthermore," she whispered, staring into his eyes, "I have decided that because of this I cannot serve another day in your house."

"*This?*" he queried softly, taking another step toward her.

Her lips parted. "I'm giving you notice, your grace. And I mean it."

His gaze flickered over her. "In your nightwear?" He reached out to trace his finger down her throat to the knotted drawstring above her breasts. "And at this ungodly hour? I'm afraid I cannot allow it."

"Well, you can't stop me this time."

"I understand."

"Then—"

"The situation cannot go on this way," he said gravely. "I will find another position for you before the end of the week."

He led her across the room and drew her down onto the carpet. For several moments they knelt, sharing feverish kisses and caressing each other through their clothes. Soon Harriet was clinging to his aroused body with a desperation that she couldn't hide. It seemed not only natural but essential to offer herself to him. She might have existed for him to pet and stroke and pleasure. His hands roamed down her back and derriere, stealing the strength from her bones. If she could bestir herself from his spell, she would touch him everywhere, too.

"Harriet," he murmured in his lilting baritone voice that mesmerized her. "Do you know I sit at my desk every night and think of being with you like this?"

She shivered. His fingers found and tenderly probed the vulnerable places of her body. Her head swam in delight. She swayed against his hard chest. She kissed his shoulder, smiling to herself. "I know you've kept those lewd pictures on purpose."

He stroked the crease of her bottom, his fingers descending in a forbidden quest that quickened her blood. When suddenly he leaned over her, she fell back onto the carpet with a moan. He bent over her pliant form. His mouth took hers in a hard kiss that left her breathless and craving more. His unremorseful gaze acknowledged her response. "I don't need those prints anymore, do I?" he asked, his hand pressing against her mound. "Besides, they hardly did you justice. Why anyone would depict this perfect body with thighs inflated like balloons is past imagining."

"And I don't have three of them, either," she said, indignant at the unfairness of how she had been portrayed for posterity.

He looked utterly blank for a moment. And then an insulting grin lifted the corners of his mouth. "That wasn't a third thigh, you milkmaid. It was the part of me that's meant to go inside you."

She levered up on one elbow, curiosity enabling her to overlook his mockery. Harriet considered herself to be anything but ignorant in the ways of the world. Her half brothers had not bothered to spare her any embarrassment when it came to the differences of their sex. That she had retained her virtue, and a certain modesty concerning earthly affairs, was no minor accomplishment. Had the duke been the devilish rake that gossip would make him, she would never have found him irresistible, let alone considered surrendering her maidenly innocence. It was, in fact, his protective nature and dedication to his aunt and niece that had captured her affection. But it was obvious that he had more experiences in carnality than she had.

And now this issue of what she had erroneously perceived to be her third appendage stirred her prurient interest.

"I don't believe you," she whispered hotly, looking him up and down as if challenging his claim.

"Harriet," he scolded, lifting his hands to her shoulders, "have you ever caught me in a lie?"

"I haven't caught you at all," she said, swallowing as she stared up into his eyes.

"But you have."

She held her breath, aware that he had loosened the cords of her nightdress and unbuttoned the long, modest sleeves. The muslin bodice abraded her aching breasts as he slipped his thumbs beneath the cambric collar. And pulled.

"Griffin."

She tried to lift her head. Too much effort. His fingers glided over the bare curves and shadowed indentations that he had exposed. For all practical purposes, her body became a map of clamoring aches that awaited his conquest. In resentful admiration, she allowed this exploration to continue. It was, after all, his area of expertise.

As a rank amateur she would be forced to submit to his demands in the foreseeable future. She did not perceive this as a sacrifice. If she applied herself—and she had the sense that she would become a devoted student under his guidance—she'd have him at *her* mercy, as she was at his, in no time.

Still, for now she was undeniably his to master. She lay with her arm half covering her face. At first she felt too overwhelmed to move. But when he kissed his way between her breasts, sucking at each elongated tip with a finesse that electrified her senses, she could not suppress the natural instincts that urged her to move.

He spread her knees father apart and studied her in absorption. The warmth of the fire, the heat in his eyes, stung her naked flesh. He slid his palms down her thighs, opening her yet wider. His thumb and forefinger gently parted her damp folds. His other hand slid under her hips.

She lifted herself, heeding instinct. She considered closing her eyes, pretending blithe ignorance of whatever acts she allowed him to pursue. But watching his face aroused her beyond what she could admit. Who would have guessed that she could undo the wicked duke? "You came to me tonight," he said, slowly lifting his head from her belly.

She lowered her hand. She might have said something. His dark smile sent every coherent thought from her brain. She loved this man so much that she was afraid what would happen if he did not return her love. Her family, after all, did have a penchant for hotheadedness. And if she conceived his child, there would be another family to love and worry over. Would he take care of them? What position did he intend to find for her after they had made love?

He claimed he needed her.

They needed each other.

She made another attempt to speak. This time she was distracted by the glimpse of his taut-muscled chest as he stripped his waistcoat and freshly laundered shirt from his shoulders. She forgot what she'd intended to say. Whatever it was dwindled in importance to placing her hand on his sculpted torso and feeling his skin, testing his strength for herself. She traced her fingers across the striated plane of his stomach. He caught her wrist, gathering her up against his chest. She curled her arm around his neck and gently drew his head to hers. He expelled a rough sigh against her mouth. She felt his hand between their bodies as he unbuttoned his trousers. When they broke apart to breathe, she made no secret of studying his lithe frame and thick shaft, curved like a scimitar from below his belly.

He laughed softly, letting her look her fill. "Well?"

Her gaze lifted to his. "Fine. I believe you. There was no third thigh. Your point is taken."

"Not quite." He gave her a knowing smile. "Just wait."

She drew her hand up and slowly touched the pulsing knob of his manhood with her fingertips. His shoulders jerked in a reflex that would have discouraged further intimacy had he not suddenly lowered himself over her and whispered against her mouth, "I don't trust my body tonight. It wants you too badly to do what it's told."

He kissed her, bracing his weight on both hands until she wrapped her arms around his waist and whispered, "Please. I'm not afraid, Griffin. I've never been afraid of you."

He released a breath, as if her admission had set him free. She raised her hips and felt his shaft stab gently into her passage. She closed her eyes, the pleasure so intense it was all she could do not to dig her nails into his back and draw him deeper. Her back arched.

He teased her. He penetrated her a little more each time she bucked her hips, withdrawing before she could catch her breath. Her sheath widened at the pressure, stretching beyond what she would have thought possible. At one point the friction became more than she could bear. She twisted at the waist. She moved away instinctively, only to feel his hands holding her hips still to permit his full entry.

She gritted her teeth and heard his soothing voice in her ear as he drove into her body. Too deep. He couldn't possibly go farther. He promised her he could. He did. And she liked it, rotating her hips until she took him completely inside her, until she dissolved into the heart of a storm. For several minutes she felt as if her spirit had been enchained.

She did not belong to herself. But then the blood in her veins began to flow with a renewed strength, and, after an eternity, she emerged, galvanized and acquainted with the laws of passion that had decreed her fate.

Chapter Twenty-five

"How is this? I must not be trifled with,
and I demand an answer."

MARY SHELLEY
Frankenstein

❧ ❧

The duke had made his decision, and he doubted he could wait until the end of the week to announce it to those it affected. For one thing, he could not tolerate another afternoon tea or hour of playing noughts and crosses with his aunt. He and Harriet could not live on stolen moments forever. One of these nights he was going to get caught sneaking into her sarcophagus suite, and no one would believe he was only playing mummy. Or Butler would creak around one of the columns and catch the master kissing the companion. Sooner or later the maids would giggle when they saw him staring at her in a desperate moment or glaring down the footmen for helping her too willingly with some small task.

Perhaps the servants had noticed already.

She was the one.

He had known it all along. He had never needed to look for anyone else. She had seen right through him from the start. She wasn't afraid of thunder or lightning, and after the last two years Griffin understood that no one could predict or prevent the storms that life held in store. But would it not be nice to have a strong woman to keep one steady during the tempestuous parts? And who would make a better wife than one who had spent most of her life fighting to come out on the right side?

Indeed, it was on the following night that this realization was put to the test by a storm that struck him without warning—before he could formally begin the proper courtship that Harriet desired. In fact, the crisis came before he could even admit to her in private that the Duke of Glenmorgan was no longer in search of a suitable wife.

Harriet thought it had been a delightful evening. Griffin had escorted her and his aunt to the theater. When the play ended, he had claimed both women by the arm to lead them through the crowd of onlookers, who thrilled to the unfoldment of another Boscastle scandal before their eyes. "You do realize what people are thinking, Griffin?" his aunt asked in a curious undertone, all the while smiling and nodding at the awestruck, as if impervious to the whispers that erupted in their wake. "The ton is now of the firm belief that you are not only a reprobate but a man who thumbs his nose at public opinion."

He shrugged, and Harriet was rather astonished to realize that he had just acknowledged their relationship to not only his aunt but to the beau monde without uttering a single word. Of course, the nature of their relationship had yet to be revealed to her. The true shock appeared to be in the making.

She had been gathering the courage to leave at the end of the week. She had also been too much of a coward to let Lady Powlis know of her decision. Perhaps she would tell her tonight. Griffin had had his chance to speak up.

As they exited the theater, someone in the crowd called out a mocking reference to the Duchess of St. Giles. Harriet had a retort on the tip of her tongue, but suddenly Griffin turned with a fury that sent the offender slinking away before he could be confronted.

"You damned swine," Griffin said, in an enraged voice that thrilled his audience to no end and sent a chill of foreboding down Harriet's back. "Why don't you come forth so that I might have the pleasure of inviting you to pistols at breakfast?"

The gathering dispersed. A few pedestrians hurried down the pavement, hesitating to cross the duke's path. The other theater guests scrambled for the line of phaetons and town carriages that awaited them. Lady Powlis and Harriet stared at each other in complete silence. The duke wheeled toward the street.

She reached back for his hand. "It's all right," she said quietly. "I've been called worse."

"Not in front of me."

"I do believe you're tempting fate tonight, your grace. Can we please go home?"

Chapter Twenty-six

We look before and after,
We pine for what is not—
Our sincerest laughter
With some pain is fraught.

PERCY BYSSHE SHELLEY
To a Skylark

❧ ❧

Harriet froze in panic when they entered the house to discover Lord Heath Boscastle, Griffin's cousin, waiting in the hall with another gentleman, who had once played a less pleasant role in her life. Sir Daniel Mallory had been her nemesis. At one time, he had served as a Bow Street detective. After his sister was murdered by a gang of street thugs, he had decided that he would rid the city of its dangerous elements, and Harriet's family fit the bill. He had retired and now served as an agent to private clients. Harriet had stayed with Lord Heath and his wife during the time he had allowed his home to be used by the academy. She had seen Sir Daniel visiting the St. James's house at odd hours.

Her last encounter with Sir Daniel, more than two years ago, was humiliating to recall. Prior to that, he had arrested her on more occasions than she could count. He had a good heart, and she'd taken advantage of it by promising repeatedly that she would stay out of trouble.

Then one night, he had been waiting for her outside a house she'd intended to burglarize with her half brothers. The useless boobies had run off as Sir Daniel dragged her cursing and crying into an elegant carriage that no detective could ever afford. "I trusted you," she shouted, bouncing up and down until she wore herself out. In secret, her instincts had recognized his goodness from the first day he had broken up a fight in a cookshop and pretended not to notice her pinching a steak pie for her supper.

"I don't wanna go to gaol!" she had bellowed, banging at the drawn blinds. "I'll be mouse meat, a little scrap like me! I'll catch some 'orrid illness, and when I die, it's your name I'll be cursin' on my lips."

He'd sworn a blue streak under his own breath. "Damn it, stop hitting the window like that. They'll think you're mad."

"I will be mad if I'm put away—"

"You are not going to gaol."

"I hate yer lousy—what?"

He exhaled loudly. "You are being taken to a private school."

She sat back, glaring at him. "To work as a maid? And who's stupid enough to trust me with their silver?"

"Your sponsor is a member of the Boscastle family. I don't suppose the name is as well known in the slums as that of Grim Jack Gardner."

She'd settled down then, her interest caught. "Wot the devil would they want with the likes of me?"

"For reasons perhaps only the devil can understand, one member of that family has accepted it as her moral duty to offer you a chance for a decent life. I warn you, Harriet, there will never come an opportunity like this again."

He had been right.

But what did he want with her now?

Had someone in her rotten family been caught in a felony? Honest to God. There was no rest for the wicked.

The gravity of his manner as he introduced himself to the duke and Lady Powlis heightened her mistrust. "Good evening, Miss Gardner. I am pleased to find you well."

She felt Griffin's hand at her shoulder, a welcome reminder that she had a staunch protector in her shade. "I think our guests and I would do better to privately discuss why they are here in the drawing room," he said stiffly. "The ladies need not be upset."

Lord Heath shook his head. "They should come, Griff."

Griffin slowly removed his evening coat. "Very well."

* * *

He offered sherry after everyone had settled in the upstairs drawing room. Only his aunt accepted. She had gone a disturbing shade of gray, and he was grateful that Harriet had taken a seat beside her on the blue silk couch.

Lord Heath did not mince words. "Your niece went missing from the academy tonight after a musical recital that only a handful of guests attended."

Griffin slid down into his chair with a groan of relief. "Is that all? Do you know how much agony she has put us through by running away?"

"I assume Charlotte and the other schoolmistresses have searched the gardens," Lady Powlis added, passing Harriet her empty glass for another drink. "That child will send us all to an early grave."

"Then perhaps this is a prank," Sir Daniel said, handing Griffin a folded letter. "This was slipped under the academy's front door an hour or so after one of the students reported that Miss Edlyn had disappeared. I wonder, your grace, if you have received a similar message?"

Lady Powlis sighed. "With all the letters that have gone ignored, it could easily have been missed. What does she say now?"

Griffin slowly shook his head. "It isn't from Edlyn at all. It appears to be a ransom note demanding the sum of thirty thousand pounds for her return."

"May I see it?" Harriet asked. "I know the penmanship of every girl in the academy." But after she read the letter over, she shook her head and felt a surge of fear. "I don't recognize the script at all."

"Did she mention meeting someone at a dance or elsewhere?" Sir Daniel asked.

"Not to me," Griffin said, his face reflective. "But I confess I am the last person she would confide in."

Lord Heath looked up. "She was last seen wearing a dove-gray dress, off the shoulders, and a black velvet band in her hair."

Harriet frowned. "Her headband had a moonstone in the middle of it."

"It belonged to her mother," Lady Powlis said quietly. "She believed it would protect her from harm."

"For God's sake," Griffin said. "Do not tell me you encouraged that nonsense. She bought the headband at the fair last year from a gypsy she paid to read her fortune. The gypsy *claimed* it had belonged to Edlyn's mother."

"You are unkind," Lady Powlis whispered.

Fierce emotions played across his face. "It is not a kindness to encourage the girl to be misled. Her mother has not come forth, nor has she been identified, in all this time. My brother refused to name her. If the woman cared, she could have contacted Edlyn during any of the past nine years."

"Perhaps she couldn't find us," Lady Powlis said, her demeanor suddenly deflated.

Griffin softened his tone. "Castle Glenmorgan

has stood in the same place for centuries. How could anyone, having left a little girl there, claim to have forgotten its location?"

"The mother could have been ill," Lady Powlis said. "Or perhaps Liam had made an arrangement that . . . It wouldn't be the first sin the men of this family have committed."

She was on the verge of tears.

Sir Daniel glanced at Griffin. "Perhaps the subject of her mother is one we ought to explore."

"What sort of person would abduct a young girl?" Lady Powlis asked in agitation, dabbing at her eyes with the handkerchief Harriet gave her.

Harriet put her arms around Primrose's shoulder. "We'll find her, I promise. Please don't cry. I know London like my own be—well, I know places that nobody even dreams exist."

"And where you are not to go," Griffin said, staring hard at Sir Daniel. "What do you want us to do? Where do we start? I feel an urgency that mere discussion cannot allay."

"There is already a search in progress, your grace. For the moment I'm going to ask you all questions that you may not immediately be able to answer. It never hurts to return to the places you took Edlyn, as if you were actors in a play. Perhaps then you will remember something unusual that she did or someone who befriended her."

Griffin stood. It wasn't enough for him to answer bloody questions. He needed to be part of the search. He was Edlyn's uncle, her guardian, and though he had never told her, nor she him, they could not afford to lose each other. She had been his sullen fairy from the first time he had hoisted her on his shoulders to let her swing on the castle's wrought-iron chandelier.

Now he realized that she had been keeping secrets, and he was startled when he saw Sir Daniel lean forward to address Harriet in a low voice that suggested familiarity. Griffin was afraid to ask what the exact nature of their association had been.

"Miss Boscastle said that Miss Edlyn might have confided her thoughts in you," Sir Daniel said.

"I shall do my best to remember," Harriet replied, "but there were only a few times that she seemed to speak her mind."

Harriet wondered if she could keep her promise to the duke. Once she could have drawn out maps of London's underworld wards and secret courts where only the hardest of criminals would venture. Few outsiders had the right of entry. Fewer still emerged alive.

There were hundreds of places to hide an abducted girl in London. And countless more for a girl who might not want to be found. Still, Harriet and Sir Daniel agreed that Edlyn had likely been taken against her will.

She frowned, suddenly realizing that Griffin and Lord Heath had not only risen but were making their way to the door. "We're going for a ride with Drake and Devon," the duke explained at her questioning look. "Stay with Primrose." He looked back at the tall man who had not moved from his chair. "I trust you will be safe for now with Sir Daniel."

Harriet wanted to go with him. The pain in his eyes reminded her of a beast who had taken a hunter's arrow to the heart. If she tried to pull out the arrow, he might bleed to death. Or lash out at her as he struggled to survive. He would not rest until he found his niece.

It seemed as if all the men she had ever known were half made up of darkness. Her father. Her brothers. One day they would fight to protect her. The next she might well be fighting them to protect herself.

"Let us know if there is news," she said. "Send word no matter what time it is."

Chapter Twenty-seven

I was moved. I shuddered when I thought
of the possible consequences of my consent.

MARY SHELLEY
Frankenstein

❧ ❧

Edlyn stared out the cracked window at the gin shop on the corner. It was dark outside, and she doubted anyone could see her from the street.

"I tell you, Rosalie, that girl is a witch. The picture did not fall off the wall by itself. She made it happen." The man wiped a dribble of wine from his chin. "It's the Welsh blood that makes her wicked."

"And the Boscastle blood that makes her wealthy," his companion, a woman in her thirties, said in a flat voice. "Remember that, and pray do not spit when you talk."

Jonathan Harvey watched Edlyn from a safe distance across the room. He wore an ill-fitting jacket, with a soiled cravat and fustian trousers. He and his lover, Rosalie Porter, lived in this unappealing tenement off what Edlyn had deduced was Hanging Sword Alley.

If she was going to be held for ransom, Edlyn

vowed to wreak the revenge that only a girl of her age could carry out.

Rosalie Porter gave her a narrow glance. "You aren't a witch, dear, are you?"

Edlyn smiled.

The gray cat preening on the hearth stretched suddenly and sauntered to Edlyn's side. She knelt to stroke his ears. His purrs vibrated in the silence of the shabby parlor.

"What did I tell you?" Jonathan sputtered, moving behind the oak settle for good measure.

"Get away from that window." Mrs. Porter rushed across the room, the hem of her dressing robe disturbing the dust on the floor. "You don't want anyone to see that pretty face. Might give our neighbors some ideas."

Edlyn pressed her bitten nails down on the windowsill. Mrs. Porter might not want anyone to see *her* face, either, smeared as it was with her *Parisienne* pomatum that promised to remove freckles, warts, and spots. Before she went to bed, Mrs. Porter would discover her costly elixir had removed something else, too. When sent to fetch the pomatum, Edlyn had come upon another jar of salve in the cupboard, which claimed to be Cleopatra's secret formula for lifting off hair.

She swallowed bitterly. She had been a fool to believe Mrs. Porter's story about her mother. She'd been a fool to sneak out of the castle one night to watch a troupe of traveling actors perform in the village. How the woman must have laughed at her naïveté, a duke's daughter asking over and over if any of the players had met a woman who could be Edlyn's mother during their travels.

She had given Rosalie Porter the idea for her abduction. She had believed the letters Mrs. Porter had sent from London convincing her that she had found Edlyn's mother but that it must be kept a secret from the Boscastle family.

Edlyn's entire past seemed to be a secret, which had begun the night her mother rowed her across a choppy lake to land on the shores of Castle Glenmorgan. She barely remembered the older man in the boat, her grandfather, his bearded face solemn. He had kissed her before lifting her out of the water. And Edlyn had stood, her teeth chattering with the horror of being abandoned. She had tried to believe she was only going to stay at the castle for a short while, and that in the sunlight it looked like heaven.

She had stared up, clutching her cloak.

The turrets of the castle touched the evening clouds, but it didn't look heavenly at all, only dark and imposing. Still, gold light shone in the windows. And as she trudged up the drawbridge, she heard laughing voices, warm and lilting, and smelled the enticing fragrance of griddle cakes and leek soup. But then her mother had turned away.

She panicked. "You're coming back for me, Mama?"

Her mother's face looked ghostly pale. "When I

can," she'd whispered, and squeezed Edlyn's hand so tightly they both started to cry.

"Mama?"

"Edlyn, I will find you again."

"Please, don't make me go."

"They'll be good to you. These people are kind, I promise. One day I'll find you. I promise."

Six years. And then nine. Edlyn looked from the tower first thing every morning and last thing at night for her mother to keep her promise. She was afraid that Mama and her grandfather had drowned rowing back across to the cove. No one had heard of the man and woman she described, not even when the duke, her alleged father, had ridden with his brothers and guards into every border town to find out who had left a little girl with unearthly-blue eyes at the castle drawbridge.

Had her mother been a gypsy? A debutante? A vicar's daughter? A love-struck girl at a masquerade ball? Liam Boscastle had made pleasure his life's pursuit. He fell in love with whomever happened to be in his bed. And forgot her in the morning, riding off into the woods without a thought.

Whether or not Edlyn was his love child, he had accepted her. But after a while, he said he did not want to hear another word about Edlyn's mother. Ever. And Edlyn had to forget her, for she had obviously done the same.

Now, because she had disobeyed him, she'd walked into a trap. She cringed as Mrs. Porter came up behind her, smelling of grease and greed.

"You didn't open that window, did you? It was never so cold in here until you came."

"What have I been telling you, woman?" Jonathan asked with a grim nod. "We've been bewitched. We can't keep her. She's gonna bring us down, I swear it."

"She is only a girl," Rosalie said, turning toward him. "And she is going to bring us a fortune, unless you ruin—"

He reared back, blinking rapidly and making gurgling sounds in his throat.

Rosalie sighed in exasperation. "What is it now?"

"Your—your—" He gestured at her forehead.

"Yes, it is my cream. You've seen it on my face a hundred times before."

He nodded, finally recovering his power of speech. "Maybe so. But I've never seen your face without its eyebrows before."

Griffin came home to find Harriet asleep on the sofa in his library. He bent and lifted her into his arms. She nestled closer to his chest, hooking one arm around his neck. "Did you find her?" she whispered, opening her drowsy eyes.

He swallowed. The warmth of her body stole over him. He wanted to hold her until he could think again. His mind was exhausted.

He carried her upstairs to her bed, glancing around the room to make certain no chambermaid sat in wait for news of Edlyn's abduction. Would she be found? Would it turn out to be a hoax? He knew the questions being asked. Unfortunately, he did not know the answers.

"It must be five o'clock in the morning," Harriet whispered as he sat down on the bed beside her. "Did you learn anything at all?"

He shook his head, staring across the room until she sat up and wrapped her arms around him.

"It'll all be fine." She put her head on his shoulder. "I know it will."

He meant only to kiss her. But then she drew him down beside her, her eyes inviting him. He circled his hand down her back, over her hips, to the hollow behind her knees. "I should know that I can't help myself whenever I touch you—"

"I want you to touch me," she whispered. "I don't want you to be able to stop."

He closed his eyes, sinking onto the bed beside her. Her skin smelled of soap. He reached for her again, his fingers loosening her heavy braid.

Marry me, he thought as numbness crept over him, not knowing whether she was awake or not. *When this is over, please be my wife.* It was light when he opened his eyes. With concern not to disturb her, he furtively slid one stockinged foot to the floor and repaired his attire as best he could. He found his boots at the door. He hoped that Harriet would sleep another hour. He hoped she at least would be refreshed this morning. But as he stole into the hall, he heard such a bone-chilling scream come from her room that he dropped both of his boots on the floor.

Damn propriety. Damn what would be said. He returned without an instant's delay to her side, taking her into his arms with an instinct that would not be denied.

"Harriet, what is the matter?"

She stared over his shoulder with a vacant detachment that raised the hairs on his nape. He shook her gently. "Harriet, was someone here?" he asked when he knew it was impossible.

He heard doors opening in the house, voices talking all at once. "You screamed," he said under his breath. "What happened?"

"I screamed?"

He shook her again. "Don't you remember?"

Her gaze came into focus. She regarded him in panic. "Why are you still here? We're going to be found out."

The door flew open. He leapt up and went to the window, searching the garden below for the cause of her disturbance. "What is going on?" Primrose whispered in a trembling voice behind him. "What are you doing in here, Griffin? What happened to make Harriet scream like that?"

Harriet drew the bedcovers up to her chin, wide awake and whispering in a sorrowful voice. "Oh, madam, please, I didn't mean to scare everyone. It was a nightmare. I haven't had one in ages. But I must have been so tired and worried and—I'm sorry."

"A nightmare?" Griffin said with a relief he could not conceal. "*A nightmare?*"

She put her face in her hands. Griffin went to her side, his aunt watching in distress.

"What were you dreaming about, my dear?" she asked.

"My father," Harriet whispered. "I was standing over the mean sod's grave—" She paused. "I mean, I was praying for his poor departed soul, and there was a gravedigger flinging sod in every direction."

"How awful, but not uncommon," Primrose said in sympathy, "to dream of one who has recently died."

Harriet shook her head. "I wasn't screaming because he was dead. I thought he'd come back to life from the grave. I felt this cold hand catch me by the ankle, and when I looked down—you know how you can't stop yourself from looking at something horrible—I saw him grinning up at me like a ghoul."

She lowered her hands. Griffin thought he might expire himself. "It's too much to bear, Harriet," he heard his aunt say like a dirge. "It is all too much to bear."

He walked from the bed toward the door. His aunt reached for his hand.

"I forgot until now," he said. He turned back slowly. "You left a string of glass beads in my carriage. I kept them, not knowing what they might mean to you."

"They're nothing. Toss them."

He frowned. "They were from your father?"

He wondered if she might be crying. But when she looked up, she was composed. "He never gave me anything but grief in his life. Go back to bed, the both of you."

Chapter Twenty-eight

He is a presence to be felt and known
In darkness and in light.

PERCY BYSSHE SHELLEY
Adonais

❧ ❦

She slept for three more hours. Once she thought she heard a soft knock upon her door, but she couldn't muster the energy to crack open her eyes, let alone call out to ask if anyone was there. By late morning she wondered if it had been the rain that disturbed her. When she dressed and went downstairs, the house was full of Boscastle cousins who had come to offer their support. The ladies comforted Lady Powlis in the drawing room. The male members of the clan had sequestered themselves in the library with the duke.

She listened for a long time to the low drift of their voices. She couldn't bear feeling useless. How could pouring tea find a missing girl? Lady Powlis's paid companion, a graduate of an elite lady's academy in London, had promised that she would not put herself at risk during this personal crisis. But Harriet had given the duke notice.

She slipped out the kitchen door to the garden.

The grass glistened with drops of rain. She'd be back before anyone even knew she had gone.

She didn't look around. She blended in with the pedestrians hurrying to and fro, a young woman of modest appearance on an errand for her employer. She walked past the lavender sellers, who stood discussing the fate of the duke's abducted niece and wondering how girls like them could expect to be safe when a proper lady could be stolen from a private school.

"Harriet?" one of them said in a startled voice, breaking away from her competitors. "Harriet, is that you?"

Harriet put her finger to her lips. The girl shrugged, muttering, "Sorry, I thought I knew you," and Harriet continued briskly down the street. By the time the hackney coach she hailed deposited her a few streets from her old home, she wished she'd had the foresight to buy a bunch of lavender to hold to her nose. She was more concerned about stepping in a puddle of slop than about her personal safety.

There were few enough people to worry about, anyway, at this time of day, even though the overleaning dwellings shadowed the street in a perpetual twilight. She recognized the elderly surgeon standing outside the public house. He stared at her without a trace of acknowledgment.

A group of boys and girls in ragged clothing clustered around her. "Got 'alfpence to spare, milady?"

"You ought to be at school, you little beggars," she scolded, slapping the grimy hands that tugged at her skirt.

Nicholas Rydell lived in the cellar of a back lane lodging house. The windows had been boarded up, but she knew the moment she opened the door that she had been followed. She hunched her shoulders to climb down the steps that led to his room. He was feigning sleep on the floor pallet beneath a pile of stolen fur-lined cloaks. Harriet detected the scent of cheap perfume in the air, the clatter of heels echoing from the room above.

She stood over his bed, a pistol gripped in her right hand. "I know you've got a knife under your pillow, Nick, and I truly do not trust you. But I've a favor to ask, and you owe me one for digging that bullet out of your leg when you were careless enough to get shot."

He laughed, his dark eyes slowly opening. He had long black hair and a hard-angled face, both cheeks bisected with knife scars. Half the girls on the street imagined themselves in love with him and believed he could be redeemed. Harriet knew otherwise. She knew what had made him who he was. His soul was dead. "You never needed an invite to my bed, love," he said amiably. He folded his arms under his head. "What's the matter, then? The duke ain't livin' up to your dreams?"

"I could shoot you dead, and your own mother would probably cheer. Now I just want to know one thing—do you or my father have anything to do with that girl's abduction?"

"I wish I'd thought of it."

Her nape tingled. A step creaked in the stairwell behind. Nick lowered his arms. "Your father's dead," he said, staring at the broken looking glass collecting dust in the corner. "What makes you think 'e'd be clever enough to pull off a kidnapping, anyway?"

"It isn't cleverness. It's spite. He never forgave me for leaving. He made no secret of the fact. And as you and I both know, he's as alive as one of the rats scratching inside these walls at night."

He frowned. "I dunno where 'e is. Maybe 'e's really gone this time. You can move in 'ere if you're lonesome."

"Lonesome?"

He laughed. "Oh, I'm good company in the dark."

She backed away from the pallet. He sat up, his hand sliding under the pillow. "There's a reward for that girl's return," he said with a shrewd look.

"You don't know her family like I do. If you've got even a finger in this, they'll hunt you down. And I'll do everything in my power to help."

She was gone before he could stop her, climbing up toward the figure who blocked the stairwell. The duke's eyes glowed in anger. "I have more than enough to worry about without losing you."

"I'm not afraid to walk in this neighborhood."

"But I am afraid for you. Give me your word that you will not come here again."

She hesitated, pushing against his tall, unyielding form. He stood his ground. She realized in resignation that he meant to exact the promise from her before he'd allow her past. "We cannot stay here like this forever," she whispered.

"Then give me your word," he said coldly. "It is a simple thing."

She looked up into his eyes. "I don't know if I can. Could we make a compromise?"

He cursed softly. "Of what sort?"

"I'll come only with your permission."

He gave her a grim look. "Absolutely not."

"Then . . ." She hesitated. She knew that Nick could hear everything being said. "Fine. Then what if I promise that I will not come here unless you escort me?"

His mouth thinned. "That I will consider, but not right now."

The man who was watching them in the mirror gave a quiet laugh. "I never laid a hand on 'er, your grace. But if you need my 'elp with your other problem, I'd be more than glad to give it."

It was still early enough when they returned to the town house to revisit the afternoon that Edlyn had spent in the park. By unspoken accord, Griffin, Harriet, and his aunt decided to exclude Lady Constance from this encore performance. She would most likely have refused to cooperate, anyway. Yesterday evening, before the news of Edlyn's abduction became public knowledge, Lord Chatterton had announced her betrothal to an elderly earl who doted on her.

"Isn't that a shocker?" Griffin murmured after he read the newspaper report aloud in the carriage. "I wonder if she will invite us to the wedding."

They reached the park at precisely the same hour as they had on their previous outing. Griffin recalled watching Harriet tumble out of the carriage before she and his aunt had abandoned him to Constance. Edlyn had wandered off like a wisp of smoke. He had not kept her long in his view. Two governesses had been rescuing their charges from a cocker spaniel that had escaped its owner.

Or was he wrong? He frowned.

Perhaps only one of the bonneted, heavily cloaked women had been a governess. The other had been standing rather close to Edlyn. The more he thought about it, the more he realized that he had been paying too much attention to Harriet to notice anything else. And he could not even pretend to remember what Edlyn had been doing when Harriet's half brother sprang out from behind the tree to cut Constance's purse.

His aunt recalled little of what transpired that day. She became annoyed when Griffin pointed out that she was muddling the proper sequence of events. She blamed Constance's prittle-prattle for impairing her memory and scoffed at his suggestion of old age.

Harriet thought to mention that there had been three phaetons sitting at the corner of the park. As to be expected, Sir Daniel had already questioned the drivers and a dozen or so pedestrians. None offered any pertinent information except to mention that the cutpurse had struck so fast, he could be described only by the color of his hair.

Evening arrived. Sir Daniel sent a brief message, reassuring the duke that a widespread search was under way.

"Edlyn's disappearance could yet prove to be a prank," Griffin reminded his aunt.

She rallied at the thought, then said, "I tell myself that every minute, but I'm not sure even she is that cruel."

Harriet was fully aware that the duke said little else and that her own efforts to raise hope had not dispelled the mood of grim uncertainty that had settled upon his house.

"I think we might all feel better after a good dinner," she said. "Something warm and savory, like roast beef with pudding. I'll talk to Cook right this minute."

But they only picked at their meal, dispirited, deprived of adequate sleep. Still, there was work to be done, and shortly after sherry and biscuits they set out again. The Marquess of Sedgecroft had invited them to his Park Lane mansion to review what had happened during the two soirées he had hosted in Griffin's honor. Without the benefit of cheerful music and the glittering array of guests, the ballroom took on a disquieting emptiness that Harriet had not expected.

Their voices echoed eerily in the vast space. She felt as though she was tiptoeing through a cemetery and conjuring up ghosts, instead of remembering the few hours she had thought to treasure in her heart.

"The guest lists from both affairs have been checked," Griffin said, walking behind her. "The young gentleman who danced with Edlyn is apparently distraught by what has happened."

Harriet wandered toward the antechamber. Weed and several other footmen stood at the buffet table laid with light refreshments. For a moment she and the senior footman stared at each other in a thoughtful scrutiny, as if by doing so one of them might dredge up some forgotten detail that would prove helpful.

"Edlyn was sitting in those chairs by the door," Griffin said. "There were people standing by her, but she—"

"—was drinking punch, I think," Harriet said, "and talking with a woman who had her back to us."

Weed followed them, bowing deeply. "Your grace, if I may speak?"

The duke turned.

"I was present when Sir Daniel interviewed the guests who had gathered in this chamber on both occasions. None of them admitted to conversing with Miss Edlyn. But I do believe Miss Gardner is correct. There *was* a woman, your grace, and I cannot place her name to the guest list."

Griffin nodded. "I think you are both right, but I shall be damned if I can describe her at all."

"She was wearing a green dress," Harriet said, contemplating the empty row of chairs. "And she might not have wanted us to see her. She left through that side door as soon as we entered the room."

Weed paled. "Despite the staff's stringent efforts, one or two intruders often manage to sneak into the marquess's home during these affairs." He paused. If Harriet was afraid he might mention her, he quickly proved he was too professional to be misguided from his current duty. "I shall question the servants at length, your grace."

"All I remember," Griffin said as he and Harriet walked back across the ballroom to his aunt and the marchioness, "is that I thought Edlyn was safe. And that—that you were the one in danger."

Harriet slowed to look up at him. "From you?"

His lips tightened. "I wasn't wrong, was I?"

"I expect we won't know what was right or wrong until we're able to think properly."

He smiled tiredly. "Yes, and that time cannot come soon enough."

Chapter Twenty-nine

His words had a strange effect upon me.
I compassionated him
and sometimes felt a wish to console him.

MARY SHELLEY
Frankenstein

❧ ❧

The strain had dampened everyone's spirits. Lady Powlis appeared to be on the verge of an emotional crisis and had to be taken upstairs by the marchioness to await the family's Scottish physician, who dosed her ladyship with laudanum and advised a night of unbroken rest.

Her ladyship's collapse turned out to be a blessing in disguise. No sooner had the duke and Harriet returned to the town house than a messenger boy ran up the front steps behind them, gripping his knees to catch his breath. "Your grace?" he asked, half-bowing as Griffin looked around in surprise.

Harriet caught his arm. The boy appeared to be half her age, too young to conceal his own dismay at delivering unwelcome news. No doubt he ran fast and was agile enough to dodge the seedy characters who infested the streets at night.

"What is it?" Griffin asked, stepping in front of

Harriet with the unthinking gallantry that never failed to move her.

"P'rhaps the lady ought not—"

"Go ahead," Griffin said in resignation. "I won't be able to keep it from her, anyway."

The boy finally straightened, holding his cap to his heart in unspoken sorrow. "There's a lady been found, beaten up outside the 'ood and Grapes. I've been directed to take you there."

"I know where it is," Harriet said. "Please let me go with you, your grace."

She saw the hesitation in his eyes. But then he nodded and called out to the driver, who had been about to turn back toward the carriage house. It was a tense ride to the tavern, Harriet chewing her lip and not daring to break the duke's silence. When at last they reached the Hood and Grapes, not tarrying in the taproom's smoky gloom, it was only to meet Sir Daniel on the stairs. He stopped to stare as if he could not believe his eyes.

"How did you know to come here?" he asked in astonishment.

Griffin shook his head. "You sent for—was it—is it Edlyn?"

Sir Daniel blinked. "No. It was a shopkeeper's assistant who had been sent to deliver a packet of thread. She will recover. But how on earth did you find out when I have only been here a minute or so myself?"

"Your messenger brought us here." Griffin

scrubbed his hand over his face with a relief that Harriet more than shared.

"I sent no messenger," Sir Daniel said, his gaze searching the taproom below. His eyes lifted suspiciously to Harriet. "It would have been unconscionable to bring you here until I reviewed the incident myself."

Harriet sighed. What might be seen as unconscionable to a gentleman of Sir Daniel's integrity would not disturb a miscreant like Nick Rydell, who thrived on the misfortune of others. But at least it proved he was on the job, even if he only wanted the reward.

"I do hope you find the person who attacked that young girl tonight," Griffin said heavily.

"So do I, your grace," Sir Daniel said with a veiled look at Harriet. "It is a regrettable truth of London life that the ladies we cherish should be guarded at all times."

"I could not agree with you more," Griffin said, and did not bother at all to veil the meaningful stare he gave Harriet.

Harriet had not realized how deeply she cared for Lady Powlis until the following day. An undisturbed stretch of sleep had done Primrose a world of good. She was subdued, but with still enough wind in her sails to insist she accompany Harriet and Griffin back to the scene of the Mayfair breakfast party they had attended.

Harriet found it hard to maintain hope that

Edlyn was playing a hoax. A disappearance going on almost two days was sufficient time to punish one's family. The girl had to realize that her great-aunt was getting on in years. In fact, Harriet was so worried about the dear harridan's health that she was torn between staying with her beneath the fig tree where they had sat or accompanying the duke on his investigation of the park.

"Go with him, Harriet," Lady Powlis said, waving her off with her cane. "I sent you searching after Edlyn that day, as I recall."

"But, madam, you don't look at all well."

"I wasn't well then," Lady Powlis snapped, proving that she was stronger than she appeared. "I'd eaten off mutton, and, believe me, there are few things worse."

"Harriet," Griffin called, motioning at her from the small ornamental bridge over the pond, "are you walking with me or not?"

"I didn't walk with you that day at all," Harriet muttered as she hastened across the lawn to join him. "As a matter of fact, I distinctly remember that you ignored me."

"I did anything but." He grasped her hand to guide her across the bridge. "Be careful where you step. The ground is wet here."

She caught her skirt in one hand, frowning as his gaze lowered pointedly to her ankles. "You did not spend a single moment in my company."

"That is different from ignoring you," he said with a wry look.

She sighed in exasperation. "Well, if that is your memory of that day, I doubt you will recall anything to be of help."

She walked around him, doing her best to envision what she had done after leaving Lady Powlis at the fig tree. Hang it. This was all wrong. She had *not* crossed the bridge. She had not come this way at all, because the bridge had been crowded with ladies watching the archery contest. Or, rather, watching the duke, she thought sourly.

She had walked around the dancers, one eye on Edlyn, the other on the contest. But then Edlyn disappeared into the rotunda. The duke had removed his frock coat to join the competition. Harriet smiled as she pictured his muscular shoulder drawn back, elbow bent against the sleeve of his fine linen shirt. When he'd hit the target dead center, Harriet had almost clapped in pride, not that he would have noticed her praise amid the audience of admiring young ladies cheering his skills and begging for another display.

The rotunda. She turned toward the domed retreat at the bottom of the garden. Edlyn had climbed the steps and vanished between the ivy-draped columns a moment or so before the duke had taken aim. Harriet had hastened to join her, intent on thwarting an impromptu tryst with some wayward rake who might be waiting for a lonely girl. But Edlyn had emerged from the other side, alone. And Harriet had noticed that she looked considerably brighter than she had in days.

The only other person in the vicinity had been a modestly attired woman in a bonnet. And if Harriet concentrated hard enough, she might be able to grasp at another detail—

"I can't remember a blessed thing," the duke said over her shoulder, not only startling the daylights out of her but yanking her straight back to the present time.

She gave a groan of frustration. The images in her mind dissolved like mist. She willed them back, to no avail. A lady in a bonnet that overshadowed her face was hardly enough for Sir Daniel to go on.

"It can't be a coincidence." She shook her head. "We both saw a woman talking to Edlyn at the party. You thought you might have seen her standing beside a woman in the park. And I am almost positive that it was this same person who met Edlyn in the rotunda."

Griffin nodded, avoiding her gaze.

"Well, say something, please. Tell me that this is not suspicious."

"Everything is suspicious. Primrose thinks she was deliberately poisoned that day. I don't believe that for an instant, but then, I still cannot believe that anyone would hold Edlyn for ransom."

Harriet frowned. "Try to think back to when you won the archery contest. The woman in the bonnet must have walked around the target at some point."

"She might well have."

She waited. He stared past her at the rotunda.

"And?" she prompted, following the path of his gaze until he looked back rather blankly at her. "You don't remember seeing her at all? You lowered your bow. The crowd cheered. You went to the sidelines and watched the next contestant—"

"No." He shook his head ruefully. "I went to the sidelines and watched you. In fact, I was watching *you* all day long. I wanted you to see me shoot. And that is the truth of it. I have noticed no other woman since I met you, Harriet. And—" He broke off.

"Go on," she whispered, her throat closing.

He glanced up at the sky. "Dear God. Unless I am mistaken, that was lightning I saw above the trees."

A little thing like lightning would not have stopped Harriet from listening to the rest of his confession. She gave him her hand as they recrossed the bridge. The week had almost come to an end. He had not mentioned his promise to find her another position, and she was certainly not of a mood to remind him until the crisis they faced was solved.

Chapter Thirty

Thy look of love has power to calm
The stormiest passion of my soul.

PERCY BYSSHE SHELLEY
To Harriet (Thy Look of Love . . .)

❧　❧

A small box had arrived for the duke while they were gone. Griffin handed it absentmindedly to Lady Powlis, who took it upstairs to open while waiting for her tea. She enjoyed admiring the little gifts that Lady Hermia Dalrymple liked to send her. Griffin peeled off his wet greatcoat and helped Harriet remove her cloak. Butler took the damp garments away to dry. A maidservant efficiently mopped up the puddles that glistened on the marble floor.

The front door, not properly on the latch, flew open. Harriet closed it before a restless spirit could sneak in with the wind. She didn't actually believe in ghosts, but sometimes she liked to give herself a scare. Either way, there was no point in risking a cold.

"How will Sir Daniel conduct a search in this weather?" the duke asked in frustration.

He began to sort through the post on the hallstand salver. Harriet knew by his terse expression that he was half expecting to come upon a letter from Edlyn and that it was a discouraging sign that no one had heard from her.

"Sir Daniel could find a lost kitten in the London fog," she said quietly. "I hate to tell you all the times he hunted down certain people who shall remain nameless, if you take my meaning. You wouldn't believe the man's instincts, the places he could find a person."

He turned and regarded her with an inscrutable look that closed her throat. She forgot that the maid was mopping circles around them, that another waited patiently to ask whether the duke preferred tea and brandy in the upstairs drawing room with her ladyship or in the library by himself.

"You," he said, in a clear, grateful voice that everyone in the hall could hear, "are good for the soul, Miss Gardner. I'm very much afraid, therefore, that I have reconsidered your request to leave and cannot allow it. You will just have to trust me a little longer to arrange the particulars. But you are not to leave this house, ever."

It was a tribute to her academy training that Harriet did not overstep the boundary between her position and what her instincts urged her to do. If she had, she would have asked the servants for a moment's privacy so that she could force him into explaining exactly what it was he intended to do.

And just as she smiled at him, and he smiled back at her, there arose an anguished cry from above—

stairs that sent every thought of romancing the duke straight out of her head.

Edlyn was going to make her captors sorry for what they had done. Spite had fired her blood for as long as she could remember. She had made everyone in Castle Glenmorgan as miserable as she could. But it had always been Griffin who came to her defense against her father during their frequent arguments in the great hall.

Would he defend her now?

She remembered the day Griffin and her great-aunts had stood up to her father in the great hall. After she had stormed away, she watched them from the music gallery above, giggling through her tears and promising that they'd be sorry when she found her mother, although maybe, *maybe,* she'd forgive them later on.

She loved them. And they had loved her.

The same could not be said of the amoral man and woman who had imprisoned her in this dark, moldy attic that stank of steak and fish. She stared down into the dripping street, the cat preening at her feet. She'd never be found once they got her out of London, and she had heard them making plans to buy passage on the Thames.

"There's someone lying in that wheelbarrow down there," she whispered, straining to see through the rain. "I wonder if he's dead."

Mrs. Porter walked in to the room. The cat disappeared. "Who were you talking to?" she asked, staring out the barred window.

"I was saying my prayers," Edlyn said meekly.

"Then you'd better pray a little harder."

"Has my uncle agreed to your terms?"

"He has one day left before we tell him where to bring the money. I daresay he shall no doubt know that we are serious when he sees your headband."

"Oh, dear," Edlyn said, crossing her closed hands over her heart. "I very much doubt he'll want me back at all. You see, I haven't always been a nice girl."

Mrs. Porter studied her carefully. "What are you holding in your hands?"

"Nothing."

"It's not nothing. Show me."

Mrs. Porter called to the man hovering in the door. "Get over here. Make sure she hasn't gotten hold of a weapon."

Edlyn raised her otherworldly eyes. "Do you mean like a sword? But my hands are too small."

"Show me what you are holding."

And when she pried Edlyn's fingers apart, she screamed and screamed as half a dozen brown spiders went scurrying up her arms to her neck into the bodice and sleeves of her dress.

Harriet thought she might be the only rational person in the house that night. Lady Powlis had gone into understandable hysterics when she discovered Edlyn's headband in the box. The maids and even one of the footmen had wept in fear and held one another, clearly convinced that Edlyn would never come back. The duke had withdrawn into his library in the worst mood she'd witnessed since knowing him, and that was saying something, as he'd never been all rainbows and roses to begin with. He was afraid, and feeling helpless made it worse.

She was relieved when he went out prowling at half past seven with Lord Heath and one of the night Runners who'd worked for Sir Daniel before he officially retired from service. Griffin would go mad if he sat here twiddling his thumbs all night. If she hadn't promised to stay home, she'd have been tempted to visit one of the flash houses in Spitalfields or Whitechapel herself. But if Nick Rydell had put out the word, he'd have every thief, prostitute, and parish watchman in London who owed him a favor on the job. She could have helped, though. She had her own friends. But Nick had taken over. He was the one everyone owed.

Edlyn had the best of the beau monde and the city's underworld joining forces to find her. Her abductors obviously had no idea whom they were up against, and Harriet didn't give a toss who got the credit. She only wanted Lady Powlis to stop crying and the duke to stop carrying the weight of the world on his well-formed shoulders.

Chapter Thirty-one

So much has been done, exclaimed
the soul of Frankenstein—
more, far more, will I achieve.

MARY SHELLEY
Frankenstein

❧ ❧

The town house was as quiet as a tomb when Griffin came home nearly eight hours later. He went straight to the library, lighting a candle before he realized that Harriet had fallen asleep on the chaise. The coals had burned out. He pulled off his jacket and covered her shoulders. There was no point in disturbing her.

He had nothing to say that could not wait until morning. Every beggar and youngblood in the city claimed to have seen a lady of Edlyn's description, and every one of their claims had led, sometimes literally, into a blind alley.

He looked out the window, half wishing Harriet would wake up. He wouldn't mind talking about where he'd been. And if he carried her upstairs to bed, he'd likely still be there in the morning. He walked around his desk and stared without interest at the books arranged neatly on the shelves. Had his brother actually read when he visited London?

Had he ever stood on this very spot and reached for—Harriet's book? No.

Griffin had placed it there himself the last night Edlyn had visited here. And even though he didn't think the story had been written that could hold his interest tonight, he found himself suddenly sitting at his desk and leafing through the well-worn pages of *Frankenstein*.

A random passage caught his eye.

"You must create a female for me, with whom I can live in the interchange of those sympathies necessary for my being."

He settled into his chair.

A compelling theme. To be created and destined to be alone.

To be considered so loathsome that no ordinary female would fall in love with you. To be forced to beg a mate from the creator who considered you a fiend, too ugly for the human eye to behold.

He turned to another page, his interest unwittingly aroused.

" *'Shall each man,'* " he read aloud, " *'find a wife for his bosom, and each beast have his mate, and I be alone?'* "

He wondered how many times Harriet had lost herself in this tale of horror and unhappy romance. And what page had she deemed important enough to mark with a torn remnant of an old letter? He glanced at her sleeping form on the sofa. It could not be considered an invasion of privacy, surely, to read what she had written. After all, she had offered the book to him and Edlyn, and in all likelihood he would find nothing more revealing than one of Harriet's lists dictated by his aunt.

The partial letter was not written in Harriet's spidery scrawl. He smoothed the scrap of paper out on the desk, recognizing Edlyn's script from one of her journal entries.

I met Rosalie Porter tonight at the ball. We were interrupted by my uncle, who would not have noticed had I been talking to a goat, and by that pretty companion who notices too . . .

That was all.

Was it enough? Did it mean anything?

At least now there was a name to investigate. Of course, the woman could be innocent of any wrongdoing, in which case she should be easily found. She might have been one of the guests at Grayson's ball who had already been questioned. She might have a daughter Edlyn's age, a student at the academy. He could not let his hopes soar. It was only a name. But it was something for Sir Daniel to go on.

Could Harriet have seen it, too?

He rose and strode to the sofa, shaking her gently by the shoulder. Her eyes flickered open. She gave him a groggy smile, muttered an incomprehensible greeting, and burrowed back between the cushions.

"Harriet, wake up, please." He shook her again, to no avail. "I need to—"

"We can't keep doing this sort of thing whenever you have the urge—" She stuck her hand up toward his face. "Be gone."

He drew his jacket from her shoulders. "I need to ask you something about *Frankenstein*."

She rolled over, one arm dangling off the chaise like deadweight. Her white cotton stockings were sagging, her plain brown muslin gown wrinkled and caught between her knees. He pushed back the curtain of softly curling hair from her face.

"*I need you*, Harriet."

She half opened her eyes. "Here? Right this minute? I don't—"

He pulled her upright, propping her against the back of the chaise. "I want to ask you about the name I found inside your book."

She frowned. "Why am I wearing your jacket?" she whispered, her head dropping back. "I can't keep my eyes . . ."

He slid his arm around her shoulders to support her weight. "What have you been drinking?" he asked urgently.

"Nothing. Oh, that—your aunt made me taste her medicine before she would take it."

"Good God."

"It wasn't half bad, though."

"I'm going to put that woman out in the old priory when we get home," he muttered.

She laughed. "Stop teasing, duke. I'm tired out."

"You are drugged, Harriet," he said in annoyance. "And absolutely useless to converse with in your condition."

"What did you say?"

"It doesn't matter."

"You called me useless. I'll try to remember that in the morning."

He shook his head. "It is doubtful you will even remember that this conversation took place. I might as well take you up to bed."

She gasped as he lifted her from the chaise. "What is it you wanted to talk about?" she whispered, pressing her cheek to the hollow of his throat.

He clasped her closer as he ascended the staircase. "Rosalie Porter. It was a name on a partial journal entry that Edlyn must have tucked inside your book."

"Rosalie Porter?"

He kicked open her bedroom door, blinking in distaste at the Egyptian motif. She looked up at his face as he dropped her on the bed. He turned, then hesitated as her eyes opened again.

She pushed up on her elbow, in that hazy realm between wakefulness and sleep. "There's no character of that name in *Frankenstein*."

He sat on the edge of the bed, unbuttoning his white silk waistcoat and pulling his boots off by the heels. "It is not a character *in* the book, for heaven's sake. It is the name of a woman that Edlyn wrote in her journal."

She subsided with a thoughtful sigh. "Porter. Rosalyn—"

"Rosalie." He stretched out beside her, his shoulders propped against the hideous mahogany headboard. "Maybe when you're not groggy it will ring a bell."

"I'm waking up," she whispered. "Give me a chance. What else did she write?"

He gave a deep sigh. "Something to the effect that I wouldn't have noticed if she were talking to a goat. She hinted that you were more attentive. And pretty."

"She said that *I* was pretty?"

He turned his head in surprise to stare at her. "Surely you know that."

"How would I know?" She wriggled up beside him, her manner now completely alert. "Tell me what you mean."

He laughed reluctantly. "There's a looking glass somewhere in this lurid chamber. You only have to employ it to confirm your beauty."

"Beauty now, am I?" She dropped her head on his shoulder. "If you think so, your grace." She drew her fingers through her hair. "We have to let Sir Daniel know."

He swallowed dryly. Her hair glinted in the dark, and he was in her bed. "I'm leaving any moment to tell him. Are my legs on the floor yet?"

"You'd better be careful you-know-who doesn't catch you sneaking out of this room."

His gaze wandered over her. She was brushing

her fingers through her hair like a self-conscious siren. It was a common female act that aroused him. But when Harriet did it with that come-hither smile of hers, his blood came to a boil. "It's the end of the week," he mused. "Do you remember what was meant to happen?"

"Of course I do," she whispered, her fingers falling still. "And I've found myself a position, by the way, so you don't have to bother. I realize that you've been preoccupied, but I took the initiative."

"What position?" he asked, bending over her.

"I thought I might go to Cornwall."

"What?"

She managed a weak nod. "To a place called Lizard's Point."

"What in the name of God?"

"Well, it's got stormy seas and shipwrecks. It seemed like an ideal place to recover from regret."

He smiled slowly. "Perhaps we can both go there soon."

"You don't understand," she said in hesitation, making most of it up as she went. "I am going to offer my services as a governess to some brooding widower. He—"

"—won't live long, either."

"—will be withdrawn and temperamental. He might leave me alone to raise his children. But then again, he might just sneak into my chamber one night and take advantage of my fallen status."

He laughed. "He'll have a hard time doing that with me in your bed."

"Get out," she said suddenly, pushing her hands against his chest.

"I was going to wait," he said, catching her hands in his. "But now I'm persuaded that planning a wedding will be more of a pleasant distraction for Primrose than anything inappropriate."

"Whose wedding?" she demanded, her face white in a veil of flowing flame-red hair.

"Frankenstein's creation and his mate," he answered dryly. "Give me some credit for scruples, Harriet. I would hardly be sitting in your bed with my aunt liable to burst in at any time. This room, as you know, has no lock. And you must also have known that I would never have held your hand in public had I not harbored honorable intentions."

She glanced away.

"I have gone so far as to obtain a special license for our wedding. What do you think of that?"

He saw the smile she tried unsuccessfully to suppress.

"You—" He pulled her up from the bed. "You knew. How?" He demanded. "When?"

She started to laugh. "I found out only tonight, I swear it. I didn't mean to go prying in your desk, but when I saw the special license sitting between those vulgar pictures of us, I just knew."

"Well, that takes the surprise out of a proposal, doesn't it?"

She framed his face in her hands and kissed him until he was laughing, too. "Does Primrose know as well?" he asked gruffly.

"No," she whispered, her eyes glistening with mischief. "But I have a sense she won't be entirely surprised herself."

He held her in silence for only another moment more. "I'd wed you today if our house weren't in crisis."

"A duke can't just get married without involving his family." She eased from his arms. "Go on before we are caught. Sir Daniel will find out if that name means anything."

She was right.

He had to catch the detective before another day went by.

Chapter Thirty-two

It might make one in love with death,
to think that one should be buried in so sweet a place.

PERCY BYSSHE SHELLEY
Adonais

❧ ❧

The woman's screams tore right through Grim Jack Gardner's vitals. He must be dead this time. Only a creature from hell could shriek to raise a body from its resting place. Which made him wonder what sort of coffin he had been laid in. He sniffed, his nostrils quivering in offense.

Criminy, the indignity he had been done—buried in a bleedin' wheelbarrow, under a shroud of fetid straw, soggy turnips, and God only knew what else.

A miserable drizzling mist fell from above.

The screaming had stopped, but not before his gaze lifted to the white face in the attic window of the alley lodging house. The angel of death was beckoning him with her hand.

He shook his head, mouthing an apology for having to miss their appointment. If Mistress Hades wanted Jack that badly, she'd have to chase him down like everyone else.

In the blink of an eye she disappeared. Vanished, as if she'd decided his soul wasn't worth the price of pursuit.

Perhaps she had been an angel of mercy. It was about time someone up above showed Grim Jack a little understanding. Whatever she was, he had no intention of waiting for her in a wheelbarrow.

He lurched to his feet and stumbled into the dark. Where was he? He thought he recognized an apothecary shop. There was a sign on the door.

Five Hundred Pounds

REWARD

FOR THE APPREHENSION
OF THE
MONSTER

Jack squinted to read the finer print before giving up and tearing the damned thing down to stick inside his begrimed coat. "Five 'undred pounds," he mused. "Who'd 'ave thought it?" He could turn himself in, bribe ten magistrates and near every gaoler in Newgate, and still come out with enough cash to retire. He might have a bit of change for the grandson Grim Jack had been forbidden to visit. Or he could drink himself to death, a task half done according to the surgeon who had stitched him up like a spinster's corset after his last run-in with the wrong end of a blade.

God, he ached. He stank. And he was still uncon-
vinced he wasn't wandering the crooked streets of
hell. He had to have a drink. But he decided that
the death angel in the window was as real as the
voices wafting from the tavern from which he had
been tossed by Nick Rydell a month or so ago.

He crossed the street as a whore came out from
the pub with a drunken gent weaving circles
around her. He ducked into a shadowed doorway
of a harness shop before he could be noticed. The
fog began to lift from his head, and as it did he
realized with a sense of disappointment that no one
in their right mind would pay a duke's ransom to
have his rotten carcass returned.

A duke's ransom.

There was another poster.

Whitechapel, April 1818

WHEREAS AN ABDUCTION
Has Been Made of a
YOUNG LADY
FROM THE PRIVATE ACADEMY
IN WHICH SHE RESIDED

Pain shot through his eyes. His body shook with
such violence that the words on the poster pranced
up and down like puppets in a Punchinello show.
Abduction? Private academy?

Damned if his own traitorous daughter hadn't
been working in a fancy school the last he'd heard

of her. She was clever, Grim Jack's girl, and even though she'd turned her back on her family, the day anyone abducted his little Harriet—who looked so like her dead mother, Jack couldn't stand the sight of her—was the day he'd rise out of his grave and take revenge.

If not that fine reward.

There was no question of a proper wedding, not until Edlyn was found. No one had the heart for a celebration under these circumstances. But the news might help his aunt forget their troubles for a while.

He would tell her first thing in the morning.

She was standing in the middle of the hall in her frilly nightcap and flannel wrapper. He might have managed to fob her off with some excuse about hearing a noise in Harriet's room had he not been carrying his boots and probably looking as guilty as he felt.

"I know you have a perfectly innocent reason for coming out of my companion's bedchamber in this incriminating state of undress," she said in a voice that could have frozen the entire Thames on an August afternoon.

"I do." He nodded vigorously. "A perfectly good reason."

It was remarkable how she could look so frail and helpless at one minute and rather like a storybook witch the next. "And that reason is?"

"I found the name of a woman written in Edlyn's

hand last night, and I—oh, what's the bloody point?—I woke up Harriet to ask her if she was familiar with it."

Her lips flattened. "And were you familiar with—you truly have a name?"

He nodded, leaning against the wall to put on his boots. "I'm out the door right now to catch her, if the inquisition can wait."

She trailed him to the staircase. "What is this woman's name?"

"Rosalie Porter, and if I miss Sir Daniel in passing, be sure that you or Harriet tell him."

She hesitated, clearly not convinced his motives for spending the night in her companion's bed were as innocent as he claimed. "I want you to know that this is *not* the end of the matter."

"Of course it isn't," he muttered, grabbing his hat and gloves from the same spot on the floor where he'd dropped them last night. "It won't be the end of it until Edlyn is a bridesmaid at my wedding. To Harriet."

Having dropped that bombshell, he took advantage of his aunt's astonished silence to slip out the front door. Coming up the steps as he started down was one of Sir Daniel's young early-bird assistants, apparently with news of his own to impart.

Chapter Thirty-three

I must perform my engagement
and let the monster depart with his mate.

MARY SHELLEY
Frankenstein

❧ ❧

Harriet rose two hours after Griffin slipped from her bed. She fetched several pitchers of cold water from below for a bracing hip bath and washed in preparation of another day waiting for Edlyn to be found unharmed, her uncle at her side.

Until then no one would be in a mood to celebrate.

It was the wrong time to announce a proposal and follow it with the usual kisses and congratulations. She was happy enough to wait for him to share their engagement with his aunt and let Lady P break the news. She could imagine her ladyship claiming she had arranged the match like a master chess player.

And perhaps she had. Harriet would not put it past the conniver, and she meant that as the highest form of tribute a girl who'd once lived to outwit others could give another. But it did seem that since she had gotten to know her ladyship, Harriet's im-

probable romance with the duke had taken root.
The old darling might not have dug the plant into
the soil. But she'd made sure to water it and sprin-
kle encouragement its way.

She could only hope that Lady Powlis did not pry
into the personal details of the duke's covert moments of amour that had occurred behind the
scenes of their rushed courtship. Harriet blushed at
the memory of how incautiously she had abandoned herself to his persuasion. She ought to be
ashamed for letting him lure her off the path of
proper behavior. Still, as long as that path ended at
the wedding altar, all would be well.

If only Edlyn were found.

She prayed that the name of the woman Edlyn
had written about would give Sir Daniel a worthy
lead to pursue. She dressed in the dark, shivering
and not bothering with the fire. She could hear pots
and pans banging below with the customary morning cheer.

*Pots. Potter. Porter. Rosalyn Porter. Rosalie. Pot-
ted roses.*

She tied a blue silk ribbon into the wayward hair
twisted on her nape.

"Rosie Porter," she said aloud, staring at her reflection. The duke thought she was beautiful. But
today her face showed strain and—she blinked.
Suddenly she was standing at a mirror in a green
room as a gorgeous actress threw herself against
the door. "It can't be. It *can't* be her."

She spun around, startled, as her bedchamber

door creaked open. "Good gracious, Harriet," Lady Powlis said. "I have been tapping at your door for—"

"Oh, madam, *do* get out of the way for once."

Lady Powlis gasped. "I beg your pardon."

Harriet bobbed a belated curtsy, eyeing her employer like the kingpin in a street game of skittles. "And I'm sure I'll be begging yours for the rest of our lives, but for the love of good St. George, if you don't move your bum, I'm going—"

Lady Powlis planted herself across the doorway. "Duchess or not, you shall not knock me down."

"It's about Edlyn," Harriet said urgently. "I *know* the woman who has taken her, and if you don't understand what I'm talking about, I shall have to explain it later. The person in question was a player at the theater when I started out. Rosie Porter, she called herself, and the besom couldn't act her way out of a chair."

Lady Powlis leaned back against the door. "How long ago was this?"

"Five years or so. She left with a traveling troupe of players when the director told her she sang like a sick cow."

"We had a troupe perform at the castle two years ago," Lady Powlis said, paling at the realization. "Edlyn was enamored of the actress who played Queen Titania. I thought she was positively dreadful."

"That'd be Rosie," Harriet said.

"She must have been in contact with Edlyn all

this time," Lady Powlis said in a faint voice. "I never thought to ask about her letters. I thought corresponding was good for her." She shook her head in horror. "The entire time we were arranging to come to London, that woman was making plans to abduct my niece."

Harriet slipped on a pair of sturdy half boots. "I think the first thing to do is ask at the theater."

"No," Lady Powlis said quickly. "I am afraid to be alone. You can't go, Harriet. What if the kidnappers come back for me, too? To double the ransom they're asking. They might be watching the house to see when I'm left alone."

Harriet wavered. It was on the tip of her tongue to point out that dragging Lady Powlis anywhere against her will was liable to attract the attention of every spy, soldier, Horse Guard, Bow Street Runner, and concerned citizen in the metropolis. But fear was a powerful force, and Harriet would not be responsible for anything that might happen if she left.

"I have to get word to Sir Daniel. That's the important thing. He has to know where to look. We shall have to send Trenton to Lord Heath's, Raskin after Sir Daniel, and the coachman to Lord Drake's for good measure."

"Won't that leave us rather unguarded?" Lady Powlis asked hesitantly.

"Madam, you have me to defend you. And Butler."

"Oh, dear."

This was hardly the time for Harriet to expound upon her past career, so she curbed herself and said, "Think calmly. What are the chances that a criminal is going to break in to this house before the duke comes home?"

Lady Powlis looked unpersuaded. "I'd feel better if we brought Griffin's brace of pistols to the drawing room while we wait."

"Fine, madam. If that gives you comfort."

"Oh, I have a pistol in my reticule, too. Fetch it for me, dear, with my cashmere shawl."

"Yes, madam."

Lady Powlis put her hand over Harriet's. "While this is not the moment of happy celebration I have dreamed of, let me offer my congratulations. It was obvious to me that you and Griffin had fallen in love."

Harriet paused. "You wouldn't have given his grace a little nudge in my direction?"

"Of course I would. I told you that I'd do anything to make sure he didn't marry the wrong woman."

Which wasn't exactly the same thing as being reassured that she was the right woman to become duchess. Still, Harriet decided it was good enough. And with any luck, she and her future aunt-in-law would celebrate the impending nuptials over a glass or two of sherry without firing a shot.

Chapter Thirty-four

The day is come, and thou wilt fly with me.

PERCY BYSSHE SHELLEY
Epipsychidion

❧❧

It was amazing how love could energize a man. Griffin had been going night and day on raw nerves. Whenever his energy flagged, he had only to think of Harriet, warm and tousled, in her bed, and he found his strength bolstered. He was going to find Edlyn so that they could become a proper family. Or as close as a Boscastle could aspire to propriety when seeking that happy state.

Fortunately, the footman whom Harriet sent from the house had located Sir Daniel without delay. And one of the Runners who wrote down the name immediately remembered an actress called Rosie Porter, a comely lady who flashed her legs at the audience and assaulted her leading man. He thought she might have run off with another woman's husband.

It was the best lead the private detective had been given. Still, no one had seen Mrs. Porter in years.

Griffin sat drinking hot coffee at the station with

Sir Daniel as he interviewed dozens of past and former members of the King's Theatre where Rosalie Porter had performed.

Harriet Gardner's name came up a few times, too, with a fondness that irritated Griffin to no end. He listened in stony silence whenever an actor or agent digressed and wondered aloud what had happened to the pretty red-haired actress who'd made them laugh.

Still, in the end, hours of lengthy interviews and poring over musty records retrieved from the Fleet Street police station tendered no helpful clues to Mrs. Porter's current whereabouts.

By late afternoon, a gang of would-be reward collectors had congregated at the station door in the hope of overhearing a helpful tip.

"Go back home," Sir Daniel told Griffin, pulling on his coat. "I'll walk in the opposite direction. The reward seekers are more liable to cause harm than help."

"You'll send for me if anything happens?"

Sir Daniel nodded. "I might visit your house in a short while. It should be time for Mrs. Porter to make her last appeal."

"Or not," Griffin said, suddenly realizing that a woman who had plotted a crime for years was capable of things he was afraid to contemplate.

Why had Edlyn not trusted him?

He knew the answer. The truth wouldn't change. She blamed him for killing her father. She had never accused him, but, in fact, it was remarkable that during one of their countless quarrels, she had not thrown that suspicion in his face.

He walked home, heading north on Drury Lane, past the academy, to Oxford Street, and from there to Berkeley Square. His cousins had begun teaching him his way around London. He passed the Bruton Street brothel at which the Boscastle men had a standing invitation and laughed. Harriet would roast him over a spit if he mentioned a seraglio in her presence.

He slowed his pace as he approached Bedford Square. It only now occurred to him to wonder why Sir Daniel meant to come to the house. Had he been hinting that Lady Powlis and her companion could be in danger? Griffin had never once considered that Edlyn's abductors might grow desperate and—

He turned on impulse and walked around the square to the back walk of his house. The sunken gate to the garden was closed. Or was it? He did not even remember if he had checked. But he *had* ordered the gates and doors to remain locked at all times, and someone had stuck a knife in the latch. His heart skipped a beat. It was five thirty. The street was still busy enough.

He pushed the gate open and heard footsteps on the pavement behind him. One of Sir Daniel's men strolled by with a walking stick. Had the man noticed the knife?

"Out for an after-dinner stroll?" he called to the tall-hatted figure.

The detective's man paused. He knew who Griffin was, and he knew they were not to acknowledge each other in public. "This isn't your knife in the latch, is it, by any chance?" Griffin asked after a hopeful pause.

The man removed his hat. Griffin noticed three other gentleman pedestrians, one with a hound, advancing on the pavement.

"Your grace," the agent said in a low voice. "This is a sign of criminal entry. I advise you to stay here until the house is searched."

Griffin slowly shook his head. "I am going into my house through the servants' entrance. In the event that I come upon any criminals, I shall deal with them as I must."

"Your grace, if I may at least accompany you?"

"Yes. But you had best go to the front door. My aunt and her companion are not exactly what one would refer to as shrinking violets. And I must warn you that in all probability they are both armed."

Chapter Thirty-five

Nothing, at this moment,
could have given me greater pleasure
than the arrival of my father.

MARY SHELLEY
Frankenstein

❦ ❧

Harriet trained her pistol on the gaunt figure that had appeared like a ghost in the doorway. Dear God. She could have shot him for a stranger. He had tied his unkempt blond hair back with a bit of string. His coat and trousers stank to heaven. She was a little stunned to realize that from a distance one might actually consider him to be handsome.

"Should I shoot him first, Harriet?" Lady Powlis asked in a quavering whisper from behind the sofa.

"Don't shoot at all. In fact—" Harriet bit her cheek, stepping around the sofa to remove the dueling pistols from Primrose's unsteady grasp. Her ladyship was liable to shoot Harriet or herself the way those guns were bobbing up and down. "If anyone shoots our nasty visitor, it'll be me."

Grim Jack held his battered hat to his heart. "Is that any way to talk to your beloved sire?"

Lady Powlis's eyes widened. "*What* did he say?"

"Nothing," Harriet snapped. "He's just some

confused street gent who wandered in here by mistake. And he's going to leave—"

Grim Jack brushed around her. "Madam, you've naught to fear from 'arry's dad. We're all friends, ain't we?"

"Your—" Lady Powlis sniffed the air like a pointer. "What is that unusually pungent odor?"

"That would be my father," Harriet said, passing Lady Powlis a scented handkerchief. "You've met him. Now he's getting out, or I'm calling the constable."

" 'ang on a minute," Grim Jack said, eyeing the fine Japanese vase on the mantelpiece. "I've risked life imprisonment, transportation, maybe even 'anging to come 'ere."

"Nice of you to bother," Harriet snapped, prodding his hand away from the table with her pistol. "You're supposed to be dead. You killed someone—"

"In self-defense." He stepped back, suddenly gaping at her as if *he* had seen a ghost. "It's been a long time, 'arry. You look so much like her. I—I—"

"What do you want?"

"I know where she is—that duke's girl that got abducted—-if you'd give me a chance to slip in a word."

"You dirty lying bag of—"

"Why don't you let the man finish, Harriet?" Lady Powlis asked through her handkerchief. "And open a window while you're at it."

"Madam." He bowed to her. "I apologize for my

indecorous aroma. But I was in dire straits, and I've risked capture to be of service to the duke, when 'e's at 'ome."

Harriet walked him to the window, her voice shaking with contempt. "You know where Edlyn is? Is that what you want us to believe? Where is she? You, who couldn't find a chamber pot if you stepped in it. You—"

"I saw 'er face," he said. "I swear it. She was behind a barred window in 'anging Sword Alley. She even 'eld out a hand to me. I thought at first she were an angel. Then I saw all them posters."

"What did she look like?" Lady Powlis whispered.

"White as a bloody corpse. Sorry, my lady. It was dark, and I thought I was seein' things."

"Could you find her again?" Harriet asked, dimly aware of a door opening in the servants' quarters.

"Yeah. But it ain't where I'd go. I went back there, see, right back to that lodgin' 'ouse, after I realized who she was. Then I remembered that it'd been some bloody awful screamin' that woke me up in that wheelbarrow."

"Screaming?" Lady Powlis said faintly. "My niece was screaming?"

Jack frowned. "No. But some ravin' shrew behind 'er was." He bent his head to Harriet's. "I watched a bit. The young lady never came back to the window, but after a while a man came out, so I followed 'im, careful like, to Blackfriars Bridge."

"And he didn't notice you?" Harriet whispered after a skeptical pause.

He scoffed, stopping himself before he swatted her with his hat. "I saw 'im meet up with a bargeman. I couldn't 'ear everything, but I put together they was makin' plans to sail tonight, if they ain't already done so."

Harriet regarded him without a hint of affection. "If you're lying, so help me God, I'll not only watch you swing, I'll hang on to your ankles and turn somersaults between your feet."

"I think he's telling the truth," Lady Powlis said, looking as if she were going to be sick, whether from Jack's story or his smell, Harriet did not know.

She did know, however, that she'd never felt so relieved to see anyone as when suddenly the duke entered the room, the look of unmasked emotion on his face the stuff of fainting damsels and impossible dreams. His eyes dropped to the pistol she was holding at her side. She shook her head. His aunt started to cry.

"It's all right," Harriet said, swallowing over a knot in her throat. "But there's no time to waste. This man—my father—thinks he knows where Edlyn is."

He nodded tersely. His gaze holding hers, he strode past Jack and motioned from the window. Harriet noticed a man across the street, another appearing on the corner. There could have been a hundred armed guards about the place. It was Griffin's presence that made her feel safe. She had known other gentlemen willing to overlook her imperfections, to offer themselves as her protector. But she had never met a man who needed her to protect him as desperately as he did.

He took the two dueling pistols Harriet had hidden behind the teapot, tucking one into his belt and handing the other to her father. "Can you take me to the house where you saw her?"

"I could, but someone's gotta be on the bridge, just in case."

Harriet had to turn away for a moment. She had seen the surprise on her father's face at the implicit trust that Griffin had given him. She thought then of her mother, of how Jack would talk about her when he got drunk, and how he cursed the world for taking her when he'd have gladly gone in her place.

She had never considered that she might have been a product of love and that there had been goodness in Jack Gardner before he became the brutal man she remembered. Who would have guessed he'd turn hero at the last hour?

He put his hand out to hers. "I've been thinkin'—"

She blinked.

"—you could always see better than anyone in the dark, 'arry. We could watch each other's backs, just like in the good—"

"Absolutely not," Griffin and Primrose said in unison.

"In fact," the duke added, "I am having two of Sir Daniel's men posted *inside* this house while I'm gone."

Jack shifted his feet. "Let's 'ope they do a better job guarding the ladies than they did of keepin' me out."

Harriet vented a sigh. "I have never felt this utterly useless before."

"Now you know how a woman of my capacity feels when she begins to grow old," Lady Powlis murmured, misty-eyed again.

Griffin caught Harriet under her elbow and drew her against him for a last word of caution, if not an embrace. "Be good. Don't give Sir Daniel another reason to arrest you."

"I love you, Griffin," she whispered.

He broke away, gesturing for Jack to follow. Harriet stood, offering Lady Powlis reassurances she wished to believe herself. She had always dreaded the day that Griffin would meet her father. Her mind had played out many humiliating scenarios. She had not once, however, imagined the pair of them forming an alliance that would fill her with pride.

Chapter Thirty-six

The magic car no longer moved;
The Daemon and the Spirit
Entered the eternal gates.

PERCY BYSSHE SHELLEY
The Daemon of the World

❦ ❦

Given a good tide, a waterman could ferry his customers from London to Gravesend in a matter of hours. From this port in Kent, one could secure a ship to France or vanish into any number of quiet villages. Even as twilight fell, the River Thames pulsed through England like a vital artery.

At Grim Jack's urging, Griffin had abandoned his carriage on a stone bridge clogged with the traffic of carts and coaches carrying city merchants home. He had no choice but to trust Harriet's sire, a confidence he realized that Jack did not necessarily share.

Without warning, Jack halted in a hidden alley that led to the waterfront. On the damp steps below, street vendors cried their wares and bargemen exchanged ribald insults that echoed in the air.

"I'm not takin' another step, duke or not, until you answer me one thing."

Griffin cursed. "Yes, the reward is yours."

"I don't mean that." Jack paused as a low whistle came from a corner behind them. "I want to know that you'll take care of me daughter."

"I'm going to marry her."

Jack grinned in disbelief. "Aye, then. Best of bloody luck to you both. Come on."

"Jack!" a woman's voice exclaimed from the door of the chophouse they hurried past. "Bless my soul, I knew you wasn't dead."

A minute later Jack tipped an off-duty waterman for the usage of his small wharf. Griffin thanked God that he had spoken with Sir Daniel's men before venturing on this quest.

They waited on the wharf forever. They waited until Griffin was convinced that this was the last place in London that he would find his niece. How many barges traveled the river at any given time? How many secret stairs served as launching places for illicit deeds that only the river would ever know?

He had taken the word of a criminal, a professional liar, a father who still gave his grown daughter nightmares. She had escaped evil. Griffin had walked openly into its arms.

He pulled his pocket watch from his waistcoat. "It's almost seven," he said under his breath.

Grim Jack glanced appraisingly at his rather battered timepiece.

A small flat-bottomed barge drifted toward the adjacent dock. Griffin stared absently at the three passengers hurrying down the pier. A gentleman carrying a portmanteau, his wife nudging a slender hooded figure who might have been an invalid or—

She turned her head. He couldn't make out her face. But he'd known her from the day she appeared like a changeling on the castle drawbridge. He had carried her on his shoulders and caught her when she tired of swinging from the chandelier. He thought she called his name. The woman at her side raised a pistol to Edlyn's head.

His mind froze. Jack shoved him aside and Griffin shoved him right back, shouting out the one word of warning that he knew Edlyn would understand.

"Drop!"

Four shots erupted, two from the cabin of a shallop drifting by, another from a boarded-up window in the deserted tenement that overlooked the wharf. The fourth came from his own gun.

Rosalie Porter fell in her final performance, her male accomplice crumbling in her shadow. And Edlyn dropped with the death-defying grace of her former self, only to be surrounded by more bodyguards than Griffin could begin to number.

"Oh, God," he said, aware of footsteps pounding down the pier and a jubilant shout from the captain of the shallop. And . . . surely that was not the Boscastle battle cry, resounding from the cabin of the shallop that had floated by? "Jack Gardner, I will seek your pardon if it costs me a dukedom. And if any man brings evidence against you—"

He turned.

Grim Jack was gone, and so was the enameled pocket watch and gold-link chain that had been attached to Griffin's waistcoat pocket. The mate to his dueling pistol, however, lay at his feet.

He carried Edlyn back to his carriage on the bridge, escorted by an entourage of well-wishers, mudlarks, and river policemen. She was crying against his neck, and nothing he said could have stopped her.

"You're all right, Edlyn. It's over. It's done. If they hurt you . . . well, that will never happen again. We'll be together. It's going to be fine now."

He could have sworn that his first footman, Trenton, was fighting tears himself as he opened the carriage door. "I want to tell you something," Edlyn whispered, her hands knotted around his neck. "I was on the turret when my father took that jump. I knew it was an accident, and I didn't tell. I let everyone blame you, Uncle Griff. I saw that it wasn't your fault, and I never told. I wanted to find my mother, and no one helped me."

He nodded. "We shall search for her together."

He deposited her on the seat. He knew that Edlyn expected him to be angry at what she had confessed. But he could not find it in him. He should also have known that the woman who had seen him at his worst, and loved him anyway, would be waiting in the carriage. And that he wanted her, needed her, to be there.

"Thunder all you like," Harriet said, gripping

Edlyn to her with one hand, the other grasping the cuff of his coat. "I've heard it all before, duke."

"Doubtless you shall hear it for a long time to come."

She stroked Edlyn's hair. "My heart stopped when I saw you both standing on the pier and heard that gunfire."

He bent his head to kiss her. "Is it beating now?" he asked, lacing his fingers through hers.

"Harder, I fear, than I can stand."

His thumb sculpted the fine bones of her face. "Then I shall take it into my safekeeping so that nothing can ever threaten it again. I am yours, Harriet. And you are mine."

Chapter Thirty-seven

He had vowed to be with me on my wedding-night,
yet he did not consider that threat
as binding him to peace in the meantime.

MARY SHELLEY
Frankenstein

❧ ❧

The Duke of Glenmorgan got arrested on the night before his wedding.

He'd considered refusing when two of his Boscastle cousins, Lords Drake and Devon, appeared on his doorstep that evening and innocently announced that, as he would be taking a wife tomorrow, they would escort him for a last night on the Town.

He shrugged. Why not? Harriet, Aunt Primrose, and Edlyn had been whisked off in an impressive coach-and-six by a bewigged driver and a haughty assembly of footmen, who closed the carriage door before Harriet could blow her betrothed a kiss. The ladies would spend the night at Lady Sedgecroft's Park Lane mansion, discussing . . . he didn't know. The mysteries of the marriage bed? That Primrose should have an opinion on such matters chilled his blood. As long as it did not involve raising an Egyptian pharaoh from the dressing closet, he assumed he would be able to deal with it.

"Are we taking my carriage or yours?" he asked as he walked out the front door, where the two blue-eyed brothers awaited him.

"Neither," Drake said, staring up at the cloudy sky. "We're walking."

Shoulder to shoulder, the Boscastle men owned the streets. Only a fool would cross a member of the legendary brood and hope to escape unscathed as well as with all his teeth intact.

Still, more fools come out at night than do stars, and it was only a matter of time before the boys ended up at a low-stakes silver hell, where Lord Devon not only lost his proverbial shirt but sheepishly realized he didn't have a sixpence on his person to pay up.

The other player, who was not only missing a few teeth but had obviously never heard of the Boscastle family, reached across the table to grab Devon by the lapels of his double-breasted gray frock coat.

Devon's hand shot up and caught the man's wrist in a paralyzing hold. "Ask him to pay," he said, grinning in Griffin's direction. "He's a duke."

The man spat a stream of spittle on the table, shaking his wrist as it was released. "Dook, my arse."

The clink of glasses, the rattle of dice, and uninhibited conversation ceased. Lord Drake Boscastle looked up from his hand of cards with a half smile.

The guard who stood at the iron-grilled door turned in expectation.

Griffin bestirred himself from his private musings of bedding Harriet and glanced around the smoke-filled den. For a moment he wondered if some bawdy toast was about to be made in his dishonor. But suddenly the player who'd beaten Devon lifted a stool over his head.

"Be ye deaf, boy?" he shouted at Griffin. "I said, 'Dook, my arse.' "

Griffin smiled, rolling up his sleeves. "I could do that."

And so he did, with Drake and Devon at his back joking that this hell was nothing compared to what they would go through when they returned in a disheveled state to their wives.

Griffin tore off his coat, flung it into a leering face, and threw a punch at another. "If this is your idea of a bachelor party," he said with a laugh, "I bloody well hope I wake up tomorrow for my own wedding."

Drake upended a table as the last of three entry doors splintered open and the guard yelled, "Raid!" The den swarmed with bludgeon-armed Bow men who had only yesterday been on Griffin's side. Gamblers scrambled for secret passageways, their cards and dice boxes swooped up before Griffin could even find his coat.

"All right." A club prodded his ribs. "Party's up. There's a penalty for illegal gambling, as if you didn't know."

"Oh, for the love of God. I'm the Duke of Glenmorgan."

The constable shifted his gaze to the two other men leaning idly against the wall. "Right. And those would be your duchess and her hairdresser, I suppose?"

Who would have dreamed that the wicked Duke of Glenmorgan would learn everything he needed to know about love in a gaol cell, from one of London's premier rakes? A helpless audience, he slumped on the hard wooden bench he shared with Devon's lanky frame, while Drake paced and waxed philosophical in the dark. Griffin felt his skull throb with what might evolve into the worst hangover of his life. At least he would meet Harriet on the morrow with all his teeth.

"I will give you only one piece of advice," Drake said, pausing as if he were about to reveal the mystical powers of the Holy Grail. "It is something that Grayson, our Marquess of Scoundrels, once confessed to me during a family crisis."

Devon thumped his head against the wall. "Here we go."

Griffin shoved his foot into Devon's back. The gaol had not been built that could house three Boscastle men at the same time.

" 'Love is horrible, Drake,' " Drake quoted. " 'Horrible,' he said. 'Don't let it happen to you.' And then, in the next breath, I vow, when I had just escaped into the hall, he said, 'I was wrong. Don't listen to me. Love is a wonderful thing.' "

"Indeed, it is," said the mordant voice of Sir Daniel Mallory, to the accompanying rattle of keys in the prison door. "And let it not be said that those of us who sacrifice our lives in the name of justice would ever dare obstruct its path."

Chapter Thirty-eight

And every beast of beating heart grew bold,
Such gentleness and power even to behold.

PERCY BYSSHE SHELLEY
The Witch of Atlas

%❧ ❧%

It was to have been a private wedding.

If both parties had obeyed the protocol set down by the stone-faced senior footman, Weed, the nuptials might have taken place in the secrecy befitting the ritual of holy matrimony. At nine o'clock that morning, to the distress of those who observed tradition even if it killed them, a horde of aristocrats and street people alike jostled elbows for a coveted place at the ornamental gates of the Park Lane mansion.

Lord Sedgecroft's well-trained staff might have dispersed the crowd had the future duchess not appeared at an upstairs window a few minutes before the ceremony to shake her wedding veil in victory.

"Wish me luck," she whispered to the blur of faces. "I'm in love with everyone today."

The ceremony went off as planned, with another duchess—Harriet's personal creator, Emma Boscastle—dabbing away tears of pride at appropriate intervals, with a delicate brush of a white-gloved hand. Never before had the academy produced such a perfect diamond from the dust.

The girls of the elite school watched their beloved Miss Harriet and her handsome duke exchange vows in an enrapt silence. The male guests, including Harriet's half brothers, whistled and stamped their feet in irreverent disregard for what no man should put asunder.

The Marquess of Sedgecroft gave the bride away. Harriet thought of her father for only a moment. God only knew when, or if, she would ever see the old louse again.

Still, in his way, Jack had proved that he loved her and taught her to stand up for those she loved.

Harriet abandoned the rules of etiquette on her wedding night and let her instincts lead her where they would. Gone for the evening, if not for the rest of her life, was the dependable companion who had been forced to stay in the background and disregard her personal needs. From the coffin of her former being rose a young duchess who shivered in delight as her husband divested her of her wedding garments.

Thus beheld by him in her rawest state, Harriet could hardly be expected to fade into the background. And as to disregarding her personal needs, the duke seemed devoted to encouraging just the opposite. She doubted he would leave an inch of her not completely kissed and conquered before he was done. His tapered fingers made a leisurely study of her back, stroking across her bottom, then sweeping up again to her breasts. She would have expressed her enjoyment quite eloquently had he not rendered her too aroused to articulate a sentence.

Indeed, he paid her unclad form such tribute that she became impatient for the chance to return the favor. At length, with one arm wrapped around the bedpost, she brought the other up to the hair knotted at her nape and pulled out all the pins.

He drew back.

The dark flare in his eyes acknowledged her desire to participate. She unwound her arm from the post and brought her hands to his chest. His eyes widened in pleasure.

"I have never let a woman undress me before tonight," he confessed as she went to work on his coat, waistcoat, neckcloth, and shirt.

She smoothed her fingers over his well-muscled chest. "And I never knew you were a champion archer until the breakfast party."

He bent his head, his kiss leaving her dizzy and breathless. "It's a damned good thing you didn't walk past me as I took aim."

He caught her hand on its way into his waistband. "I shall take care of that. Lie down, my love, and let me gaze at you while I do it."

She reclined back on the bed, grateful that this was his suite and there were no hideous decorations on the headboard to wake up to in the morning. She still couldn't believe she would sleep beside him and see his face whenever she opened her eyes.

She could see far more than his face right now, and her heart pounded at the beauty of his lithe virility. In fact, the warm reality of his body filled her with a wonderful desperation. She parted her thighs without prompting as he slid up the bed between her legs. His mouth grazed her soft white breasts. Her nipples darkened and stiffened instantly. With nary a thought to propriety, she reached up and allowed herself full knowledge of her husband's amorous skills. The world fell away as she applied herself to unparalleled midnight pleasures and acts of creation that were anything but polite.

She hooked her legs over his backside. He groaned, slipping his hands under her rump until the head of his erection pushed deeply into her passage. She ran her hands down his back and felt his beautiful body tremble.

" *'Fear not,'* " her wicked husband quoted as he possessed her in the throes of uncontrollable passion, " *'that I shall be the instrument of future mischief. My work is nearly complete.'* "

Great God! What a scene has just taken place! . . . I demand a creature of another sex, but as hideous as myself. . . . It is true we shall be monsters . . . but on that account we shall be more attached to one another.

Author's Note

Frankenstein was published anonymously in 1818 in three volumes (not as a single novel) and became an instant bestseller. Thirteen years later Mary Shelley admitted authorship and confessed to the public that her groundbreaking novel had been conceived one rainy summer in Geneva during a competition against three other novelists to produce the best ghost story.

Mary won, still a teenager, and invented the science-fiction genre. I became fascinated with her life and work over a decade ago while researching a short novel I was writing about a horror novelist.

Mary was sixteen when she ran away with poet Percy Bysshe Shelley. Their marriage was plagued with scandals and personal tragedy and reads nothing like a modern-day romance. Percy drowned in 1822. Mary died of a brain tumor when she was fifty-three.

For errors made and liberties taken, I hope that Mary and my readers will "compassionate" me. If not, let Percy have the last word:

"What!"—Cried he, "this is my reward
For nights of thought, and days of toil?
Do poets, but to be abhorred
By men of whom they never heard,
Consume their spirit's oil?"

I hope you will be inspired to read *Frankenstein*
if you have not done so, and discover Mary Shelley's brilliance and her fascinating life as a writer
and feminist.

Cheers,
JILLIAN HUNTER